The Quinton Quads and the Mystery of Malprentice Manor

Steve Ince

ISBN: 9798668757688

Imprint: Independently published

www.steve-ince.co.uk

Cover and interior illustrations by Steve Ince

Dedication

For my grandchildren,
Caitlin, Leilani, Selene, Louie, Freya and Ariana.

May your adventures always be fun.

CONTENTS

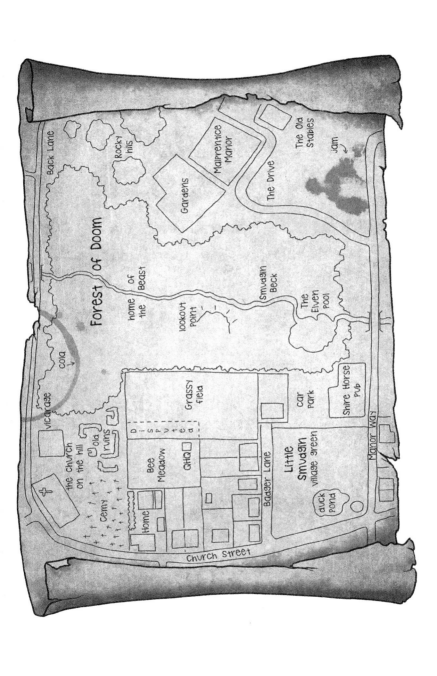

Prologue

The old woman's face twisted into a snarl ugly enough to scare even the bravest of people. Surprisingly, this was the closest she ever came to a smile, but for anyone unlucky enough to encounter Edith, this was a rare occurrence. She practically never smiled.

Although she struggled to read the ancient piece of paper in the dim light of the cellar, she could at least make out that it was some kind of map and was delighted to hold it in her grasp, hence the rare, scary smile. She lifted her head with a more serious look on her face and pointed a long, bony finger at the big man in front of her.

"We have no time to waste," she declared in a voice that grated like fingernails on a blackboard. "We must find it as quickly as possible."

Gus folded his mighty arms and huffed with frustration. "Where do we even begin to look for something like that? If the thing's as valuable as you think, it's going to be well hidden."

"Of course, you fool. That's why no one's found it so far." The woman's eyes narrowed and her gaze turned to ice. "But it will be mine, no matter what it takes."

In spite of his hardened appearance, the man shivered at her determined words. But if she was right about what this scrap of paper meant...

"Yeah, whatever it takes," he agreed and smiled in his own, nasty way. "Where do we start?"

"Find a few men who are willing to get their hands dirty but who will ask no questions. The less they know the better." She folded the old paper carefully along its original creases and clutched it in both hands protectively. "I must study this map for clues." She started to leave the gloomy cellar but stopped when the big man spoke again.

"Don't forget who found it," Gus said.

"You'll be amply rewarded, have no fear of that." Edith turned and locked her gaze with his. "This mystery has remained unsolved for generations. Once it's revealed I'll have everything that's rightfully mine. No one will keep me from that!"

CHAPTER ONE

Worms for Breakfast

"We need to go outside," Caz yelled as she hurtled down the stairs and exploded into the kitchen. "Mum's in one of her moods again."

Caz was one of the Quinton Quads, four sisters who had a reputation for mischief, even though such behaviour was never intentional. Any trouble that came about did so as a purely accidental consequence of their adventurous and imaginative natures, which took them along paths determined by their curiosity. At least, that's how they saw it, but others, like their Mum, always seemed to take a different view.

"What have you done this time?" Sally asked. "It's only the first day of the summer holidays and she's already mad at us?"

Of the four, Sally was the eldest by about five

minutes (followed by Caz, Poppy and Em in turn) and liked to think of herself as the leader of their little band. It wasn't that she was overly bossy or tried to assert her seniority to the detriment of the others, but out of all of them she was most like their Mum and she was the bossiest person the girls had ever known. Unfortunately, Sally did have a tendency to keep the others organised with an unwelcome flair for creating detailed schedules.

"Actually, Mum might only be mad at her," Em piped up, speaking around a mouthful of toast. She was the most thoughtful and academic of the four and was generally slower at eating because her mind always strayed onto thoughts about science or nature. The others suspected that Mum liked Em best simply for the fact that she made far less noise than they did. But such was their united nature that none of them had ever discussed it openly or made any kind of deal about it.

"You know how it always works, Em," Poppy said. "If one of us is in bother, we all share the trouble."

Although the girls were pretty positive overall, Poppy was the most optimistic of the quads and could generally see the bright side of most situations. She'd always look for the good in people, too, and tried to make sure that everyone would be friends with one another. She preferred having fun through spontaneous play rather than any strict organisation and planning, but her positive nature meant that she didn't like to upset Sally by saying something about the latter's schedules.

"If we're in trouble it's more than likely to be something Caz did," Sally added.

"Hey!" Caz yelled. "That's unfair." But her sisters

stared at her with looks that showed they knew it to be true. "Okay, little Tommy got into my jar of worms and started eating them..."

"Ewww...!" the other three said in unison, pulling faces to match. "Worms for breakfast!"

"...but I don't see how it's only my fault." Caz folded her arms and frowned.

She was right, of course. While it had been her idea to collect the worms, all four of the quads had helped her do so, even though none of them had any idea what they were going to do with the collection once they'd filled the jar.

The quads hadn't even considered that Tommy, their brother, would get into the jar let alone decide that earthworms were worthy of eating. But being fourteen months old and rapidly becoming an expert in walking and climbing where he shouldn't, keeping an eye on him had become a full time job for Mum, even though the girls were supposed to help out.

They'd recently had their tenth birthday — just a couple of months earlier — but when their mother was at her most exasperated she claimed the girls combined had given her forty years of stress. Clearly, bringing the girls up to be strong and independent was a mixed blessing.

"Where's Dad?" Em asked.

"He's got a business meeting on the golf course," Poppy answered. They all nodded knowingly.

It wasn't that Dad shirked his family responsibilities in any way, but there were times he felt outnumbered and needed to get his head together by getting angry at his golf clubs and a series of small, dimpled balls. Weird that. The only time that Dad seemed to love golf was when he wasn't actually playing the game.

"See, it's not me she's really mad at," said Caz and her three sisters shrugged.

Suddenly there was a scream from upstairs followed immediately by Mum yelling, "If I catch those kids I'm going to have their guts for garters!"

"Time to get some fresh air," Poppy said and they headed for the kitchen door as one. They jostled through it as smoothly as a shoal of fish squeezing between jagged coral while avoiding a dangerous predator. They shot out of the house and hurtled down the garden path.

"Hi, girls," Uncle Rosko called from the doorway of the old stables, which had been converted into living quarters for him a couple of years earlier. He was Mum's uncle on her mother's side but everyone in the family called him "Uncle" at his insistence. He disliked the idea of being referred to as "Great Uncle Rosko" by the girls. Such was his insistence in this matter that even some of their friends called him Uncle.

The quads waved and called a quick greeting but passed him by in a flash, such was their urgency to flee their mother's angry mood. Rosko chuckled to himself and watched as the girls ran through the patch of garden where their Dad grew his vegetables then clambered over the fence and into the field beyond.

Bee Meadow was an uneven, rocky field that had come with the house when their parents had moved in fifteen years ago. But rather than remove the rocks and develop it, they'd encouraged wild flowers and plants to grow, which helped all kinds of wildlife in return. Whenever there was a school project that involved the study of nature, the girls had a great source of flora and fauna they could study, sketch and photograph.

Although the meadow was the domain of nature, there was plenty of room to play, too. The quads ran in single file along the narrow paths that had evolved over the years and which twisted through the long grass and summer flowers. They ignored the many bees that gave the field its name and the insects payed them little notice in return, as was their nature. The girls trotted along like jungle explorers fleeing a dangerous, carnivorous beast.

They stopped for breath beneath their tree-house at the far end of the meadow where it bordered the Malprentice land; unfortunately, a long-disputed border. A previous generation of that family had allegedly moved the boundary fence and shortened Bee Meadow by at least twenty feet. This happened long before the quads were born but they regarded themselves as guardians of the border and the tree-house was their frontier outpost.

"Shall we take refuge?" Poppy asked. While the girls were all equally curious about most things, it was usually Poppy that asked questions first. "Up in QHQ."

The four girls loved to give inventive or grand names to things and it hadn't taken them long after Dad had built the tree-house to begin calling it Quads' Headquarters, which they then shortened to QHQ.

"That depends on how bad Mum's mood is," Sally replied and looked at Caz, who shrugged.

"Pretty bad, I suppose," she said.

They all looked back at the house, now in the mid-distance, and could see their Mum heading in their direction with Tommy supported on her hip. Her body language spoke volumes of a tale of pent up fury.

"Sally! Caz! Poppy! Em!" she shouted, doing so in the order of their birth as she always seemed to do. "Come here, now!"

Em gulped. "I think we need to put a lot more distance between us and Mum."

"Yeah. Time to scarper," Sally urged.

Without a moment's hesitation, all four of them clambered over the old fence and dashed across the grassy field towards the Forest of Doom. Although they could still hear Mum calling after them, they weren't able to make out what she said because of the sound of their pounding feet and the swoosh of the long grass as their legs pushed through it.

Leaping over a second fence, they used the abrupt shadow from the tree canopy above to their advantage. They hunkered down in a patch of bracken to hide from Mum and catch their breath. In the relative silence they could no longer hear her calling after them.

"She's given up," Caz said.

"For now, yes," Poppy responded.

"We'll be in for it when we go home for lunch," Em said with a pout on her lips.

"At least we have a few hours hours of freedom," said Sally. "Before we're grounded for the rest of our lives."

"Mum's not that bad." Poppy smiled at the others. "I bet we're only grounded for a week." They laughed.

"But it's the first week of the holidays," Caz said and sighed.

"And next week we're visiting Gran," added Em.

"It sounds like this morning could be the most important few hours of the summer," Poppy declared. "We'd better make the most of the time."

"It's a shame we didn't grab the bag," Caz said. "We could have gone swimming in the Elven Pool."

They rose from the bracken with a sigh then turned so they faced into the woods. Em asked, "Which way?"

Sally looked to her left and pointed up the slope. "This way."

The ground rose slowly as they picked their way between the trees and trudged uphill through the undergrowth.

Their heads shot upwards in reaction to a sudden sound in the leafy canopy above their heads, fearful that the local tales might be true after all.

"What is it?" whispered Em.

"Can you see anything?" asked Sally.

"Perhaps it's the beast," Caz suggested.

"Look! There!" Poppy pointed to a particular spot in the greenery above.

A fat wood pigeon was perched on a branch and flapped its wings among the leaves. Then a second pigeon flew in and the two seemed to dance around on the branch making even more noise before they flew off altogether. With the noisy pigeons gone, the girls now heard the sweet sound of other birdsong and a couple of crows calling out in the distance.

Sally looked around to get her bearings once again then began walking deeper into the Forest with the others right behind her.

Although the girls called it the Forest of Doom, its real name was Manor Wood. But when the quads were a little younger and had explored the woods for the first time, they felt it needed a name that better suited the excited way they felt. So far there had been no actual doom, but the fact that it belonged to Evil Edith meant that simply walking through it wasn't without an element of risk.

Malprentice Manor and the land around it — including this wood — was owned by Edith Malprentice, a woman with a nasty streak the width of a motorway and a withering gaze that could turn milk sour. The quads were sure that making it illegal for kids to even exist would be high on her list of things to do if she ever became Prime Minister. She always seemed determined to spoil all their fun, so they'd given her the name, Evil Edith. It turned out they hadn't been the first to call her this.

"As this is going to be our last chance for a couple of weeks at least," Em abruptly said. "We should try and find evidence the beast exists."

"Cool idea," said Caz. "It could make us famous. And rich."

"We should do it for important, scientific reasons." Em folded her arms in a bit of a huff.

"But rich could be good, too." Caz grinned.

"Ooh, yes!" Poppy clapped her hands. "Think of all the animals or homeless people we could help."

Sally held up her hands. "Don't count your chickens before they hatch, as Gran would say." Gran loved her little sayings and it was rare that she didn't have one prepared for just about every type of situation. Even if they didn't always fit as well as she hoped.

"Trouble is," Sally continued. "If we're hunting the beast we'll have to do it without our regular kit. Everything is in the bag we left behind."

"Okay," Poppy said. "How do we start?"

Em looked around as the others waited for her to come up with some kind of scientific approach. "We should spread out in a line then make our way up the hill. But go slowly and search the ground for any signs of the beast."

"Great plan," Sally said. "Let's get started."

As they moved apart to put a few metres between each of them, Caz picked up a fallen branch about a metre in length. To her, wielding some kind of stick was a vital part of exploring the Forest of Doom.

Em looked in the direction of the old manor house, but couldn't see it through the trees. A little relieved, she gave the signal and they started their search.

Malprentice Manor was a bit of a mystery to most people in the area. Evil Edith never let anyone into the grounds who didn't work there and potential visitors were discouraged by Gus, the brute of a man she employed for such things. As far as the girls had been able to tell she had no friends or family, which didn't really surprise them. But the tales about the house fascinated the girls and inspired regular surveillance from their tree-house.

There were stories of giant rats in the cellars; of ghouls trapped in the attic that were fed the giant rats; of ghosts that roamed the halls, wailing at midnight; of a beast that lived in the woods and came out whenever there was a full moon. Stories that no one claimed to believe, although the quads were absolutely convinced of their authenticity. And while it might appear a little crazy to be hunting a dangerous beast, they were certain of their safety since it wasn't night and the full moon was a week away.

"Over here!" Em called. "Quick!"

The other three dashed over to where she stood and she pointed down at a muddy patch still wet from the heavy downpour of two days earlier. In the middle was a large depression, about thirty centimetres in length.

"Wow, it's a footprint!" Poppy cried out. "You found it, Em."

"Well," Em responded. "I only found a footprint."

"But it's a start," Caz said. "It's evidence."

"Yeah," Sally added. "What a pity we don't have a camera with us."

"We could memorise it," Em suggested. "Then draw it when we get back home."

They crouched down to study the footprint more closely.

Crack-Crash!

A loud and unexpected noise came from over the

brow of the hill and made the girls jump with surprise. They looked at each other, suddenly afraid.

"It's the beast!" Sally said. "It must be coming back."

CHAPTER TWO

The Grisly Beast

The quads looked at each other, frozen to the spot. Their natural fear fought a desperate battle with their almost unlimited curiosity and the latter won out after only a few seconds. Somehow, they each knew what the others were thinking.

"We must be mad," Poppy said as all four of them stared in the direction the sound had come from — up the slope.

"Or on the verge of a great discovery," Caz replied.

"Hush!" whispered Em. "We don't want to scare it."

"Us? Scare the beast?!" Sally was astonished.

"It's been hiding in the Forest of Doom," Poppy said. "Maybe it's frightened of humans."

Without another word they started up the slope but almost immediately stopped when they heard a drawn-out buzzing roar.

"Do you think it's in pain?" Em asked.

"Let's find out," Sally replied and started running up the hill through the trees with the others quickly on her heels.

As they crested the brow of the hill, the buzzing roar stopped and it was followed by another crashing sound, so close the quads almost jumped out of their skins, but instead they dropped to the ground to hide in the undergrowth. They looked at each other with wide, staring eyes and expressions that spoke volumes — they all hoped the beast hadn't seen them. They breathed as quietly as possible as they listened for clues to the creature's location.

Instead of the beast, though, they heard the sound of a man shouting, though his words were unclear.

"Someone else is after the beast," whispered Em. "Do you think they want to kill it?"

"That would explain why it hides so well — it wants to avoid being hunted." Sally slowly raised her head as she spoke, but halted when the strange roar started up again.

"It's definitely in pain," Caz said.

"We've got to help it!" Poppy declared and stood up just in time to see a tree falling towards their position. "Move!" she yelled.

Poppy leapt towards a nearby oak with the others copying her action a fraction of a second later. Her swift reactions saved them all, for the tree crashed to the ground in the space they'd just been.

Unfortunately, a large branch snapped off and flew in the girls' direction. In a synchronised movement, they dived further behind the old oak and the branch hit the thick trunk, missing them by less than half a metre. It shattered on impact and the girls were showered with wood splinters, which caused Poppy to let out a short scream.

As they tried to regain control of their pounding hearts, they heard footsteps pushing through the undergrowth, rushing towards them. They shrunk right down, screwed up their eyes and covered their heads with their arms as they waited for the worst.

"What on Earth are you doing here?!" shouted a man's voice from right over them.

Sally looked up and saw the shape of a broad man silhouetted against a patch of sky. A second man, holding a chainsaw, stood at a distance behind him, a worried look on his face.

"Stupid kids," the first man said. "Get up from there."

The quads stood up and instantly recognised him as Gus, Evil Edith's butler-come-handyman. Built like a bear (and often referred to as Grisly Gus), it was said he could out-pull a plough horse and rumoured that he often ate kids for breakfast. The girls gathered themselves into a small group and became unnaturally silent.

"You could have been killed, you idiots!" Gus snarled at them. "And you're trespassing."

"We were only looking for the beast," Sally responded, a nervous tremor in her voice.

"There's no beast in these woods."

"There is, too," Em said. "We found a big footprint in the mud."

"Really?" Gus put his hands on his hips and stared at them with fierce eyes. The girls nodded weakly.

Gus lifted up his left foot and gestured towards it to suggest the sisters take a good look. His huge wellington boot was caked in mud and the girls immediately realised that the footprint they found belonged to Gus.

"You're the beast!" Poppy exclaimed.

In spite of the anger written all over him, Gus

suddenly burst into laughter and slapped his thigh. He leaned against a tree to try and control his mirth but that only seemed to make it worse and he screwed up his eyes to prevent tears from forming.

The quads took this as their opportunity to escape and ran off in the direction they'd come from. They pelted through the undergrowth and down the slope as if their lives depended on it.

Gus stopped laughing, opened his eyes and saw the girls had gone, so he cupped his hands around his mouth and shouted after them. "I'm the beast and I'm going to eat you for breakfast!"

Although the girls were out of sight over the crest of the hill, Gus heard them let out a squeal of fear. Chuckling to himself he turned away and headed back to his companion just as Edith Malprentice arrived on the scene.

"Who were you talking to?" she demanded.

"Just those quadruplets from the village," Gus replied. "They're gone, now."

"I told you to inform me if you caught them trespassing."

"Give me a chance; I've only just seen them." He chuckled again. "I don't think they'll be back in a hurry."

"It would have been better if you'd captured them," Edith snarled. "Then we could have dealt with them properly."

Gus shrugged and turned to the other man who waited with the chainsaw ready to continue. His eyes were wide and fearful as he stared at Edith.

"What do you think you're doing here, anyway?" Edith sneered with her usual level of contempt.

With the toe of his boot, Gus prodded the stump of the tree they'd just cut down. "These old trees are overdue for felling and we need the timber down in..."

"Not here!" Edith snapped. "Hurry up and finish then return to the house. I must deal with those infuriating trespassers and I'll not leave the manor unattended." She turned on her heel and stormed off in the direction of the house.

Gus watched her walk away for a while then muttered to himself when she was out of earshot. "One of these days..."

He turned to the man with the chainsaw and made a zipping motion along his lips. The man shrugged in a way that said it had nothing to do with him.

The sisters didn't stop running until they were back in Bee Meadow, then they dropped to the ground and sprawled out in the long grass beneath QHQ. They panted fiercely to try and get their breaths back, unable to speak for a few minutes.

"I'm starving," Caz eventually said.

"Is that all you can think of?" Em asked, sitting up. "We've just found out that Grisly Gus is the Beast of the Forest."

"The Grisly Beast!" Poppy said. "He probably changes into something gruesome at nightfall."

"He's already something gruesome," Caz said. The others nodded in agreement.

"I don't think he really changes," Sally chimed in, which was followed by three looks of disappointment from her sisters. "I think he's hiding something and doesn't want us to find the real beast."

"Ooh, you could be right," Caz said. "Maybe the beast is his pet."

"Why can't he have a hamster like normal people?" Poppy asked.

"Does he look like normal people?" Sally responded.

"What I want to know," Em said. "Is what kind of things he feeds to the beast."

"Kids, probably," Caz said. "We were lucky to escape with our lives."

They fell into silence, staring up at the blue sky dotted with small, white clouds. It was a beautiful day to lie in the meadow and do nothing, but this lasted all of ten minutes before Caz's stomach made a gentle growling sound.

"Do you think it's lunchtime yet?" she asked.

Em looked at the shadows cast by the nearby

fence posts. "No, it's only about eleven o'clock."

Caz sighed like she was going to implode if she didn't have something to eat. Over an hour to lunch was too long to wait.

"Let's get a banana or an apple," Sally said. "Mum doesn't mind if we eat fruit between meals."

"Let's hope she's forgiven us for the worms," Poppy said.

"I hope Tommy's okay," Em added.

They picked themselves up and wandered in the direction of the house. As they passed Big Rock, named because it was the largest rock in the field, Caz clambered on top of it and looked back towards the Forest of Doom. She squinted against the glare of the day then shook her head in relief and clambered down.

"There's no sign of the beast," she said. "Or Gus."

In the garden, Tommy sat in the middle of the lawn inside his large play-pen, along with a huge number of toys. A garden umbrella had been erected to shield him from direct sunlight. Nearby was a chair, a half glass of lemonade and a book — it seemed as though their mother had just popped inside for a moment.

As soon as Tommy saw the sisters he stood up a little shakily and reached out to them through the bars of the play-pen. "Cods!" he shouted gleefully with a big smile on his face. He hadn't quite mastered the word, Quads.

"Hello, Tommy," Sally said with a big grin and reached into the play-pen to lift him out. She gave him a cuddle and he drooled into her ear. "Ugh, Tommy!" she cried out but laughed anyway.

The four girls fussed over him like crazy for a few minutes — they adored their little brother.

"I hope you didn't eat all our worms," Caz said and

tweaked his nose. He slapped her on the head in response and laughed as if he'd done the funniest thing ever.

"Biscuit," he said.

"No, Tommy," Poppy said. "We can't have biscuits between meals."

"What about some fruit?" Em asked him.

"Juice," he replied and the girls laughed.

They turned when they heard a noise at the kitchen door and saw their mother who looked behind her as she came out.

"Please come through," she said. "I've left Tommy in the garden." She turned as she stepped through the door and spotted the quads. "Oh, they're here..."

The look on Mum's face was a little fierce but behind her came a sight to chill the blood — Evil Edith emerged from the kitchen with an expression like a dozen thunderstorms.

Both women marched up to the girls but before either of them could speak, Tommy caught sight of Edith and abruptly burst out crying.

"Oh, you have another brat, do you?" Edith said, eyeing the baby with disdain.

"I beg your pardon," Mum said. "My children are not brats! There are times when they are wilful, disobedient, mischievous, contrary and downright irritating, but they are not brats."

"They say a mother's love is blind..."

Mum took a quick, deep breath and forced herself to control her temper. "What is it they're supposed to have done?"

"There is no suppose in the matter," Edith said, her nose raised sniffily in the air. "They have trespassed on my land and I insist that you control them better than you do."

"We were only playing in the Forest of Doom," Caz said. "We didn't do any harm."

"The Forest of Doom?" Edith looked as though she'd never heard anything so ridiculous.

"It's just their name for Manor Wood," Mum explained.

"We were only having fun," Poppy said.

"I suppose it's fun to nearly get killed, is it?"

"What?!" Mum exclaimed. "What happened?"

All four quads tried to talk at once but Edith cut them off instantly.

"They wandered into an area where trees were being felled," she said. "Children do not recover from a tree dropping on their heads I can assure you."

"It was an accident," Em said. "We were tracking the beast."

"That's enough!" Mum said. "Rein in your imaginations immediately."

All four fell silent and stared at the two grown-ups with sulky expressions. They knew better than to disobey their mother at a moment like this.

Mum looked at Edith. "Were they really in danger?"

"Indeed. I'm sure neither of us want to be faced with dead children."

Mum's hands went to her face — the dreadful reality of the situation hitting home hard. She turned to the children, horror and anger fighting each other for dominance. The quads looked down at their feet and fidgeted uncomfortably.

"Juice," said Tommy and Sally tried to shush him.

Mum took a deep breath and turned back to Edith. "Mrs. Malprentice, I think the girls probably have something to say to you." She glared at the four of them.

As one, they took a breath and spoke in unison. "We're sorry, Mrs. Malprentice."

"And I'm sorry, too," Mum added. "They won't do that ever again."

Evil Edith narrowed her eyes. "If they so much as set foot on my land, I'll not only have the police arrest them, I'll make sure the courts make an example of all four."

"Don't you think that's a little harsh? They're only children."

Edith almost poked Mum with her bony finger as she pointed and hissed at her. "I'll not have anyone sticking their noses into my business, especially not those who are little better than street urchins. You should have brought them up better."

"Now just you wait!" Mum snarled. But rather than follow up on this opening, she simply seethed, ground her teeth and clenched her fists, determined to control her anger.

"I shall see myself out." Edith turned about and strode toward the kitchen door. Tommy chose this precise moment to fill his nappy and did so with a rather noisy farting sound, which caused him to giggle.

Edith came to a halt, sure that the noise had been an insult directed at her. She spun around and stormed back to them, her finger pointing like a rapier, once again ready to let rip with her venomous tongue... Then the smell hit her.

While the Quinton family weren't exactly used to the smells that little Tommy could generate, they at least knew what to expect from his noxious bottom. Edith was so taken by surprise at the strength of the stench that her eyes watered and she gagged as if she was going to be sick. She fled through the house as if a demon was chasing her.

As soon as she was gone the quads burst out laughing and even their mother joined in. However, she became serious again almost immediately and took Tommy from Sally.

"Stay right there!" Mum ordered. "When I've changed his nappy we're going to have a serious talk." She took the little boy indoors and the girls were left to ponder on the type of punishment coming their way.

Although Mum had been far more troubled by the idea of them nearly dying than she was the trespassing, she'd still meted out serious punishment. By her standards at least. Although she could be bossy and was often rather serious, she was also very fair and understanding.

The girls were banished to their room for the rest of the day, they couldn't leave the house or garden for the rest of the week and had to wash all the pots and pans by hand — not using the dishwasher — for the whole of the summer holidays.

"This is so unfair," Em said. "We were only trying to advance human knowledge." She punched her pillow in frustration as she lay on her lower bunk. The quads shared a single room that contained two sets of bunk beds. Sally and Caz had one set with Poppy and Em on the other.

"Yeah," Sally agreed. She sat on her top bunk while writing in her journal. She didn't like to call it a diary because that made it seem trivial, in her opinion. "How do you spell vindictive?"

"Does it matter?" said Caz from the bunk below.

"You never show your journal to anyone. But Em's right, it is unfair."

"Actually," Poppy said, staring at the stars painted on the ceiling above her. "We were lucky not to have got it worse. Whatever we think, we should accept our punishment and make the most of the situation. We still have each other to play with."

"Which is all we need most of the time, anyway," Em added and Sally nodded in agreement.

Caz grinned. "Pirates!" she yelled and ran over to the huge chest below the window.

It took all four of them no time at all to don pirate hats, eye patches and plastic cutlasses. The two sets of bunks became rival pirate ships attacking each other, crewed by marauding pirates.

"Prepare to board, me 'arties," yelled Sally and grabbed The Plank from the tight gap between the bunk bed and the wall.

The Plank was one of those multi-use items they could never imagine being without, often using it for a makeshift see-saw, slide, picnic table and display shelf, among many other things. Now the girls used it as the means to pass from one pirate vessel to the other, spanning the gap between the two top bunks.

Sally and Poppy advanced towards each other across The Plank with swords drawn. They snarled piratey insults at each other, but had to crouch quite a bit so their heads didn't bump the ceiling.

"You scurvy dog! Prepare to die!" shouted Sally.

"Never, you bag of fish-heads!" retorted Poppy. "We be the most savage pirates to sail the seven seas."

"Fire all cannons, matey!" Sally cried out.

"Aye, aye, Cap'n," Caz shouted from the lower bunk. She had the waste basket on its side as a makeshift cannon. "Boom!" she yelled and threw a screwed-up-paper cannonball at Em.

"We've been holed! We're taking in water!" Em knelt in the bunk below Poppy and pretended to bail out the seawater pouring in.

"Plug the hole and make it good, bosun," Poppy ordered as she clashed swords with Sally.

The bedroom door abruptly opened and Mum walked in. "For goodness' sake! Will you please make a little less noise!"

"Arr, matey," Caz said, looking up at her mother from the lower bunk.

Mum glared at her with her hands on her hips. "I'm trying to get Tommy to have his afternoon nap."

"Sorry, Mum," Caz replied. The pirate game came to a complete end and the quads flopped onto their respective beds with a collective sigh.

"You may think this punishment is unfair but you have to learn about boundaries and respecting other people's property."

"But we..." Sally began, but Mum held up her hand.

"I know you didn't do any harm to the woods," she said. "But that's not the point. They're not your woods to play in as you like."

"Why can't woods like that belong to everyone?" Em asked.

"Oh, I wish that were possible. The world would be a much better place." Mum spread her arms in a slightly exasperated manner, somewhat sympathetic of the quads' plight, then left the room.

The girls looked at each other and sighed — it was going to be a long day.

They each grabbed one of the many books

crammed into the room's numerous nooks and crannies and began to read.

CHAPTER THREE

Market Day

Poppy opened a bleary eye, still tired, and discovered the bedroom was filled with bright light. Last night she'd stayed awake much later than the others, gripped by the exciting story in one of her favourite books. Now she regretted doing so as she now felt exhausted, but the sun was well up. She peered over the edge of her mattress and saw that her three sisters were lying on the floor playing a board game.

"At last!" Caz said when she spotted Poppy was awake. "We thought you were going to snore all day."

"I don't snore!" Poppy replied and threw a pillow at Caz. A second later all four were on their feet and laughing as they engaged in an all-out pillow fight.

Unfortunately, the fun came to an abrupt halt when Em stood on one of the game pieces with her bare foot then bumped heads with Sally as she fell over.

In spite of the pain she was in, Em fell into a helpless fit of giggles. So infectious was her laughter that the other three were soon laughing uncontrollably, too.

"Cods!" Tommy shouted from the doorway where he was held in the arms of his mother. He clapped his hands and giggled then fought to be released so he could join the girls in whatever fun it was that made them laugh so much.

Mum held on tight and spoke seriously through the girls' giggles. "I want you ready in five minutes. Today's market day in the village and I want to make sure we get there early."

Caz's laughter stopped instantly. "But we haven't had breakfast," she complained.

"Okay, ten minutes," Mum said then left with Tommy.

Caz gave out a big sigh and Sally nudged her. "Stop complaining, Caz. At least we get to leave the house."

"Have we got any pocket money left to spend in the market?" Poppy asked.

"We used last week's on that end-of-term gift for our teacher," Em replied. "And it's two days before we get this week's money."

"If we get it," Sally said. "We're being punished at the moment, remember."

Caz sighed again, but pulled on her trainers and dashed into the bathroom. "Last one down's a frog-faced, bogey monster."

Four minutes later, Poppy entered the kitchen a full minute after the others, but as she'd woken later than them she'd had to change out of her pyjamas before cleaning her teeth and brushing her hair.

"Here you go, frog-face," Caz said and threw Poppy a banana. She was taken by surprise, but after a couple of seconds of nifty juggling she held it firmly and began to peel it. Sally had already poured four glasses of orange juice.

As they half expected, they had finished eating and drinking before Mum was ready. Whenever Mum gave a time to be ready by, it always required a good degree of flexibility due to the variable nature of Tommy's needs.

As Em cleared away the glasses, the back door opened and Uncle Rosko entered the kitchen with a grin. The girls greeted him and hugged him as one.

"Hi girls. I have a new knot for you to learn," he said, his large moustache dancing as he spoke. "The bowline."

Uncle Rosko took a length of rope from his pocket and demonstrated the knot slowly, ending up with a loop that he slipped over his hand and onto his arm. "It's useful for securing the end of a line."

The girls took turns trying the knot and Rosko talked to them while they did so.

"I hear you had a bit of bother with Edith Malprentice," he said.

"Yeah," Caz responded as she watched Sally make a success of tying the knot.

"We were only looking for the Beast," Em said. "To advance scientific knowledge."

Rosko chuckled. "I hate to disappoint you, but the Beast doesn't exist."

"How do you know?" Poppy asked.

"Edith and I made it up when we were kids." His eyes lost focus as his mind wandered through his memories. "We used to play in Manor Wood all the time, even though we weren't supposed to."

"Why?" Sally asked. "It's her wood."

"It wasn't back then." Rosko looked away for a moment. "Edith married into the Malprentice family in her early twenties."

"So she used to trespass, too!" Sally exclaimed.

"If the Beast isn't real, what about the Mystery of the Manor?" Caz asked, struggling with her turn at the knot.

"That definitely exists," Rosko replied, much to the surprise of the girls. Adults usually spoilt all of the good stories about such places.

"What is it?" Em asked with her eyes like saucers.

"If we all knew it wouldn't be a mystery," Uncle Rosko chuckled. "But I'll get to the bottom of it eventually."

Sally nodded then frowned at the piece of rope. "What if you can't slip the knot's loop over the end of a post or something?" she asked.

"Good point," Rosko said. He knelt down by one of the table legs and showed them how to tie the knot directly onto it.

Sally smiled. "Cool. I like it."

Caz took the rope from Uncle Rosko and tried to tie the knot around the leg but she slipped up somewhere and it came apart.

"Come on, Cods," Tommy yelled from the hallway and Caz didn't have a chance to try again.

"We've got to go help Mum," she said, a little annoyed with her failure.

"You'll get it," Rosko said. "Practice later."

He left by the back door and the girls went through to the hallway where their little brother was already in his buggy. Mum put on a pair of sunglasses, checked her appearance in the hall mirror and opened the front door.

"Sally," she said. "You push the buggy. Caz, you can get the trolley."

"Oh, no!" Caz exclaimed. She hated that trolley.

The summer sunshine and the school holidays had brought the locals out in force and the market place, at the southern end of Little Smudgin, was much busier than usual. A number of shoppers had children in tow and some kids were hanging around in the hope of finding something interesting to do.

"Don't forget," Mum said. "You're currently grounded, so I don't want you talking to any of your friends." She picked up a basket at the fruit and veg stall, handed it to Em then started poring over the tomatoes.

As far as Caz was concerned, she had no interest in talking to anyone while she was in charge of the shopping trolley and currently trailed at the back of the group.

It was a contraption so lacking in style the quads had dubbed it The Nana Nightmare. Not only was it the kind of thing old ladies often used, it was covered with a particularly unpleasant tartan pattern no Scot would ever be associated with. It's only redeeming feature was that Mum had obtained it from a car boot sale for only two pounds. Dad had joked that they should have paid Mum to take it off their hands.

The discomfort on Caz's face turned to an expression of horror when she saw one of the coolest boys in her class — Tim Redfern, the school cross-country champion.

She immediately let go of the trolley, allowing it to

stand on its own, and moved a couple of steps away. She pretended to look at the items on the nearest stall, only realising too late that she appeared to be checking out piles of cheap insoles and old-fashioned slippers that smelled unpleasantly of rubber heated by the sun.

Tim whizzed by on his bike, weaving in and out of the various shoppers, and gave her a beaming grin, his white teeth a striking contrast to his dark skin. A moment later he'd made his way through the throng of people and disappeared from view.

Caz wished for the ground to swallow her up, but knew that her only hope of any salvation was that Tim would forget all about the trolley by the time they all returned to school in September.

"Poppy, potato bag!" Mum called out over the general noise of the crowd.

Poppy stepped over to the shopping trolley and rummaged inside. After a moment she pulled out a canvas bag on which Mum had written "potatoes" with a permanent marker pen. Poppy skipped over to her mother with a beaming smile on her face — anything that helped towards protecting the environment pleased her. When the woman on the stall weighed out the potatoes Mum wanted, they went straight into the bag without the wasteful need of any additional packaging.

The woman gave Poppy a wink and the girl smiled in return. No one seemed to know the woman's real name but everyone called her Pep and had done so for decades, judging by the weather-carved lines on her face. Poppy loved the way she always seemed cheerful no matter the weather, shouting out the prices of this week's bargains in between serving customers.

"Caz!" Poppy yelled. "Bring the trolley over here."

Caz grabbed its handle and dragged it over to the fruit and veg stall. She swung it around and almost caught Mum's leg, but quickly opened the top, pulled out more canvas bags and let Poppy put the potato bag into the bottom.

"I'm bored," Caz said but Poppy nudged her and pointed towards the far side of the market. Caz turned to see what had caught her sister's eye and was surprised to see that Uncle Rosko was talking to Evil Edith.

"What do you think they're chatting about?" Poppy asked. They were too far away to hear anything.

"Who knows," Caz replied. "They've known each other for a hundred years."

"Don't exaggerate, Caz."

They continued watching and whatever was said between them caused Uncle Rosko to laugh out loud, which made Edith so angry that she raised her hand to slap his face. Then she remembered where she was, held herself in check and spoke through clenched teeth as she pointed at him with her dagger-like finger.

They saw nothing more of this exchange as a group of people abruptly filled their field of view. By the time they'd moved and the girls could see through to the other side of the market again, both Rosko and Edith had gone.

"We've got to ask Uncle Rosko what that was about," Caz said.

"Wouldn't that be rather rude?" Poppy asked. "He might think we were spying on him."

"Maybe," Caz responded. "We'll tell the others later and see what they think."

The rest of the shopping trip was uneventful, apart from when Tommy dropped his ice-cream onto the pavement and screamed as if he'd been stung by a dozen wasps and took a full ten minutes to calm down. The family group finally trudged up the gently sloping hill of Church Street that took them home. Once the groceries had been put away it was time for lunch.

"Pizza!" Tommy cried out when Mum asked what they wanted and the girls giggled.

"No, Tommy," Mum said. "You can have a sandwich. Cheese and lettuce?"

"Jees and less," he said, trying to copy his mother's words. For some reason this was his favourite sandwich and Mum set about preparing it.

Because Mum had things to do in the office after lunch, the quads spent most of the afternoon playing with Tommy in the garden, which meant the time flew by and they completely forgot about their punishment. It only re-entered their heads when their friend, Molly, called them on the phone to ask if they all wanted to come over for tea and Sally, who took the call, had to explain that they were grounded.

The quads looked at each other with glum faces as they stood in the hall by the phone and Caz gave a sigh big enough for all of them.

"It's going to be a long week," Em said.

"Ow!" Poppy cried out. Tommy had slapped her on the top of her head as she held him. He giggled and she pretended to steal his nose.

The phone rang again and made them jump, but Sally was fast enough to pick up the receiver in the middle of the second ring. "Hello, Quinton residence," she said then listened to the caller for a few seconds. She then covered the microphone end of the receiver and shouted at the top of her voice. "Mum! It's for you!"

The office door opened and Mum strode over to the phone, which Sally handed over.

"Hello," Mum said into the phone. "Yes, speaking." The girls watched as Mum listened — her expression changed to serious then worried. "Just a moment." She turned to them with her hand over the receiver. "Have you seen Uncle Rosko?"

"Not since he was in the kitchen this morning," Sally replied.

"Caz and I saw him in the market," Poppy added. "But not after that."

Mum spoke into the phone again. "I'm afraid we don't know where he is. I'm sorry he didn't come in."

Putting the phone down, Mum turned to Caz. "Check he isn't home, will you?"

"We haven't seen him come back," Caz replied.

"Just do it. Uncle Rosko didn't turn up for his

doctor appointment, which isn't like him."

Caz sped out of the house and over to the old stable Rosko used as his home. She was back within thirty seconds. "It's all locked up and I can't see anything through the window."

"Where could he be?" Mum wondered aloud, then, "What was he doing when you saw him in the market?"

"He was talking to Evil Edith," Poppy said.

"Arguing, more like," Caz added.

"Stop calling her that," Mum said. "Still, it doesn't explain why he's missed his appointment."

"Unless Edith kidnapped him," Sally suggested.

"This is serious, Sally!" Mum snapped. "I don't have time for your fanciful ideas. Now make yourself useful and get Tommy his tea. I'm going to make some calls."

As the quads wandered into the kitchen, Sally muttered, "Well, he could have been kidnapped."

"Uncle Rosko is twice Edith's size," Em said. "She can't just knock him out and throw him over her shoulder."

Poppy and Caz laughed at the thought and Sally shrugged her reluctant agreement. "I suppose."

When their mother came off the phone and entered the kitchen, Sally and Poppy were helping Tommy eat his tea while Caz and Em peeled potatoes and carrots for their evening meal, which they usually ate later when their Dad came home from work.

Mum sat down at the table. "I've phoned everyone I can think of, even Mrs. Malprentice, but no one has seen him since this morning."

The evening had been a sombre affair, with everyone waiting for the phone to ring with good news about Uncle Rosko, but it never came. Once Tommy was in bed and the evening meal eaten, Sally washed the dishes, Caz and Poppy dried them and Em put them away. Dad had eaten his food quickly then gone out in the car in the hope of spotting Uncle Rosko somewhere in the locality.

When the girls had finished, they tried to play a board game, then tried to read, then tried to do some drawing. But nothing would hold their attention because of the concern they each felt.

Eventually, Mum sent them to bed in spite of their protests and told them that she would worry enough for all of them. They'd only just changed into their pyjamas when the phone rang and they thundered downstairs faster than they'd ever done before.

Mum was even quicker and snatched up the receiver before the girls finished descending the stairs. "Hello. Quinton residence."

The girls stared at their Mum in silence as she listened to the person who'd called. Whoever it was spoke very loudly and Mum had to move the receiver from her ear and they could all hear that the caller was a woman in some distress.

"Just a minute, Mrs. Redfern," Mum said when she was able to get a word in. "I'll see if the girls know anything." She looked at the four worried, upturned faces. "Have any of you seen Tim Redfern today?"

"Tim?" Sally was puzzled. "What does he have to do with Uncle Rosko?"

"Nothing," Mum replied. "But Tim has gone missing, too."

"I saw him this morning," Caz said. "He rode his bike through the market."

"Did he say anything?" Poppy asked?

Caz shook her head. "He rode past and was gone."

Mum relayed this information to the missing boy's mother and after a few seconds the call ended.

"What on Earth is going on?" Mum said to no one in particular.

"Do you think they've both been kidnapped?" Em asked.

Mum sat on the stool beside the phone and put her face in her hands. "I honestly don't know what to think."

The girls looked at each other a little afraid — they'd never seen Mum like this before.

CHAPTER FOUR

What a Dilemma

The next day the quads awoke particularly early, in spite of getting to sleep very late. Worrying about Uncle Rosko had kept slumber at bay until well into the early hours. They sneaked downstairs quietly so they didn't wake Mum and were surprised to find their father was already up. He was feeding Tommy his breakfast at the same time as reading the news on his laptop.

"Girls!" Dad looked up and beamed at them. "It's lovely to see you before I go to work." The quads surrounded him and gave him a group hug, to which he responded warmly.

"Did you find Uncle Rosko?" Poppy asked as they pulled out of the embrace.

"I'm afraid not," Dad replied. "There's been no sign of him. Your Mum's been up all night and has only just gone to bed exhausted. I don't want you to disturb her unless there's news about Uncle Rosko."

"All right," Sally said. "Do you want us to look after Tommy?"

"I've arranged a child minder. I'm going to drop him off on my way to work."

"But we can look after him," Caz said.

"I'm sure you can, but the law doesn't allow it. You're too young." He smiled at them fondly.

"If you take us all together," Em said. "We have forty years of experience."

Dad laughed. "I'm afraid it doesn't work like that. You each have the same ten years of experience. But don't worry, I'm sure your mother will need you to help her when she wakes. Just let her sleep for now."

"We'll play in QHQ until she gets up," Poppy said.

"Don't go any further than that until we know why Rosko and Tim have disappeared."

"We can't anyway," Caz said. "We're being punished."

"Oh, yes," Dad said and frowned. "I haven't had the chance to speak to you about that so far. Your Mum said you were nearly killed in the woods."

The girls looked a little sheepish. Dad gave a little stern stare to each of them in turn, though he struggled to keep his expression serious.

"The tree landed nowhere near us," Sally said, not quite telling the truth but sparing Dad additional worry. The other three nodded in agreement.

"Still, it sounded like you put yourself in a dangerous situation." Dad's serious tone was genuine, now.

"There's always going to be some danger if we hope to find the Beast of the Forest," Em said. "We were doing it for science."

Dad smiled at her fondly but it didn't reduce the importance of his words. "You're all wonderful girls with the greatest imaginations I've known, but sometimes a line has to be drawn. There is no beast in Manor Wood."

"That's what Uncle Rosko said," Poppy responded.

"What about Grisly Gus?" Caz asked.

Dad chuckled. "Yes, he's a bit of a beast at times, but he's still just a man."

"Even though he works for Evil Edith?" asked Poppy.

"Yes, even though." Dad stood up, closed his laptop and tucked it under his arm. "I don't want to stop you having fun, but you still have to be careful you don't put yourselves in danger. Now I have to go to work. Can you girls get Tommy cleaned up while I finish getting ready?"

"Yeah, Dad," Sally replied.

By the time he returned in his suit and tie, carrying his briefcase, they'd tidied away Tommy's breakfast things and cleaned his face and hands.

"Juice," Tommy said.

"Not in the car, Tommy," Dad said. He slung Tommy's baby bag over his shoulder and picked him up.

With a little difficulty, he bent and kissed each of the quads on the tops of their heads. "Be good and take care. I'll see you tonight."

The girls looked at each other after Dad had left the room. There was nothing to be said so each of them gave a serious nod then immediately set about making breakfast.

They finished washing and drying the dishes as quietly as they could so as not to disturb Mum. Although they disliked their punishment, there was no point causing more trouble by not doing it, particularly with the crisis the family was going through.

"What are we going to do?" Caz asked.

"Let's go to QHQ," Sally responded. "That way Mum can sleep as long as possible."

"We won't hear the phone," Poppy said.

"There's an extension in Mum's bedroom," Em reminded her. "She won't miss any news about Uncle Rosko."

Em put the last of the dishes away, Poppy hung the tea-towels on the rail and they all made their way towards the back door.

But they immediately stopped when Sally hissed, "Wait. Supplies!"

Like a well-oiled machine, the four of them grabbed various items — a half-prepared backpack from the under-stairs cupboard, a bag of apples, a multi-pack of crisps, half a loaf from the bread-bin, a jar of jam and some peanut butter, along with bottles of water from the fridge, kept in there for emergency picnics. They left the house ten seconds later and set off down the garden path.

They stopped as they passed the old stables, but when they peered through the windows and tried the door there was still no sign of Uncle Rosko. They continued down the garden towards Bee Meadow.

As they climbed the low fence, Poppy paused, sitting on the top plank. "What are we going to do all day?"

"We'll think of something," Caz replied. "We usually do."

"I wish we could search for Uncle Rosko," Sally said. "But Mum would go spare if we left the meadow."

Em crouched beside a patch of long grass and summer flowers. "We could go on a nature hunt." She stood up holding a beetle in the palm of her hand, it's wing casings shining beautifully. "Look what I just found."

The beetle decided to fly off at that moment and the four girls watched it disappear deeper into the long grass.

"To do it properly," Sally said, "We'd need to get nets and collecting jars and notebooks and we can't disturb Mum."

"Let's go to the tree-house and invent a new game," Poppy suggested with a weak grin.

They trotted down to the far end of the field and climbed the ladder. The girls flopped on the cushions and battered chairs and enjoyed the privacy the tree-house offered them. It was almost as big as their bedroom but felt bigger because space wasn't taken up with bunk-beds. Whatever you might say about Dad, he knew how to build a great tree-house and they usually spent more time here during summer than they did in the main house.

"I think we should draw up an agenda," Sally said and the others groaned. Although they didn't usually mind the way she thought of herself in charge, sometimes she simply went too far.

"Why on earth would we want one of those?" Caz asked. "It's the summer holidays — we do stuff and have fun. We don't need an agenda for that."

"But we always have so much we want to do, how do we know we're going to fit it all into the next six weeks?" Sally looked hopefully at the others.

"She does have a point," said Em. "Don't forget, Uncle Rosko's taking us to see Gran next week."

With that the mood became glum once more and Poppy began to cry. "What if no one finds him?" she sobbed.

The others crowded close to console her with a hug but her tears were infectious and all four were soon gently weeping.

Then Sally broke away and wiped at her tears, leaving grubby streaks across her cheeks. "No!" she yelled. "He's going to be all right."

"Yeah," Caz agreed, rubbing at her own face. "He knows all kinds of survival stuff."

"And he loves to teach us things," Em said. She blew her nose on a handkerchief and shoved it back into her pocket.

"But..." Poppy started to say.

"We have to stay positive for Mum's sake," Sally commanded. "We don't know what's happened so don't assume the worst."

Poppy fought back the tears and nodded. They did gentle fist-bumps to confirm their agreement.

"Let's help find Uncle Rosko!" Caz said.

"Yeah!" agreed Sally.

"How?" Poppy asked. "We can't leave here."

"We can take it in turns to keep a lookout," Em suggested and began rummaging in the storage box in the corner.

"And the rest of us can think up ideas for Poppy's new game," Sally said.

Unfortunately, it now seemed that their minds had abruptly emptied of fun ideas and the three stared at each other feeling somewhat at a loss. So Caz started playing with a spider on the floor, Sally pulled at some leaves that had pushed through some small gaps in the walls and Poppy grabbed some paper from the stack on the shelf. But all three became lost in their thoughts. Em found what she'd been looking for — a pair of binoculars — and stood up, looping the strap over her head.

With windows on each of the four sides, the tree-house gave them a great vantage point to see in all directions. To the north was the Church on the Hill, to the west was their house with the farmland beyond and to the south was the village of Little Smudgin.

To the east there was a clear line of sight across the wooded valley to the home of Evil Edith — Malprentice Manor. The large house was situated part way up the rise with rugged, rocky hills behind.

The girls often liked to take turns spying on the manor house using Dad's binoculars, which they'd borrowed a couple of years earlier and had forgotten to give back ever since. Unfortunately, their spying never turned up anything of interest, unless you call Evil Edith going out in the car, driven by Grisly Gus interesting.

Em gazed through the binoculars and first looked to the South in the hope of catching sight of Uncle Rosko in the village. She then moved to the west window and focused on their own house and the stable, before turning her attention to the church and finally the manor house.

She was just about to look away and start the cycle again when something caught her eye. It took a moment to see it again, but there was definitely something at one of the attic windows.

It was difficult to be sure because of the light reflecting off the glass, but it looked like someone was banging on the window pane. Someone who appeared to be trapped inside. However, this was nothing compared to what Em saw next and she gasped in shock.

"There's been a murder!" she exclaimed and almost choked when Caz dashed over and grabbed the binoculars from Em's hands causing the strap to pull at her neck. She freed herself and let Caz take the binoculars.

"Where?" Caz said as she scanned the grounds around the house, then, "Oh, wow!"

She passed the binoculars to the others in turn and each saw the same thing: two boys, about their age, wearing shorts and T-shirts. They carried something rolled up in an old carpet.

"There's someone trapped in the attic, too," Em said. "But I can't tell who it is because of light reflecting on the glass."

"Do you think it's Uncle Rosko?" Poppy asked.

"What about Tim?" Caz asked. No one voiced the unpleasant possibility they were each thinking about what could be rolled inside the carpet the boys were carrying.

"I bet they solved the Mystery of the Manor," Sally said, putting a more pleasant spin on things. "Perhaps they found the lost treasure."

There were many tales about the manor house, but the most intriguing — and the real mystery of Malprentice Manor — was the one that told of an enormous horde of treasure buried somewhere on the grounds. With its location lost for centuries, the treasure had never been found.

"But who are those boys?" Poppy asked. "This doesn't make sense."

"They're not from round here." Em shrugged, feeling a little helpless. "What should we do?"

"I say we investigate!" declared Sally. "We'll rescue Uncle Rosko and bring these killers to justice."

"Perhaps we can solve the Mystery of the Manor while doing so," Poppy said.

"Shouldn't we just call the police?" Em asked.

Caz snorted her derision. "When have they ever taken notice of us? We reported those UFOs last year and they had the cheek to say we were wasting police time."

"And it was the same when we called about the invisible man," added Poppy.

"And the spies trying to hack Dad's computer!" Sally added. "Although that actually proved to be a virus we accidentally downloaded while trying to find free software."

Em sighed. "You're right. If this murder is going to get solved it's down to us to do it." She lifted the binoculars to her eyes again. "They're taking the carpet into the old stables."

"Then that's the place to start," Caz said and grabbed the backpack they'd brought with them. "We'll head through the woods, go straight over to the stables and look for clues."

"Does anyone have a camera?" Sally asked. "We'll need to photograph the evidence."

Poppy held up a battered-looking camera she'd rescued from the bin when her dad upgraded to a better one last year. "What about plastic bags and cotton buds? On TV they're always dabbing at things with cotton buds."

"We're detectives, not forensic scientists," Caz said.

"Actually, I'd rather like to be a scientist," Em said and Poppy nodded her agreement.

"Okay, me and Sally will be the detectives," said Caz.

"Can we try not to get caught this time?" Em asked. "The last thing we need is the old woman calling the police on us!"

"Yeah," said Sally. "Sergeant Varma was really annoyed when that drowned body in the duck pond turned out to be a plastic bag of rubbish."

"Never mind that," Poppy said. "We can't waste any more time. Let's go."

"Just a minute." Caz opened the backpack and began to gather other items from around the tree house — a box of matches, a battery-powered torch, a screwdriver, a small ball of string, a roll of sticky tape and a notebook. She dropped the things on top of the food and water they'd put in it earlier.

"Ready," Caz said and let down the rope ladder. She swung her feet over the edge ready to climb to the ground.

"Stop!" Em said. "We can't do it. Mum said this is the furthest we're allowed to go for the rest of the week."

The quads became instantly deflated, their chance to become detectives defeated by the punishment they'd been given. Sally spread her arms in exasperation and faced each of the others in turn but unable to think of anything to say.

She grabbed the binoculars again and observed the scene across the valley for a few seconds. "Those boys have left the body in the stables."

"Well I say we investigate anyway," Caz said. "Murder and kidnapping are dreadful crimes and we can't let them get away with it."

"And we have to help Uncle Rosko!" Em yelled.

"What a dilemma!" Poppy cried out, her fists clenching in frustration. "Do we do what Mum said or do we investigate the murder?"

"Look at it this way," Sally said. "Whatever extra punishment Mum gives us, she won't kill us. But someone has been killed over there."

She quickly glanced around at the others. "All right, let's have a vote. Those in favour..."

Everyone's hands shot up before Sally could finish speaking. Caz grinned and started climbing down the rope ladder. Sally, Em and Poppy quickly followed.

Before they clambered over the fence onto Malprentice land, they looked back towards their house.

"I don't want to go, but I think we have to," Poppy said quite plainly. "We must think of the greater good!"

Her words firmed their resolve and they almost leapt over the fence in their eagerness to investigate the crime.

CHAPTER FIVE

The Old Carpet

The four girls dashed across the field towards the Forest of Doom, desperate not to be out in the open any longer than necessary. The pack pounded against Caz's back and the long grass whipped around their ankles.

They clambered over the second fence with only the faintest hint of trepidation and were soon making their way through the half-light beneath the trees. They walked quickly but carefully so they didn't trip on hidden roots.

"We'll be in for it when Mum finds out," Em said with a slightly regretful pout on her lips.

"Maybe we can solve the murder and get back before she even realises we're gone." Poppy's optimism made them all smile.

"Maybe that won't matter," Sally said and grinned wider. "If we solve it we'll become heroes."

"Maybe there'll be a reward," Caz suggested. "What should we spend it on?"

"How can you think about spending money we don't have?" Em was a little annoyed. "It's a waste of thinking time."

"I agree," said Poppy. "We shouldn't get ahead of ourselves. Besides, we're not doing this for a reward, we're doing it because it's the right thing to do."

She stuck out her hand and the other three placed theirs on top in a strong show of solidarity. Whatever their small differences and however their discussions might go, they always regarded themselves as a team.

As they trudged along, Em broke the silence. "Do we have a plan? Do we just gather evidence to give to the police?"

"We should find those boys and make a citizens' arrest," Sally declared.

"They just killed someone!" Poppy exclaimed. "They might kill us, too."

"There's only two of them," Caz sneered. "The four of us can easily deal with two boys."

"It sounds dangerous to me," Em gulped.

Sally stopped and turned to the others, striking a dramatic pose as she did so. "We can't let fear stand in our way when we're on the path to justice!"

"Yeah!" the other three shouted as one. A crow called out as if disagreeing with them but they ignored it and marched off again. Everyone knew that crows were smart, but that didn't mean they knew everything.

Caz caught up with Sally and whispered. "You read that justice thing somewhere, right?"

Sally shrugged. "Actually, I do so much reading I'm not really sure."

Caz nudged her in a friendly way and the two put

an arm around each other's shoulders and walked along that way until they came to the bank of the stream that ran down the centre of the valley in which the woods were located.

They paused and looked ahead of them. Although they were lower down than Lookout Point, they could see through a small break in the trees and up the hill at the other side of the valley. The manor house was clearly visible and, using the binoculars, they checked it out in more detail once again.

"There's no sign of anyone," Em said after her turn. "But we can't see the stables from down here. They're further back over the rise."

"Well, they've already dealt with the body," Caz remarked. "They're probably doing something else just as nasty."

"At least that means we can investigate the carpet in the stables without being disturbed," Sally added.

"Let's hope it's as easy as that," Poppy said with a wry look.

They slid down the bank to the edge of the water and crossed Smudgin Beck by a series of flat stepping-stones that stood above the surface of the water by a few centimetres. During wetter weather, when the flow of the stream was greater, the water rose over the stones and it was impossible for a person to cross without their feet getting soaked.

A little further downstream were the remains of the dam they'd built the previous year. It had lasted for the whole summer holidays and was only washed away when torrential rain had lashed the area at the end of September. Although they had discussed rebuilding it on a number of occasions, this wasn't the time to do so.

They helped each other clamber up the far bank,

then ascended the slope on the Manor side of the valley, working through the trees in almost complete silence. The sense of urgency weighed upon them and they didn't want waste any time with needless chat.

The slope of the valley side soon became more gentle and they reached the far side of the Forest of Doom. However, although the trees ended, this side of the woods were bordered by a wild hedge of hawthorn and brambles and it stood between them and their objective. It presented a seemingly impenetrable barrier to the four girls. But they turned to their right and trotted along the space between the trees and the hedge with Sally in the lead.

"Oh, no!" she declared with some dismay as she came to a halt. "Look!"

"The gap in the hedge has gone!" exclaimed Em. "It's like it was never here."

"It isn't that long since we were last here," said Caz.

"We haven't been to the Manor through here since Easter," Sally said.

"And you know what brambles are like," Em added.

"Yeah," Poppy said. "They're delicious and Mum makes great pies with them."

Em put her hands on her hips. "I meant that they grow so fast it's not surprising the hole has gone."

"Oh, of course," Poppy whispered, a little red in the face.

"We don't have any shears to cut through the new growth," Sally fumed. "Or the time to go back for them."

"Perhaps there's another gap further along," Caz suggested.

"I'm sure there will be," Poppy said. "We can't stop now." She immediately set off to look, unusually eager to take the lead.

Unfortunately, she was looking so intently at the hedge for a way through that she didn't watch where she put her feet and tripped over an exposed root. She sprawled headlong into a patch of bracken.

The others rushed over, picked her up and brushed her down. She was more embarrassed than hurt and she smiled a little self-consciously.

"I'm such a fool," she said. "I can never do anything right."

"What a load of baloney!" Sally said, using one of Uncle Rosko's regular sayings. "You're as good as anyone else in the world."

"Definitely!" added Caz. "All you did was trip up. It was an accident."

Em crouched down to look at the root. "Which might turn out to be a very happy one."

"What do you mean?" Poppy asked and Em pointed at the ground.

At the base of the hedge, between two of the hawthorns, an animal had scraped out a small gap, which is why the root was exposed.

"What could have done that, Em?" Caz asked.

"A fox or a badger, probably," she replied. "Judging by the size of it."

"Pity it isn't bigger," Sally said. "Then we could crawl through."

"So let's make it bigger," Poppy said. "We just need to find a couple of sticks to dig with."

"Great idea." Sally grinned and high-fived with Poppy.

They spread out and searched around the base of

the trees for fallen branches and it didn't take long before they had a couple that were long enough to dig with and had the strength not to break.

They dug in pairs, taking turns, and soon had the hollow scraped out with plenty of depth for them to squeeze under the hedge.

Caz went first and wriggled through on her back to avoid the needle-like thorns that stuck out from every branch and twig in the hedge. In spite of the care she took, pulling her stomach in to make herself thinner, she caught her arm on one of the thorns. Although it only gave her a light scratch it still stung, but that was to be expected. Hardly a summer day went by without the four of them winding up with minor scrapes and scratches. Such things were all part of their adventures and usually looked far worse than they actually were.

Once Caz was through, Sally pushed the backpack after her then followed through herself, allowing Caz to help by pulling on her arms.

When all four of them had squeezed through, they looked at one another and burst into laughter — they were filthy and brushed each other down as best they could but couldn't get rid of all the dirt.

"Bringing people to justice is dirty business," Poppy said and they all laughed again, though they quickly became serious once more as they remembered what they were doing.

"Come on, we need to hurry," Em said. "Let's head straight to the stables."

Unfortunately, an unexpected crash startled them and they dropped to the ground, pressing themselves flat into the long grass that covered the ground at this side of the hedge. They were out of sight of anyone in the grounds, but if someone looked out of the upper windows of the manor they'd be spotted now they were on this side of the hedge.

"What was that?" Em hissed.

"Sounded like some kind of death machine to me," Caz replied.

"Oh, yeah," said Sally. "Like two kids are going to have a death machine."

"Maybe they just dropped some pots and pans?" Poppy suggested.

"That sounded like an awful lot of pans." Caz frowned. "Come on."

They moved to the right and worked their way around the bottom of the slope that led up to the manor house. They'd sneaked in here on a number of occasions and knew that the best way to approach the house was to circle around to the south and come up behind the old stables. The hill was a little steeper at that point and offered more cover to hide their approach.

There was no way into the stables at the back, but the dilapidated wall had a few missing bricks and the girls spied through the holes.

"I can see the rolled-up carpet," Poppy said, her eyes close to one of the gaps. "And it stinks like crazy in there."

"Decomposition," Em said, as if that explained everything. Then she added, "Dead things rot."

"Yeah." Caz nodded. "Remember that mouse behind the fridge."

"Ugh! Gross!" Poppy grimaced and shuddered at the thought.

"Come on," Sally urged. "We don't have time to waste."

They made their way along the back wall and

stopped at the corner to check for any sign the two boys were around.

"Is it me," Poppy whispered, "Or does it seem a lot quieter than usual?"

"And creepier," Em added.

"That's a good thing, right Sally?" Caz asked.

"Well, it probably means that those two kids aren't nearby," Sally replied. "So we're safe for now."

"Just a minute," Em said before anyone had a chance to move. "What are those two boys doing here?"

"We all saw what they were doing," Caz replied.

"No, I mean that Evil Edith hates kids," Em said. "So why are they even at the Manor?"

"Oh, no!" Poppy exclaimed. "They must have done something to her, too."

Caz shrugged. "Like that's not a good thing?"

"Don't be silly," Poppy snapped. "It means that three people are missing — Uncle Rosko, Tim Redfern and now Evil Edith."

"And one of them has been murdered!" Sally almost growled out the words.

"But who?" Em whispered, her voice cracking, her hand shooting to her mouth.

"That's what we've got to find out." Sally beckoned them to follow with a jerk of her head.

She led the way around the corner, along the end wall of the building and into the stables through a door just around the front corner. It was a large building with lots of empty stalls that once would have held horses. All they contained now were piles of rotting straw.

The quads each pulled an unpleasant face — there was an awful stench that grew stronger the further into the stables they moved. It didn't take them long to find the rolled up carpet, left at the back of one of the stalls. They were also quick to work out that this was the source of the smell.

Poppy pulled out the old camera and started taking pictures, hoping they'd come out okay in the gloom because the flash didn't work too well.

"Should we unroll it?" Caz asked, looking at Em then Sally, who shrugged then nodded. Then shrugged again. Now they were here, faced with the reality, the excitement of investigating a murder was gone and a shiver went through each of them.

Caz crouched, took a corner and shuddered. The carpet was thick, heavy, rather damp and more than a little icky to the touch. When the others grabbed onto it, too, they pulled in one combined tug to unroll it. All four hurried out of the stall, holding their noses and retching a little — the smell had grown suddenly much worse.

They cautiously peered over the low separating wall from the next stall and gasped.

"Oh, no!" exclaimed Em.

"It's not Evil Edith!" added Caz.

"It's a poor fox," Poppy said and sniffed.

"Those boys killed a fox!" Sally fumed.

"Why would they do that?" Em asked. "Foxes are cute, but Evil Edith is..."

"Evil!" Sally said. "Just like those boys. Get as many pictures as you can, Poppy; we'll report them for animal cruelty."

But as Poppy started taking pictures, Em put her hand over her mouth and dashed for the door. Unfortunately, she didn't make it very far before she threw up on the broken surface of the stable's floor.

When she finished she wiped her mouth on a handkerchief from her pocket and was about to turn back to the others when movement at the door caught her eye. She stared in shock.

"Sally. Caz. Poppy." Em backed away from the doorway. "You need to come here, now."

The other three poked their heads around the end of the stall then rushed over to Em's side.

Silhouetted in the doorway were the two boys they saw carrying the carpet earlier, the taller of the two held a menacing length of tree branch like a club and tapped it against the palm of his other hand in a threatening manner.

CHAPTER SIX

The Fox in the Stable

"You're in trouble for trespassing, you are," the taller boy said. He looked to be twelve, two years older than the quads. "You shouldn't be here."

Em stepped forward and glared up into his face with almost a snarl on her own. "We're investigating a murder."

"Murder?!" The smaller boy looked suddenly scared. "Do you know anything about a murder, Diz?" He was the same age as the girls and clearly under the influence of the older boy, who he looked up at, open mouthed .

"Take no notice, Conker," Diz said. "The little liar's making it up."

"I am not a liar!" Em yelled, her voice becoming a little shrill. "We've just seen the poor fox you murdered and we're going to tell the police and the RSPCA."

"But... But..." Conker stammered, his chubby face

becoming flushed. He twisted the bottom of his grubby T-shirt in his nervous fingers.

"Now just you wait..." Diz began to say, but Em wouldn't let him finish.

"You can't deny it," she said. "We've seen the evidence."

"Yeah," added Caz. "We saw you carrying the body in a rolled up carpet."

"That's right," Sally said and put her hands on her hips.

"If you confess, the police might go easy on you," Poppy suggested.

"We're not confessing to anything," Diz replied, his anger rising with each passing moment.

Em moved even closer, completely outraged by what had befallen the unfortunate fox. "You're going to pay for what you did."

Diz clenched the fist of his free hand and raised the branch as if he was going to hit Em with it. She raised her arms to protect herself, but Diz thought better of it and simply pushed her backwards.

Unfortunately, her feet caught on the uneven floor and she went sprawling backwards, hitting her head on the ground before her sisters could grab her.

"Ow!" she yelled.

Sally and Poppy immediately dashed to her side but Caz flew over to Diz and punched him smack in the middle of his face. He dropped his makeshift club and staggered back as blood began to flow from his nose.

"You hit me!" Diz yelled. "You hit me!"

"Maybe we should go," Conker said and pulled at Diz's arm.

But Diz shrugged him off and reached down for his club. "We're not leaving until I finish this."

"Oh, yeah?" Caz said. "You want me to punch you again?"

"Punch this, you little witch!" Diz raised the club above his head in both hands and Caz gulped.

"Stop that!" a deep, angry voice bellowed from outside. "What the heck is happening?" The owner of the voice stepped through the stable doorway and the quads instantly realised it was Grisly Gus. Their eyes widened — what could this mean?

Diz hid the club behind his back and spoke nervously. "She attacked me," he said and pointed to Caz with his free hand. "For no reason." With the back of his hand he wiped at the blood still oozing from his nose, which he then held out to show the big man. "See!"

Gus raised an eyebrow and turned a fierce, questioning gaze upon the smaller boy, Conker, who looked as if he was about to run away or cry. Maybe both.

"Well?" Gus asked.

Too afraid to speak, Conker simply shook his head very slightly and Diz glared at him.

"Get out! Both of you."

Diz and Conker stood their ground for only half a second before they abruptly turned and headed away. Diz pushed at Conker and hissed something nasty at him that no one else could hear. Gus turned back to face the girls.

"What on Earth are you doing in here after what happened in the woods?" he growled. "You know very well this is private property."

"We..." Em started to speak but her courage fizzled out. Poppy stared at her feet but Caz, fired up by her encounter with Diz, was about to burst with rage.

However, Sally stepped forward as self-appointed spokesperson. "Actually, we're investigating the murder of a fox."

"What?!" Gus was genuinely surprised. "You can't murder a fox."

"Unlawfully killed, then," Caz piped up.

"Those horrible boys rolled the body into an old carpet and put it in here," Sally said. "We have pictures as evidence."

"So," Gus said, a smirk on his face. "We have four little Miss Marples, do we?"

"Who?" Caz asked and looked at the others.

"She was a lady detective," Poppy answered. "In some of Agatha Christie's books."

"Yeah, what she said," Gus added, then frowned. "But whatever you think you've found, that fox wasn't murdered."

"Oh, really?" Em said, finding her voice again.

Gus sighed and folded his big arms, his muscles bulging under his light shirt. Poppy gulped and Sally nudged her.

"That fox got into a disused cellar," Gus said. "Then couldn't get out. We only found the poor thing when we tracked down an awful smell. The boys were acting stupid so I made them deal with it."

"Oh," Em said and all the girls looked at the ground a little embarrassed. "Are you going to call the police on us?"

"I don't have the time to bother with that," Gus replied. "But now you're finished with the crime scene I'll give you two minutes to get off the premises or else."

"You'll report us?" Em quailed.

"No, I'll have me some fresh kids for tomorrow's

breakfast!"

The quads looked at each other for the shortest of moments then all four bolted out of the stable door and started running across the courtyard. When they heard Gus's wicked laugh behind them they ran even faster.

The most direct path back to the woods took them across the large drive that swept in front of Malprentice Manor. Their combined feet crunched on the gravel in a staccato rhythm that was abruptly broken when Caz slid to a halt and gouged a shallow trough in the immaculately kept surface.

She looked back the way they'd came but saw no sign of Grisly Gus. "Come on," she said and dashed around the corner of the main house furthest from the stables. The others hesitated a moment but quickly followed her without question, then all four ducked behind a hedge that ran along the side of the house.

"Do you want to get us into more trouble?" Poppy whispered. She glanced around nervously.

"We came to investigate," Caz replied. "So that's what we're going to do."

"What?" Em asked, puzzled.

"You said you saw someone in the attic," Sally replied, catching onto Caz's reasoning. "And we know there are at least two missing people."

"That's right." Caz nodded. "There might not be a murder, but we still have a case to solve."

"And rescue whoever's in the attic," Em added, her expression changing to one of determination.

"It must be Tim and Uncle Rosko," Poppy said. "We can't leave them there."

"I agree," Sally said. "But how can we do anything with Grisly Gus hanging around?"

CHAPTER SEVEN

Searching the Manor

"We need a plan" Em said a little frantically. "We can't leave them trapped in the attic — Gus will probably eat Tim for tomorrow's breakfast."

Each of the other girls nodded their agreement but for the moment were lost for an answer until Poppy suddenly brightened then immediately changed her mind.

"What?" Caz asked.

"I thought I had an idea, but it wouldn't work." Poppy sighed and slumped against the side wall of the house.

"We can't stay here forever," Sally said. "Caz, you keep a lookout while we think of a plan."

Caz nodded then moved to the corner to look around it. There was nothing to see, but she settled into a squat to make herself comfortable. They were well hidden between the house and the hedge but it was best to be certain.

"Okay," Sally said. "Think hard."

They all fell into silent thought and the sounds of the countryside birds added to the gentle murmur of the wind through the trees. A person could almost imagine there were no problems in the world it was so beautifully peaceful.

But the quiet lasted for all of two minutes before it was broken by the sudden rumbling of Poppy's belly, which caused all four of them to burst out laughing.

"Shh...!" Sally hissed, the first to recover. "We don't want to get caught here."

"I'm starving," Poppy said. "All this excitement makes me hungry."

"We should all have something to eat," Sally suggested. "Did anyone bring a knife to spread the peanut butter and jam?" The others shook their heads — no one had thought of that.

"There's a screwdriver in the bag," Caz suggested.

"We can't use that," Em responded. "It will take forever."

"So why don't we just use our fingers?" Caz asked.

"Because they're mucky from the digging," Em replied.

"Well, Gran always says that a bit of muck never hurt anyone," Caz said and shrugged. Gran always had something to say about everything, even if some of it was downright nonsense.

"Don't forget," Poppy said. "We've all touched Evil Edith's manky carpet."

"Yuck!" exclaimed Em and the others pulled disgusted faces.

"We'll just have to wait until we can wash our hands," Sally said. "Evil Edith's germs would probably kill an elephant."

Poppy's stomach rumbled again and she sighed.

"What do you reckon Grisly Gus likes to eat when he's not having kids for breakfast?" Em asked.

"Jam sandwiches," Caz replied. "With jam made from snot." Everyone giggled.

"Scones with rabbit poo instead of raisins," suggested Sally.

"Slugs on Toast," Poppy said and the thought held her hunger at bay.

"Beetle Bogey-non," said Em. "When he invites people for tea." The thought of a group of adults eating such a meal set everyone laughing again, though Caz still kept watch throughout.

"Something's happening," she abruptly hissed and everyone fell silent. They could hear the faint sound of a car engine.

"Who is it?" Sally asked.

"I don't know," Caz replied. "I can't see anything... Oh, wait."

A very old but rather splendid car came around the far corner, between the house and the stables, then parked in front of the main doors.

"It's Gus in Evil Edith's posh car," Caz informed the others in a whisper. "And now she's come out of the house."

The old woman marched up to the vehicle and stood beside it for a moment until Gus jumped out and held the rear door open for her.

"So she hasn't been captured like the others," Poppy said.

"So why are those boys hanging around?" Em wondered aloud.

"They could be slaves," Caz suggested, then immediately shrunk back into the shadows.

The car passed close to where the group were hiding and they were lucky not to be seen. It picked up a little speed as it travelled down the slope of the drive towards the main road.

"Excellent!" Caz said. "Neither of them can stop us if they're both gone."

"Operation rescue is on!" Sally declared.

They all rose, but couldn't go above a stoop because of the hedge. They scooted along as Sally led them towards the back of the property.

The cover of the hedge ended about halfway down the side of the house and they came to an abrupt but silent stop when they spotted a gardener pottering around a vegetable patch. Thankfully, he had his back to them so they continued on their way.

Suddenly, he turned around and Em gasped quietly, sure that he'd spot them. But he was in the middle of cleaning his glasses on an old hankie and couldn't see the four of them now he wasn't wearing them. They barely breathed as they crept along but were soon around the corner, behind the house and out of his sight. They took in the rear of the manor.

"Look!" Poppy whispered and pointed. A little window had been left open a few feet above their heads, small enough that an adult couldn't get through but just large enough for the girls, they hoped.

"We need something to stand on," Caz said and looked around for something suitable. She immediately raced over to a huge earthenware plant pot that looked like it was made for the gardens of giants. Thankfully, it was empty, apart from some dead leaves, so Caz tried to lift it but it was way too heavy to do so on her own.

The other three came over and with a coordinated effort they lifted the cumbersome pot off the ground, manoeuvred it over to a position beneath the window then turned it upside down.

"Me first," Caz said and clambered onto the base of the upturned pot, which brought the window into easy reach. She gave the backpack to one of the others, squeezed her way through the opening then dropped into the room at the other side. She landed on a pile of dust sheets that lived up to their name and clouds of dust billowed into the air, which made her cough and sneeze.

Caz caught the bag as it came through the window then each of the other sisters came through in turn. For a few moments they stood in silence amid the dust motes that danced in the air.

The room looked like it might have once been a study of some kind. A desk and chairs were covered with more sheets, but the bookcases that lined the walls stood empty and uncovered. When a person thought about Edith Malprentice, it was hard to imagine what kind of books might once have rested on these shelves.

Sally led the way across the room to the door and they left a trail of footprints in the floor's thick covering of dust. The door creaked as she opened it but there was no suggestion that anyone had heard the noise.

"This place is creepy," said Em, her voice barely louder than a whisper.

"What do you expect?" Sally said. "Evil Edith lives here."

They slunk out of the room and along the corridor outside. A loud ticking came from a grandfather clock set into a small niche and they couldn't help but feel that it counted down the seconds until Gus and Edith returned.

"We need to find the stairs to the attic," Sally said as they hurried past the large, old timepiece.

The corridor turned a corner and came to a dead end, though there was an open door on the left that led to another room. Again, they entered with care and made their way through it, but halfway across the large space they each stopped and looked around.

The furniture consisted mainly of high backed chairs spread about almost randomly, though in groups of two or three and each group accompanied by a low table. But it was the wall decorations that had halted them in their tracks — the mounted heads of numerous wild animals, their lifeless expressions both sad and scary at the same time.

"Now this room is really creepy," Em said. "Why would anyone do such a dreadful thing?"

"Because they think it's sport," Poppy said and sniffed back a tear.

Caz clenched her fists and almost snarled. "It's only a sport if both sides are evenly matched."

"I hate this as much as all of you," Sally said. "But

we have a mission to complete before Gus and Edith come back."

"Yeah," Caz agreed. "We don't want her prisoners to end up like these poor creatures."

"Which way?" Poppy asked.

There were four doors in addition to the one through which they'd entered the room and Sally shrugged. Then she pointed to the one on their left and moved in that direction. "It's as good as any, I suppose."

As they left the room, Em gave a shudder and shut the door quickly behind them. They were in another corridor but ignored the doors leading off it, choosing to walk down to the end where they turned a corner to the right. A few metres further along the corridor turned right again and this section ended in another door.

This led them back into the room with the awful animal heads.

They took the next door along and this led into a small room with a spiral staircase that headed upwards, so they dashed up it and found themselves in a small bathroom with no other exit.

"Come on, we'll have to go back," Sally said and moved towards the staircase.

"Actually, I need to pee," Caz whispered, as if there was someone else around to hear her.

"Me, too," Poppy said.

"Okay," said Sally. "But don't flush or someone might hear."

So they all took it in turns to use the facilities and wash their hands before heading back down the spiral staircase. Which meant they were back in the creepy animal-head room for a third time with only one more door to choose from.

This door opened smoothly and silently, much to the girls' relief, but they found themselves in the main hall of the manor, which wasn't the ideal place to be. But at least there were stairs leading upward and they would take them nearer their goal of finding the attic.

Then right out of the blue there was a dreadful crashing sound that made them jump and grab each other for a second before racing up the stairs and along another corridor to the right. Although they had no idea where the sound had actually come from, it was better to move towards their objective than away from it.

At the end of this passageway, they slipped through an open door into a small room and took a moment to calm down again. Their hearts raced and their lungs drew in huge breaths.

Poppy wandered over to the window and peered through it carefully. "Come and look," she said after a moment.

The others crowded around the sides of the window and stared at the scene below. A man stood by a tractor that had crashed into a tree and the vehicle now steamed from the impact's damage. He scratched his head for a moment then spoke into a mobile phone.

"Can you hear what he's saying?" asked Caz.

"No," Sally replied. "But at least we know what caused that crashing sound. Come on."

She led them out of the room and along the corridor again, passing the top of the stairs before heading in the opposite direction. They still had two floors to go up before they reached the attic level.

At the end of the corridor was a plain wooden door that opened onto a narrow staircase that led upwards again. The old wood smelled of ancient varnish.

"This smell reminds me of boring old school trips to stately homes," Caz said.

"I like those places," Poppy responded with a little indignation. "Learning how people lived in the past."

"They only teach you how the rich people lived," Caz said. "The homes of the poor are never preserved and open to the public."

"Let's not get into that, now," Sally urged. "We need to find where the prisoners are being held."

"Besides," Poppy added. "We shouldn't hate people just because they're rich. I'm sure we'd all love to be rich one day."

Caz opened her mouth to reply again but Sally clamped her hand over it and said, "Hush!"

They froze in position on the stairs and listened. Quite distinctly they could hear the sound of footsteps coming from the floor below, drawing nearer. The girls looked at each other nervously, expecting to get caught at any moment.

The footsteps came to a stop, followed by the sound of door opening and someone rummaging in what might have been a cupboard or closet of some kind. Then the door closed and the footsteps made their way back from where they'd come, fading completely after a few moments. The quads breathed a sigh of relief and continued upwards.

The corridor they found themselves in was narrow with lots of doors leading off. No carpet covered the floor and the walls were decorated in a plain beige colour with no pictures for decoration.

"This is where the servants used to live," Poppy announced.

"How do you know?" Caz asked.

"Because all big houses put their servants on the upper floors. Don't you learn anything on our school trips?"

Caz shrugged. "I don't see why people need servants anyway."

Poppy put her arm around Caz's shoulders in a friendly, sisterly manner. "At least there are no servants here."

"Well, there's Gus, the butler," Em said.

"Him? A butler?" Sally was astonished. "Grisly Gus looks more like a bodyguard."

"Maybe he's good at multi-tasking," Poppy said and grinned.

"Nah, he'd need brains for that." Caz laughed at her own joke and the others joined in.

Poppy's stomach rumbled again.

"Okay," Sally said. "Let's stop and have something to eat. But let's be quick about it."

"You sound just like Mum," Caz said as she wriggled out of the bag's straps and began to open it.

"Don't say that, Caz," Poppy grinned. "She might ground you for a week."

Sally sighed but smiled along with the others and they all sat on the floor. The two jars were opened — jam and peanut butter — then each of them took a slice of bread and used their fingers to smear both spreads onto them. They licked their fingers and munched on the sandwiches in double-quick time. They finished it all off with a drink from one of the bottles of water.

Em wiped her fingers onto her shorts then spoke in a very posh voice. "I say, I never would have thought we'd have the pleasure of eating at the manor."

Sally and Poppy grinned, but Caz laughed hard

while taking a drink of water and some of it came out of her nose, which then made her cough and laugh at the same time. Eventually, Sally had to slap her on the back to help her recover.

They sat without speaking for a few moments while Caz got her breath back and blew her nose into a hanky. Then they quickly packed things away and set off again.

At the far end of the narrow passage, a small window looked out towards the south-east. It had been left open a little and a cooling breeze came through it along with a sound that chilled their bones. A car crunched the gravel as it arrived at the house and came to a halt with a short skid. The doors opened and closed and the girls could just make out the voices of the people below.

"Can I get you anything, Madame?" Gus's voice asked.

"No!" Edith's voice snapped back. "I'm going to my room and don't wish to be disturbed until lunch is ready."

Sally looked at the others. "We need to hurry."

Finding the next set of stairs didn't take long — they were just around another corner — and the girls soon reached the top of the house. They were in the attic, which was huge. Half of the space was partitioned into smaller areas, all of which were extremely dusty, and held all kinds of ancient junk from rusty suits of armour to more manky carpets. There was even an old painting of a man dressed in clothes from the nineteenth century.

"Percy Malprentice," Poppy read off the inscription at the bottom of the frame.

"He doesn't look a bit like Evil Edith," Em said.

"Maybe he's from a more pleasant line of the family," Sally suggested.

"Is that why the picture's in the attic?" Caz asked. "Because it's too nice for Evil Edith?"

"Maybe." Poppy looked closely. "I like it."

They continued moving through the attic storage areas until they'd gone as far as they could. In the middle of a rough brick wall was an old wooden door.

"Do you think Uncle Rosko's in there?" Poppy asked.

"And Tim." Caz said.

"They've got to be," Em replied. "There's nowhere else they can be."

Sally twisted the door handle both ways then did so a second time just to be sure. "It's locked."

"They wouldn't be prisoners if it wasn't," Poppy pointed out.

Sally ignored the remark and bent to look through the keyhole. "There's a pencil in here!" she exclaimed.

"And a piece of newspaper on the floor," Caz added, picking it up.

Em snapped her fingers. "I bet they pushed the key out of the lock to try and escape."

"So why is the door still locked?" Caz asked.

"Maybe it didn't land on the newspaper." Poppy got on all fours to search the floor around the base of the door. "I can't see it."

"What about that gap between the floorboards?" Sally asked, so Poppy put her eye to the gap but it was too dark to see anything.

"Torch, please." Poppy held out her hand and Caz took the torch from her bag then handed it over. Poppy shone the light down the gap and immediately saw something.

"It's there!" she shouted and stood up. "We just need something to prise up the board."

Caz grinned and immediately dashed over to one of the suits of armour that was propped against a post that held up the roof. Lying at the feet of the armour was an old sword, tarnished and rusty with age. She picked it up and tried to hold it aloft triumphantly, but it was heavier than she imagined and it fell to the floor with a clatter.

"Caz!" Sally hissed. "Be quiet!"

Caz shrugged, picked up the sword in both hands and brought it over to the others. She placed it into the gap between the boards and levered the board up quite easily, though the sword itself was left with a slightly bent tip. Caz put it to one side; quietly this time.

Two objects glinted in the space where the floorboard had been — a key and a small coin that had a strange look to it. Poppy crouched down and grabbed the coin, completely ignoring the key.

"It's an old threepenny bit," she said and showed the others. The odd little coin had twelve sides and a portcullis design on the side that faced upwards.

"It can't be a real coin," Caz said.

"It was real before the 1970s," Poppy said. "Before we got proper money." She put the coin in her pocket and they all looked back at the hole again.

Sally bent down to pick up the key and held it aloft. But just as she was about to put it into the lock Diz and Conker appeared at the other end of the attic.

"Oy!" Diz shouted. "You shouldn't be up here. And don't open that door."

Sally put her hands on her hips and glared at the taller boy. "Why should we take any notice of you?"

"You'll be sorry if you do." Diz smirked.

"It's true," Conker added. "He's not lying."

Caz clenched her fists and stepped forward but Poppy grabbed her arm to stop her.

"There's no need for violence," she said. "We should all be friends."

"With them?" Caz asked incredulously. "You've got to be joking."

"Hey!" Conker said. "There's nothing wrong with us."

"But there'll be plenty wrong with you if you open that door," Diz said. "You'll die of a dreadful disease."

Sally stepped forward and the other girls moved with her. "We know what's behind that door," she said. "That's why we're here."

Diz smacked his fist into the palm of his other hand. "Perhaps we ought to teach you a lesson."

The girls looked at each other then as one shouted, "Get 'em!"

As they dashed forward, the two boys stared with bulging eyes for a moment, then thought better of their threat and ran away. But when Diz reached the top of the stairs he paused long enough to say something.

"I'm going to tell Granny that you're trespassing," he said. He and Conker then disappeared down the stairs. The girls stopped their chase and laughed in triumph.

"Did you hear what they said?" Em asked, a little shocked. "Evil Edith must be their grandmother!"

"No wonder they're so horrible," added Poppy.

"We don't have much time if they've gone to tell on us," Caz pointed out.

They dashed back to the locked door and Sally used the key immediately. But as they pushed it open, a girl in white rushed out with a scream. She had a hockey stick grasped in her hands and as she dashed forward she raised it above her head ready to strike.

CHAPTER EIGHT

The Old Library

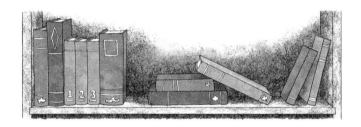

The hockey stick came down like an executioner's axe, but Sally's reactions were like lightning and the makeshift weapon only swiped through empty air as she leaped out of the way. The other three sisters stood behind where Sally had just been and stared in shock for almost half a second.

"Get her!" Caz yelled and she immediately jumped at the girl, with Poppy and Em following her immediately. The three of them made a grab for her arms but she was just as fast as Sally and she squirmed out from under their hands. The three sisters nearly fell over each other as they scrambled to change direction.

The strange girl ducked, rolled on the floor and came up with the hockey stick ready for another attack and immediately made her move. She swept it around at head level and almost caught Poppy a blow on the temple but Em dragged her out of the way and it missed by a few millimetres.

Sally was on her feet again and joined her sisters facing this wild creature that seemingly resembled a girl. The latter swung the hockey stick back in a return stroke and the quads dodged again. But as the stick reached the end of its swing it created an opening.

"Now!" yelled Caz and the sisters leapt forward in unison before the girl had the chance to bring the weapon around a third time.

She wasn't without further tricks, though, and tried to elbow Caz in the face. But it seemed that Caz read the girl's mind, ducked under her arm and grabbed her around the waist in a tackle that would have impressed the coach of the school rugby team.

The girl was knocked to the floor with Caz on top of her, which forced the breath from her lungs and the hockey stick from her hands. Sally and Em pinned her legs down and Sally grabbed her arms. She was helpless and couldn't move.

"Hey!" the girl exclaimed. "What the heck do you

think you're playing at?"

Sally was genuinely astonished. "Us?! You were the one who attacked first. If I hadn't dodged, my head would have been split open."

"Look, I'm sorry, okay?" The girl's words didn't match the angry look on her face. "I thought you were my brothers."

"Why didn't you stop when you saw that we weren't?" Caz shouted.

"Because you came for me, Dumbo." She narrowed her eyes. "I had to defend myself."

Sally and Caz looked at each other for a moment then nodded. They relaxed their holds on the girl and let her stand up, although Poppy kicked the hockey stick well out of her reach.

"Wait, are your brothers Diz and Conker?" Em asked.

"You know them?"

"Kind of," Caz replied and grinned.

"Caz punched Diz," Poppy added.

"Well, he deserved it," Caz said.

A strange look passed over the girl's face like she was trying to make up her mind about this piece of news.

"They're pretty horrid," Em said. "Are they the ones who locked you in here?"

"Er... Yeah." the girl said and became thoughtful for a few seconds. "Yeah, that's right. They trapped me up here against my will and I thought I was going to starve to death. Thanks for the rescue." She looked over at the hockey stick. "Sorry for attacking you. My name's Mildred."

The quads relaxed a little and introduced themselves. Then Poppy remembered why they'd come up here. "Hey, what about Uncle Rosko?"

"Oh, yes," Sally said. "Is there anyone else in that room?"

"No," Mildred replied. "Why would there be?"

"Two people are missing," Caz said. "Tim Redfern from our school and Uncle Rosko."

"Well, I haven't seen them," Mildred said with unnecessary indignation. "I've been locked in that place for three days."

"Wow!" Sally said. "I'm glad we were able to save you."

"Maybe you can help us find Uncle Rosko and Tim," Em suggested. "But maybe you should change first?"

Mildred, who was nine, wore light summer pyjamas made from a white cotton material. On her feet were an old pair of trainers that looked ready to fall apart. Her dark, straight hair was unkempt with a greasy texture that matched her poor complexion. Her pale skin was dotted with a number of pink spots.

"I'll be okay," she said. "Besides, I haven't got any other clothes up here."

The quads shrugged in unison, which Mildred found funny and laughed.

"We should form a gang," she said. "What should we call ourselves?"

"Why do we need to be a gang?" Poppy asked. "Can't we just be friends?"

"What about The Fearless Five?" Mildred asked, ignoring Poppy's comment.

"That's not why we're here," Sally replied, sternly. "We saw someone at the window and came on a rescue mission."

"We thought that Grisly Gus had locked someone

away so he could have them for breakfast," Caz added.

Mildred was shocked. "He wouldn't do that, would he?"

"Everyone round here knows about it," Em said. "They say he's been eating kids for years."

"That's stupid!" Mildred shouted. "Granny wouldn't let him do that. Would she?"

"Maybe Evil Edith likes to eat kids, too," Poppy suggested.

"Speaking of her," Sally said. "We should scram before she finds us up here."

The quads started moving towards the stairs that brought them up to the attic and after a moment Mildred followed them. But they'd only covered half the distance when they heard movement on the stairs and the sound of voices.

"We're too late," Em said. "We're going to get caught."

"No," Mildred said. "There's another way down."

She quickly dashed over to a corner of the large attic room and pulled up a trapdoor that had been hidden from view by the junk surrounding it. She immediately started climbing down the ladder below, followed by Sally and Poppy.

"Ooh, an encyclopedia," Em said as she spotted a pile of books next to the trapdoor.

"We don't have time for that," Caz said and urged her through the trapdoor.

Em climbed down reluctantly. "But it's about natural history."

Caz followed her and pulled the trapdoor closed behind her. "If we don't get a move on we'll be history. But there won't be anything natural about it."

Gus, Edith and the two boys entered the attic just

as the trapdoor closed with a loud enough noise to catch their attention.

"Damn!" Gus exclaimed. "They've gone through the trapdoor." He raced back down the stairs he'd just come up. "I'll try to head them off," he shouted.

Edith pointed at Diz and Conker with a gnarled finger. "You two, follow them down the trapdoor and don't let them escape. You're in enough trouble as it is. Whatever happens, we can't let Mildred out."

The two boys looked nervously at each other for a moment then did as their grandmother ordered. Even though they were scared of what the quads might do, Granny was far too fierce to disobey.

Once down the ladder, the group of girls raced off with Mildred in the lead. She seemed to know where she was going so the quads were happy to follow. Unknowingly, she led them towards the stairs Gus was descending and he suddenly appeared in the corridor ahead of them. They immediately stopped their headlong flight and returned the way they came.

"In here!" Mildred shouted and pushed through a side door into a small store room in which shelves were completely filled with crockery of all kinds. But they didn't have time to look closely as Mildred went straight through the door on the opposite wall.

They were now in a small, dimly-lit hallway that smelled of lavender furniture polish and a faint hint of grilled bacon. But smells aside, there was also a worn wooden staircase that led to the floor below. Their footsteps sounded like thunder on the old wood as they raced down, barely keeping from tripping over each other on the precarious, steep steps.

Once at the bottom, Mildred took a twisted route down further corridors and through a couple of small rooms before they found themselves in a huge library room. Mildred shut the door behind them and locked it with a key that had been left in the lock.

She immediately went over to a door at the other end of the room but when she tried it she found it was locked and this time there was no key in the lock.

"Will the key to the other door open it?" Poppy asked.

"Worth a try," Caz replied and dashed over to fetch it.

While she was doing so, Em looked around the room, in awe of the huge number of books that lined the walls. But she looked disappointed as she ran her finger along the surface of a small table. So much dust covered everything that the place can't have been used in decades.

"Oh, no!" Caz exclaimed. "The key doesn't fit. We'll have to go back."

Unfortunately, just at that moment, the handle of the other door rattled and Gus's voice came through it, muffled by the heavy wood. "Open this door, now!"

"We're trapped," Em said. "Perhaps he'll eat all of us."

Sally turned to Mildred. "Is there another way out of here?"

"No," Mildred replied and shook her head. She jumped with fright then stared at the door as Gus thumped hard on the other side.

"What if we unlock the door then grab Grisly Gus and tie him up?" Caz suggested. She instantly knew from the looks on the others' faces that none of them thought it was a good idea. She shrugged. "Ah, well..."

Sally turned to Mildred, who looked decidedly pale and distracted, and clicked her fingers in front of the younger girl's face to get her attention.

"Mildred," she said. "You must know something that can help us."

"I don't think so..." Mildred replied, a little unsure.

"Anything?"

"Well..." Mildred looked at the quads staring faces and almost didn't say anything more. But she spread her hands out and said, "There's supposed to be a secret passage in here, but no one's ever found it."

"How wonderful!" Poppy exclaimed, her face beaming with excitement. "An old library like this is the perfect place for a secret passageway."

"So why haven't I found it?" Mildred was more than a little indignant. "I've looked every time I came here."

"Maybe you just needed help," Em said, trying to placate her.

"Okay, spread out and look for anything that might be a secret switch or lever," Sally said. Mildred glowered at her, but it quickly changed into a forced smile when Sally looked in her direction.

"Just a minute," Caz said. "Gus has gone quiet. I thought he'd have tried breaking the door down."

"The doors are too heavy for that," Mildred said. "He's probably gone to fetch the spare key."

"Oh, no! We don't have much time to find the passageway," Poppy said and the girls started searching frantically.

Two minutes later they still hadn't found anything but Em had stopped searching moments earlier and now stood in the centre of the room, slowly turning around, her eyes scanning all the features on the walls, bookcases and fireplace. It was this last feature that caused her to pause.

She couldn't put her finger on it at first, but after a few additional moments of examination she clapped her hands together and said, "The fireplace isn't symmetrical!"

She rushed over to it and examined two flowers that had been carved into the support columns for the mantelpiece. The one on the left was a beautiful rose while the one on the right was a large daisy. As Em looked closely at the daisy she squealed with delight. "This is it!"

She pushed the centre of the flower and it depressed inward like a button. Something clicked and whirred behind the walls and one of the bookcases swung out. Behind it was a small area with built in seating and cushions.

"A secret reading nook!" Em exclaimed.

"It's not a secret passage," Mildred said disdainfully.

"But at least we can hide in here," Sally said and climbed inside.

Not intended for so many people, the five girls had to pack in tightly and could only just close the bookcase door behind them. They fidgeted in the small space.

"Stop moving and be quiet," Sally ordered. "We're going to get caught if you don't."

They stopped moving and the silence was complete but for the gentle sounds of their breathing. After a minute that seemed like an age, they heard the sound of a key in a lock and a door opening, followed by a number of footsteps.

"They're not here!" Evil Edith said, her voice coming through the bookcase more clearly than the girls would have expected. Gus gave a simple grunt as a reply followed by his heavy footsteps treading across the floor.

A moment later the bookcase swung open — they'd been discovered.

"How did you find us so quickly?" Sally asked.

"Easily." Gus pointed to the floor. Their footprints were clearly visible in the thick dust. The two boys rushed over to see what was behind the bookcase, pushing past the adults to get close.

Diz pointed at the girls and laughed. "You think you're so clever, but you're stupid."

"I think it's cool," Conker said and Diz nudged him hard, but he glared back. "It's a secret room. How is that not cool?"

The boys moved closer in spite of themselves, eager to get a proper look at the small space. The girls were in no rush to leave the reading nook, though, for Evil Edith glared at them over the boys' heads, a fierce expression on her face.

"Well, Mildred, are you pleased with yourself?" she asked at last.

"I don't know what you mean," her granddaughter replied.

Edith folded her arms across her chest to emphasise her annoyance. "I'm sure you do. Did you explain to these girls that you were in isolation because you have the measles and are highly contagious?"

Mildred was about to deny it when she shrugged and spread a wicked grin across her face.

"You're as bad as those two," Sally said and pointed at the boys, who leaned even closer and began to behave in a threatening manner.

"Are we going to die of measles?" Poppy asked, fighting back the urge to cry.

"Of course not," Em replied and reached out a

comforting hand to Poppy. "Mum had us vaccinated when we were young."

"A pity their mother wasn't that considerate," Edith muttered. "Then I wouldn't have to put up with them staying here for the next two weeks."

"Now get out of there," Gus growled. "Before I seal you in for good."

"And once you're out I shall call the police and my solicitor," Edith said. "I imagine your parents will be upset at the prospect of you being thrown in jail."

Before anyone could move, however, the sound of a text message coming through made them all pause. They stared at each other for a few seconds before Sally pulled out the old phone the four girls shared between them. They were only supposed to use it for emergencies, which was all it was really good for because it was such a basic model. They were more than a little surprised when it went off.

"It's Mum," Sally said as she checked the text. "Uncle Rosko's disappearance has been reported to the police and she wants us home immediately."

Caz was the first to react and attempted to push past Mildred, but the other quads also tried their hardest to leave the small nook and immediately got in each other's way. Caz reached out to find something to grab  onto so she could pull herself out and her fingers wrapped around a stone ring set halfway into a slot in the wall by the entrance.

However, instead of giving her a firm grip to heave herself out of the tangle, the ring came free of the slot with the kind of loud click that suggested some kind of mechanism had been tripped. The floor of the small room abruptly opened up and dropped the five girls down a chute.

Trying to save herself, Mildred grabbed onto her brothers' T-shirts, but the sudden action overbalanced the two boys and they tumbled forward into the chute, too.

Before Gus and Edith had the chance to react, all seven children had disappeared into the darkness beneath the manor.

CHAPTER NINE

In the Darkness

The two nasty adults stared at each other in irritated surprise, but it was Edith who recovered first and demanded answers from Gus. "Where on Earth have they gone?!"

"I have no idea," Gus replied. "I thought you understood the layout of the manor inside out — shouldn't you know where it leads?"

"Don't be impertinent! You're my butler and should know your place."

"Yeah, right," Gus grumbled. "Maybe when I get paid for doing it."

"I already told you," Edith said, pointing a thin finger at him. "When we find what we're looking for you'll get your share."

They glared at each other for a moment before Edith looked over the edge of the chute. Gus peered over her shoulder

Although the seven kids had disappeared quickly, the drop of the chute wasn't vertical, but sloped away at an angle, though steep enough that they'd be unable to climb back up.

"I'll get some ropes and follow them," Gus said, but as he turned away the old mechanism creaked for a moment then clicked again. The nook's floor swung back into place and although he rushed back it closed too fast for him to stop it.

"Damn!" Gus tried to open it again but the stone ring Caz had pulled was now missing. He inserted his finger into the slot, but whatever mechanism operated the moving floor it couldn't be triggered that way.

"I don't know how we're going to find them," he said. "Those brats could be anywhere."

"Wherever they are," Edith hissed. "My grandchildren are with them. I don't care about the quads, but my son will never forgive me if anything happens to Mildred and the boys."

"What if they find something they shouldn't?" Gus asked.

"Indeed. You need to discover their whereabouts quickly. None of them must discover what we're doing. Get to it!"

"All right," Gus responded, a little reluctantly.

From the secret nook in the library, the seven youngsters slid a long way from their starting point, well below ground level of the manor. They ended their unexpected journey in an uncomfortable heap as they slid from the end of the chute and across a stone floor. Although the stone had been worn fairly smooth, it was still coarse enough to give each of them an unpleasant scrape on any areas of exposed skin and they yelled out in surprise and pain.

They had no idea where they were because utter darkness enveloped them completely. They quickly became aware of a strange half-scream, half-wail that sounded to the quads as if ghosts and ghouls were nearby.

"Shut up, Conker," Mildred snapped. "You big cry-baby."

The sound ended as Conker choked back his fear and said, "Someone's sat on my head."

Diz laughed. "Just hope I don't fart."

Sally sighed with annoyance then asked, "Do we have a torch?"

"Of course," Caz replied. "I'll get it." She still held the stone ring she'd pulled out of the wall in the nook, so she shoved it into her backpack before groping about inside it and pulling out the torch she put in there earlier. "I hope the batteries will last."

She clicked it on and shone it on the others, who all seemed to be okay, barring minor bumps and scrapes. In spite of their predicament, she grinned and found that Sally, Poppy and Em were smiling, too.

"That was fun," Poppy said, wearing the biggest grin of everyone. "This is turning into an amazing adventure."

However, the three Malprentice kids weren't so happy and each of them scowled as if they'd been told to eat a huge plate of broccoli.

"As cool as this is, we need to get out of here so we can help search for Uncle Rosko," Em said, her expression changed to one of concern. "We still don't know what's happened to him?"

"And we won't until we find him," Sally said. "But you're right, Em, we need to look for a way out."

"What about calling Mum?" Poppy asked.

Sally stared at her hand — she was still holding the phone from when she'd read the text message a few minutes earlier. She laughed and switched it back on. "Oh, no! I can't get a signal."

"It won't be able to penetrate all the rock and earth," Em explained, more for the benefit of the other kids than her sisters.

"I'd better save the battery for later," Sally said. She powered it off completely and put it back into her pocket.

Caz stood up and shone the light around to see the extent of the room they were in. But as she turned to do so, her foot slipped off the edge of the floor they were on and began to fall.

Thankfully, Em saw this, reacted quickly and grabbed the back of Caz's clothes. For a moment it seemed that both of them may go over the edge, but Caz quickly regained her balance and stepped away from the danger.

"Blimey, that was close," Caz said. "Thanks, Em."

"No problemo," Em replied.

"Are we at the edge of a pit?" Sally asked.

Caz shone the torch at the edge she'd nearly fallen over, then at the ground beyond, which was a good six metres below. The injuries she might have sustained if she'd fallen down there didn't bear thinking about.

Exploring further with the torch, Caz quickly discovered that the ground below wasn't a pit but the main floor of the room and they were standing on a circular platform. It was a massive cylinder of rock that stood proud of the ground.

With Caz shining the light about some more, everyone could see that the room was about thirty metres across and must have been carved into the rock of the hillside on which the manor had been built. Three tunnels led out of this chamber, but in order to reach them they needed to get down to the main floor.

Poppy looked over the edge of the platform. "We were really lucky."

"Yeah," Sally agreed. "If we'd slid any further we'd have dropped down there."

"You nearly killed us!" Mildred screamed at Caz. "Give me the torch so I can be leader."

"Like that's going to happen," Caz replied with a sneer. "We have the torch so we're in charge."

Sally stood beside her and agreed. "Yeah. We rescued you, don't forget."

"Even though she didn't need rescuing," Conker piped up.

Mildred glared at him. "Shut it, Conker!" Then she looked at Diz and pointed at Caz. "Get me the torch, Diz." She clearly regarded herself as the boss of the three in spite of being the youngest.

Diz stepped forward and reached for the torch but stopped and blinked when Caz shone it in his eyes.

"You can try if you like," Caz said. "But I'll give you a fat lip to match your bloody nose."

For a very brief moment he weighed up his options then backed away. "Get it yourself if you want it."

Mildred fumed with anger and stepped over to Caz. "Gimme the torch!"

"Get lost!"

"I want that torch," Mildred said and pushed her face right up to Caz's.

Caz passed the torch to Sally without taking her

eyes off those of Mildred. "Not a chance, stinky breath."

"What?!" Mildred was genuinely surprised that Caz didn't back down.

"Your breath smells like a baboon's backside," Caz elaborated.

"Which you'd know because you look like a baboon." Mildred gave her a nasty smirk.

"Better to look like a baboon than a slimy slug."

"A slug? I don't..."

"A slimy slug with stinky, baboon-bum breath." Caz grinned. "Stinky slimy slug!"

Mildred pulled back her arm to punch Caz but never got the chance to strike as Poppy and Em stepped between them, each holding a small bundle in their arms. They'd found six old torches, the kind that burned with a flame when lit.

"Look at these," Poppy said. "We don't need to argue about our torch."

"Where did you find them?" Sally asked.

"They were on the floor near the end of the chute," Em replied.

"Gimme them!" Mildred snapped. She grabbed the three torches from Em who just shrugged and let her have them.

"There's no need to be rude," Poppy said. "There's plenty to go round."

Mildred sneered but looked pleased with herself. She gave one each to Diz and Conker then stared at her own as her expression changed to one of frustration.

"I bet you wish you had some matches," Sally said.

Poppy gave a torch to Sally and another to Em while Caz pulled out the matches and struck one.

"Now this is an adventure!" Caz exclaimed as

Sally's torch flared into life at the first touch of the match's flame. She lit Poppy's torch next but Em shook her head.

"I'll keep mine for later," she said. "In case we need it."

"Good thinking, Em," Caz said.

Caz put the battery torch away and turned to look at Mildred and her brothers. All three stared at the box of matches hopefully.

"Ask nicely," Caz said and beamed a wicked smile at them.

"Just gimme the matches," Mildred ordered. "Now!"

Caz put the matches back into her backpack, making a big deal out of the way she opened the bag. She even rattled the box a little for good measure. Conker sighed and stepped forward.

"Please," he said. "Will you light our torches?"

Caz was about to strike a match when Poppy stepped forward and lit Conker's torch from her own.

"Saves on matches," she said.

Rather than have the manners to ask for a light themselves, Diz and Mildred lit their torches from Conker's. As soon as hers was alight, Mildred started walking away.

"Come on, let's go," she said. The two boys followed her for a moment then all three came to an abrupt halt.

"How do we get down from here?" Conker asked.

Without saying anything, the quads spread out and searched along the edge of the circular platform and it wasn't long before Sally found something.

"There are some steps here," she said.

A flight of stairs was carved from the rock that formed the platform they were on and followed the curve of its side as it descended to the floor below.

"Okay, after me," Mildred ordered and made a bee-line for the stairs. Diz and Conker followed closely.

"Wait!" Sally said and the Malprentices stopped. "Do you know your way around this place?"

"Of course not," Conker replied. "Even Gran doesn't know about this."

Poppy clapped her hands in delight. "I bet this is where the lost treasure is hidden. We should look for it while we're down here."

Mildred, Diz and Conker pricked up their ears at this and in the flickering torchlight their eyes seemed to sparkle at the thought of finding a fortune.

"What treasure?" Mildred asked.

"Lost treasure, stupid," Caz replied.

"It was hidden centuries ago," Em explained. "But the location of it got lost."

"How do you know about this and we don't?" Diz asked.

"Everyone round here knows stories about the lost treasure," Sally said.

"Just imagine if we were the ones to find it." Poppy went a little dreamy at the thought.

"If we find it, it's ours!" Mildred stated then began walking down the steps. "Come on, you two. We've got treasure to find."

The quads looked at each other and shrugged. They didn't want to follow Mildred's lead but what could they do?

"We can't look for treasure," Em said. "We have to get out of this place and help find Uncle Rosko."

"Maybe we'll find the treasure on the way out," Caz said and grinned.

The steps down were so narrow and steep it was almost impossible to descend them without pressing against the curved wall of the raised platform. But even so, it wasn't long before all seven were on the main floor looking at the three tunnels.

"What do you reckon this place is?" Caz asked.

"I've heard about places like this," Em said. "They're filled with vampire bats and pet alligators gone wild and poisonous slime that glows in the dark and..."

Sally, Poppy and Caz all shouted at the same time: "Shut up, Em!"

The quads looked around nervously. The flickering light from the torch flames cast shadows that danced around in a menacing manner and caught the corner of the eye in unexpected ways.

"Those things don't exist," Sally said with a nervous tremble in her voice. "It's nonsense. Right?"

But no one was convinced enough to be completely certain. The spooky nature of the chamber they were in, combined with the torchlight, pushed their active imaginations into overdrive.

"Hah!" Mildred snorted. "Scaredy cats."

Caz clenched her fists and ground her teeth but Sally stopped her from doing anything stupid and said, "Standing around, arguing and fighting isn't going to get Uncle Rosko found."

Whatever response anyone might have made following Sally's remark, it was cut off by a dreadful wailing that came from one of the tunnels.

"See!" exclaimed Em. "I knew there'd be wild creatures down here."

"That sounds more like the screams of a demon," Sally said.

The torches flickered wildly, almost in danger of going out, their flames seeming to dance with a life of their own.

Mildred dropped her torch and screamed.

CHAPTER TEN

Separate Ways

Triggered by Mildred's surprise reaction, the two boys screamed, too, unable to control themselves. All three were frozen to the spot with fear. Although they quickly got their screams under control, they were still pretty spooked and even in the warm glow of the torchlight it was clear that the colour had drained from their faces.

"Wh... what on Earth was that?" Mildred quaked.

"The midnight beast," Caz replied.

"But it's not midnight," Mildred said, her hands shaking really badly.

"Down here it doesn't have to be," said Caz. "Not when it's always as dark as midnight."

"Caz..." Poppy started to say.

"And when the midnight beast comes," Caz continued. "The first thing it eats is your heart."

"Stop it, Caz!" cried out Em. "There's no such

thing."

Caz shrugged and pulled a scary face at Mildred.

"That sound was only the wind blowing through the tunnels," Sally said. "Didn't you notice the torch flames flickering at the same time."

"You horrid little maggot!" Mildred yelled.

"You poisonous bunch-backed toad!" Caz responded.

"Hey, that's Shakespeare," Poppy said and smiled.

"I know," Caz said with pride. "He used some great insults."

"Do another one," Em said.

Caz looked at Mildred again. "You are the rankest compound of villainous smell that ever offended nostril."

Mildred took a brief moment to work that one out.

"But I still prefer stinky slimy slug," said Caz.

"Enough!" Sally said. "We're wasting time."

"Sorry, Sal," Caz mumbled, though not really sorry.

"Let's try this way," Sally said and pointed at the left hand tunnel. "We can try them in order." She and the other three quads started moving towards it but Mildred had other ideas.

"We're not going down that tunnel!" she declared. "We're going to look for the treasure. On our own, so we don't have to share."

Sally ground her teeth and forced herself not to say something she'd later regret.

Poppy chimed in to diffuse the situation. "Okay, Mildred, you lead the way and we'll follow you."

"No!" Mildred yelled. "You're not coming with us."

"Oh, for heaven's sake!" shouted Em. "We can't keep arguing or we'll never get out of here and find our uncle."

She swapped her unlit torch with Sally's flaming one and stormed into the left tunnel. Almost immediately her sisters followed her but Poppy turned to face Mildred and her brothers for a moment.

"We really shouldn't split up," she said.

"I don't care what you think," Mildred snapped.

"But, Mildred..." Conker said.

"Shut it, Conker!" Diz ordered. "Mildred's right, we should go our own way."

Mildred was a little taken aback. She couldn't remember Diz ever agreeing with her before. It must be the thought of all that treasure.

Poppy shrugged and ran into the left hand tunnel after her sisters. Mildred, Diz and Conker stayed where they were and almost immediately started arguing about which direction to take.

Poppy caught up to the others quite quickly. "I don't think we should leave them behind."

"They made their choice," Caz said.

"Yeah," agreed Sally. "We gave them the chance to come with us."

"Anyway," Em added. "We'll make better progress without them arguing all the time."

Sally and Caz nodded but Poppy still wasn't convinced. "What if we get out but they don't?"

"We can get the police to send a search party for them," Em said.

"Oh," Poppy said. "That makes sense."

With that sorted in their minds, the quads set off and marched in relative silence, trying to cover as much ground as they could as quickly as possible.

The tunnel went straight for quite some distance before turning this way and that a few times. They descended a slope then ascended another before stopping for a breather and a mouthful of water. The tunnels were hot — not what any of them expected underground — and the smoke from the torches made their eyes sting when the tunnel ceiling became low in places.

Feeling a little recovered after the brief rest, Poppy made a suggestion: "We should sing some songs to keep our spirits up as we march along."

Sally laughed. "I bet you've been reading Enid Blyton again."

"So?" Poppy was a little indignant. "I like Enid Blyton. Besides, that doesn't stop us from singing some songs."

"I think that's a really bad idea," Caz said. "There's no telling what might be down here and we don't want to draw attention to ourselves."

"Like the midnight beast?" Em asked.

"Of course not," Caz replied. "But there could be rats and snakes and stuff. Don't forget the stories about giant rats in the manor — this could be where they come from."

"We should have brought weapons," Sally said.

"Well, we could have," Poppy responded. "If we'd known we were going to be exploring the dungeons of Malprentice Manor."

"Just imagine if we found the treasure down here," Em said in a dreamy way.

"Yeah..." was all Caz managed, her head filled with her own imaginative thoughts.

"We're not looking for the treasure," Sally said, breaking the spell. "We have to get out of here and find Uncle Rosko before we can even think of something like that."

For a moment, Caz, Em and Poppy looked a little glum but sense soon prevailed and they nodded their agreement.

"You're right, Sally," Em said. "Family before fortune."

They gave each other fist-bumps to cement their decision then Sally pulled out the phone and switched it on again. Unfortunately, the tiny display still showed no signal so she powered off and put it away again.

"Do you think the others will be all right?" Em asked. "Do you think we should go back for them?"

"It's too far back," Sally said. "It's more important that we press on."

"We won't forget them once we escape," said Poppy.

"I bet they won't remember us if they get out first," mumbled Caz.

"Maybe not," Poppy said. "But that's no reason for us to be like them."

"Besides," Sally said. "They're so useless they probably couldn't find their way out of their own back garden without a trained guide."

"What if they came across some giant rats?" Em asked.

"They'd never survive," Caz stated. "They'll be too vile to eat."

"The rats or the Malprentices?" Em asked and everyone laughed.

Mildred, Conker and Diz made only slow progress along the middle tunnel, mostly because they kept arguing about who should lead the way. In spite of the fact that Mildred saw herself as the boss of the three, she was convinced it would be better if one of her brothers led the way.

"How much further do these tunnels go?" Conker moaned. He was currently in the lead due to the fact that both Mildred and Diz had threatened to thump him if he didn't do it.

"You think I'd know something like that, stupid?" Mildred snarled in reply.

"The way you normally talk, anyone would think you knew everything."

As soon as Conker said it he realised that it was a mistake and even Diz cringed at the thought of what was to follow. Conker turned around, flinching before she'd had the chance to do anything.

"Sorry," he said quietly.

"Sorry? You'll be even sorrier in a minute, you ugly worm." She dropped her torch onto the ground and rushed at Conker, completely intent on doing him harm. Her fingers were spread and curled like claws.

Conker, though, simply stepped to the side of the tunnel at the last moment and Mildred's attack missed its mark. As she tried to correct herself she stumbled, fell and slid across the floor.

What no one had seen, because of all the bickering, was that part of the tunnel floor had collapsed at some point in the past and Mildred's momentum carried her over the edge of the hole before she could stop herself. Conker and Diz looked at each other in horror but couldn't speak out loud with the idea that their sister had just fallen to her death. What would their father say?

"Help me, you idiots!" Mildred's voice shouted from inside the hole.

The two boys dashed to the edge and saw that Mildred had managed to cling onto a protruding rock just below the hole's jagged rim, but her fingers were already starting to slip on the crumbling rock.

Diz lay flat on his belly and reached over the edge, which enabled Mildred to grab onto his arm, first with one hand, then the other. However, she still hadn't fully recovered from her measles and wasn't strong enough to pull herself up.

"Give me a hand, Conker," Diz snarled.

Jolted into action, Conker lay down beside his brother and reached over the edge, too. Between them they were able to pull Mildred up and back to safety, though she scraped her arm and leg in the process.

"Look!" she screamed, pointing to the grazes. "Look what you've done, now."

"You're welcome, don't mention it," Conker said and turned away.

"What?!" Mildred looked clueless.

"We did just save your life," Diz said.

"I'd have killed you if you hadn't." Mildred's anger showed no sign of abating and any thought of gratitude towards the two boys had passed her by completely.

Conker was trying to ignore her. He stood at the edge of the hole with his torch raised high so he could get a good look at the ground on the other side. It appeared to be solid enough from his perspective and the hole was only a bit more than two metres across. But two metres can seem like two thousand when the space between appears to be a bottomless pit. He gulped.

"Are you even listening to me?" Mildred yelled from a few metres away, scared to go near the edge of the hole again.

Conker glanced at her for a moment then threw his torch over to the other side of the hole, where it landed in a shower of sparks but remained alight.

"What are you doing, Conker?" Diz asked.

"We can't stay here," Conker replied.

He backed up about four metres and paused, then backed up some more to make sure. He stood still for a few moments, taking deep breaths and concentrating on his goal. But the longer he left it the harder it became to begin his run-up.

"Ha! You'll never be able to make that jump," Mildred sneered.

She never would have said it if she'd known, but her scathing remark was exactly the boost Conker needed. He shot off the mark like a stone leaving a catapult. His feet pounded hard on the ground and he leaped harder than he'd ever done before.

It felt like he hung in the air forever, with the bottomless depths beneath him, but when he landed on the other side he'd made the jump by a good margin, clearing the edge by over half a metre.

When he realised he was safe he leaped into the air punching his fist in celebration. "Yes!" he exclaimed. "Yes! Yes! Yes!"

In spite of himself, Diz was impressed and looked on his younger brother with new eyes. He tossed over his own torch and Conker grabbed it out of the air with fresh confidence.

Diz backed up and ran at the hole with great speed but started his jump too far short of the edge. For a moment it seemed that he wouldn't make the jump at all, but he just managed to get half a foot onto the edge at the other side, which crumbled a little. Thankfully, Conker grabbed his arm before he had a chance to slip back.

"Thanks," Diz said between panted breaths of exhilaration.

"I'm not jumping across there," Mildred said. "Not in a million years."

"Why not?" Diz asked. "I thought you were the school athletics champion."

Yeah, well..." Mildred's mind raced to find an answer. "It's the measles, see. I'm not back to my full strength yet."

"Okay," Conker said. "You stay there and we'll send help when we get back."

"Wait! You can't leave me on my own."

"It's either that or you jump across," said Diz, spreading his arms and shrugging.

"I forbid you to leave!"

"Like that's gonna stop us." Diz tutted.

The two boys started walking slowly away.

"Maybe the midnight beast will keep you company," Conker teased.

"No, please." Mildred almost seemed to be crying as she said this and the boys looked at each other, scared they'd gone too far.

Abruptly, the wailing of the wind in the tunnels sounded out again and Mildred's fear of this overcame the dread

she felt for the hole in front of her. She dashed forwards and leaped over the gap as if she were flying. She landed heavily but safely clear of the hole.

Then she dropped to the floor on her knees and cried. Her brothers had no idea what to do as they'd never seen Mildred like this before. Nor were they practiced in the art of comforting others, so they simply stood beside her until the crying stopped and Mildred got to her feet again. They steeled themselves ready for a torrent of verbal abuse but it never came.

Mildred was completely docile.

This made Diz and Conker feel even more uncomfortable than Mildred's normal, horrible moods and looked away from each other without a word. They stared at the ground for a few moments before Conker started moving off.

"Come on," he whispered. "Let's go."

The next five minutes, as they walked along the tunnels, were the longest all three had been together without arguing or calling each other names. In the lead, Conker found himself smiling, with a strong desire to whistle, though he refrained from doing so.

The corridor twisted and turned a few times before opening out into a wider area with dark, shadowy alcoves. They came to a swift halt and stood trembling at the thought of what they might contain.

"This is stupid," Diz said. "We can't stand here doing nothing."

"Yeah." Conker nodded, trying to make himself brave. He and Diz started walking again with Mildred behind them following silently.

But as the three walked past the dark alcoves, three pairs of large hands shot out, grabbed them and held onto them firmly.

Unable to stop themselves, all three screamed in fear. Then rough hands clamped over their mouths to shut them up.

"Did you hear something?" Poppy asked and the group stopped. Whatever she'd heard, there was only silence, now. Poppy shrugged, thinking she must have been hearing things.

"Could have been the wind in the tunnels again," Sally said and they continued on their way.

"Or an echo," added Em.

"Or the midnight beast capturing the Malprentice kids," Caz said and they all laughed.

A few minutes later they came to another stop when Sally turned to them. "I think we should take a break and have a snack," she said and put her torch down.

"Great idea," Caz said and unslung the backpack. She sat on the ground cross-legged with the pack in front of her and opened up the top.

However, before she could reach in and remove anything, something fast dashed out of the darkness and raced past them. It grabbed the bag as it went then disappeared down the tunnel before the girls could react or get a good look at whatever it might be.

"What was that?!" Em asked.

"It's the midnight beast!" Caz exclaimed, now really worried. Her earlier joke no longer seemed so funny.

CHAPTER ELEVEN

The Chase

Because the quads had placed their burning torches on the ground while they took a rest, the light they cast was greatly reduced and they didn't see the thief properly. They could only hear pounding footsteps rushing away from them. Sally picked up one of the torches and held it aloft, but by then the bag snatcher was already too far away.

The four looked at each other nervously then Caz leaped to her feet. "We've got to get that bag back. We need that food and water!"

"Wait!" Poppy pleaded. "If it really is a monster, we'd be stupid to chase after it."

"That's right," Sally said. "We can't just go charging through these tunnels. There might be more of them."

"Ooh," Em responded. "Wouldn't it be great if we discovered a previously unknown creature that lived in complete darkness. It probably has big, bulging eyes... or maybe no eyes at all... and... and..."

"Shut up, Em!" her three sisters said in unison.

"I was just thinking from a scientific point of view," Em explained.

Caz and Sally rolled their eyes, but Poppy looked really worried and her voice trembled. "What if it comes back?"

Then the sound of a loud but distant sneeze came out of the darkness the thief-creature had disappeared into. The girls looked at each other in surprise, which turned to astonishment when they heard a faint, "Excuse me."

"That's not a monster," Sally said. "It sounded like a boy."

"What's a boy doing down here?" Poppy asked.

"We're down here, aren't we," Em said.

"The why doesn't matter," said Caz and she grabbed one of the lit torches. "We've got to chase after him and get our bag back."

She raced along the corridor with the torch in her hand and the others quickly followed her. The floor was uneven, as they'd already experienced, so running was much more difficult than walking had been and after a few minutes it didn't seem as though they were gaining any ground in their pursuit. Then they came upon a fork in the path with tunnels leading to the left and right.

"Do we split up?" Caz asked.

"No, just be quiet a minute," Sally replied.

In the silence they could hear the boy's footsteps growing ever fainter, but they were clearly coming from the right hand tunnel.

Caz pointed in that direction. "That way!"

They set off running again, following the direction their quarry had taken. Three minutes later, the tunnel ended in a blank wall and they came to an abrupt halt.

"Where did he go?" Em asked.

"Maybe he's a ghost," Caz suggested. "And he just disappeared."

"But he couldn't have made the bag disappear," Poppy said. "And I don't see it anywhere."

"So how did he escape?" Sally mused.

The quads lapsed into silence while they gave it some thought, but it wasn't long before the quiet was interrupted by Poppy. "What if he used magic?"

"Or a secret door," Caz said.

"Let's hope it's a door," said Sally. "We don't know how to deal with magic."

"Dad says magic isn't real," Em said but the others ignored her.

"Look!" Sally pointed to the torch Caz held. Its flame flickered and writhed about, clearly affected by a breeze from somewhere.

"Where's the draught coming from?" asked Poppy.

Caz moved the torch about and was able to trace the direction of the air flow and follow it back to its source. A long, natural crack ran from the floor to the ceiling on the left hand wall and looked like it was simply a part of the rock the tunnel had been carved from. However, when they held their hands over the crack they could feel the breeze blowing through.

"If there's a door here, how do we open it?" Sally asked and the others shrugged. There was no mechanism that anyone could see.

"We could try pushing on it," Caz suggested and leaned against the section of wall to the right of the crack. When nothing happened the other three joined in but still there was no movement.

"I think we're pushing in the wrong place," Em said.

The girls moved to the left of the crack and as soon as they started pushing, part of the wall swung away from them like a huge stone door. Its movement was almost completely silent and opened with relative ease considering the size of it. The quads quickly slipped through and it closed behind them on its own.

"Wow!" Sally exclaimed as the four of them took in their new surroundings.

"Cool!" echoed Caz.

"It's beautiful," Poppy added.

"It must be some kind of bio-luminescence," Em said.

The ceiling and walls of the corridor in which they now stood, glowed with a faint light in random patterns of blue and green. The effect was quite remarkable and completely unexpected.

"Can I borrow the phone?" Em asked. "I want to take some pictures."

Sally handed it over with a warm smile and for about thirty seconds Em snapped away until the phone beeped a warning. Em looked at it then handed it back to Sally.

"The battery's low," she said and wore a guilty look.

"Don't worry," Sally responded. "It doesn't matter when we can't get a signal." But she powered it down anyway to save the little that remained.

"Hey, we're supposed to be chasing the kid who stole our bag!" Caz said and set off down the corridor at a run. Sally and Poppy raced after her but Em only jogged along, still taken by the glow that surrounded her.

"I wish I had something to collect a sample in," she muttered to herself.

She was abruptly brought back to reality by the screams of her sisters from up ahead. She picked up her pace and soon found them at the bottom of a pit, far too deep to climb out of.

"What happened? Did you fall down there? Are you hurt?" Em asked, her questions flooding out.

"We're okay," Sally replied.

"The floor just descended as we stepped on it," Poppy added. "It went down too fast for us to get out."

"What I don't understand," Caz said. "Is why that kid didn't trigger the trap when he came this way first."

"Ooh, that is odd," said Poppy.

"Maybe there's a way to reverse the trap," Em said. "It can't be a one-time thing, right?"

"Good thinking, Em," Sally called out.

Em searched the walls and floor for a sign of a reset mechanism, but there was nothing on the floor and the way the glowing matter had spread made it difficult to see any features on the walls.

From below, Poppy asked: "Do you think this glowing stuff is edible?"

"It's probably radioactive," Caz replied. "Eating it could turn us into mutant zombies or something."

"I think I'd prefer the something," Poppy said.

"Not if that something is a giant, blue slug that glows and smells of baby poo." Caz grinned.

"Yuk!" Sally said and pulled a face. "Baby poo is the worst ever smell."

"I think I've found something," Em shouted. "Just give me a minute to check."

The blue and green patterns of the glowing bio-mass spread randomly across the affected areas, but the small section of wall Em now stared at had a different look to it. The lines weren't perfect but the colours had formed into two roughly concentric circles. Such a thing was highly unlikely to have occurred naturally.

"There must be something under here," Em whispered to herself. She poked at the luminous matter, touching it cautiously for the first time as she didn't know what to expect. Nothing happened and in spite of it's beautiful glow it felt very ordinary to the touch.

Using her fingernails to start scraping it back, she quickly found that it pealed off in large pieces, much like old wallpaper when it's been given a good soaking. It felt a bit like it, too, she thought as she removed a piece about the size of a dinner plate. Although she was fascinated by it, she knew she didn't have time to study it any further. She folded the piece up and shoved it into one of her pockets.

The space left by the material she'd removed, contained a stone circle set within another circle like a large button just begging to be pressed. So she did just that.

The floor of the pit started descending further and Em's three sisters screamed at her: "Stop, Em!"

She immediately released the button and the downward movement halted. Em stepped over to the edge and looked down.

"What happened?" Sally shouted from below.

"I found this button and pressed it," Em replied. "I didn't think that would happen."

"Is there another button, Em?" Poppy asked.

"I'll take a look," Em said.

However, she could see no sign of any other circles in the blue and green patterns on the walls, or anything else that might be connected to the pit. She returned to the button and stared at it, trying to find some clue she'd missed. Unfortunately, the button, the surrounding ring or the wall immediately around it had no markings that might help. It was just a plain inner circle with a ring around it.

Then she clicked her fingers in realisation.

Using fingers on both hands, Em pushed in the ring

that surrounded the central button and the trap's floor began to rise to cheers from the three girls below. Once it was level with the corridor, which took just a few seconds, she released the ring. But the trap descended again and Em had to press the ring once more to bring it back up.

Keeping it pressed in, she said, "Get over to the other side so I can release this switch."

They did as she suggested, but with her at the wrong side of the trap, she released the ring and realised her predicament, as did the others.

"How will you get across?" Sally asked?

"I don't know. I can't jump that far," Em said. The trap was at least six metres from end to end and the full width of the passageway. She'd have to be an Olympic long jumper to cover that kind of distance.

"Maybe if you ran really fast you could get across before it dropped too low," Poppy said.

Em shrugged. She didn't really have much choice, so she backed up the corridor a good way and wished that she had the speed of The Flash. She ran as fast as she'd ever run before and soon sped through the section of floor that contained the trap. She clenched her teeth and willed herself to make it.

But nothing happened to the floor.

She'd made it across as if there was no trap to trigger. She came to an abrupt halt and hugged her sisters.

"Way to go!" Caz exclaimed.

"But why didn't it trigger?" Sally wondered.

"Maybe it's not designed to trap kids," Poppy said. "Maybe it needs the weight of an adult to trigger it."

"That would explain why that boy didn't trip it," Caz said.

"And why you three did," said Em, finishing the train of thought. "Your combined weight must be the same as an adult."

"This place gets weirder and weirder," Sally said. "Come on." She started walking along the corridor with the others behind her.

"I bet that kid's long gone by now," Caz said.

"Yeah," Em agreed.

They trudged along in silence for a short while, their heads hanging and feeling bad about the loss of the bag, paying little attention to their surroundings.

So it came as a surprise when the corridor ended and they found themselves in a large, circular chamber lit by more of the bio-luminescent matter, which covered the surface of the high ceiling. It looked magnificent and they stared upwards in awe.

Their view of the room was partly obscured by the large standing stone a few metres in front of the corridor's exit. Its surface was covered with intricate patterns and symbols, carved long ago by unknown hands.

The imposing object was one of a circle of similar stones, placed there in ancient times, each with similar markings. As they stepped around the obstruction, they could see that the ring of stones went all the way around the large room and their markings were echoed in a carved design on the floor.

Although the room looked amazing, they were more astonished to see, in the centre of the room, a large, iron cage containing a single occupant.

The circular bottom edge of the cage rested on the stone floor with heavy iron bars that went up and over to form a dome. A loosely hanging chain led from the top of the dome up to a hole in the ceiling where it disappeared into the darkness. The chain swung a little as though it had recently been activated.

The cage's prisoner was a boy of ten with dark skin, who clutched the quads' bag to his chest. He looked bewildered, confused and more than a little scared.

"That's Tim!" cried Caz, her eyes bulging wide. "Tim Redfern!"

They stared without moving for a few moments but in spite of Caz's exclamation, Tim hadn't even noticed they were here.

"How did he get down here?" Poppy asked.

"He can't have come through the manor like us," Sally said.

"Perhaps we should just ask him," Em suggested.

They ran towards the cage calling out Tim's name and he blinked his eyes as if terrified by these four girls rushing at him. He backed away to the far side of the cage and hugged the bag still tighter, fear written over his face. His dark skin shone with a film of sweat.

"Tim, it's us," Caz said. "The Quinton quads."

His face wore an expression of deep fear and confusion. Although there was a flicker of recognition at the mention of his own name, he couldn't pull his mind together. He didn't appear to be properly registering the world about him.

The girls slowly moved closer to the cage, worried they might scare him some more if they approached too quickly.

"How did he get in there?" Poppy asked. "There's no door."

"More to the point — how do we get him out?" Caz said.

Em gazed upwards, towards the ceiling, following

the chain with her eyes. Sally saw her and looked up, too.

"The cage must have dropped down from the ceiling on that chain," she said.

As the quads continued to draw nearer, Caz's foot landed on a slab that shifted slightly, accompanied by a heavy stone click. With a low, deep rumble, the circular section of floor, on which the cave stood, began to descend very slowly, taking the cage and Tim with it. High above, the chain played out from the hole in the ceiling making a rough, grating sound as it did so.

"Where's it taking him?" Em asked.

"Wherever it is, it's not going to be anywhere good," Sally replied.

"It probably leads to certain death," Caz said.

"Stop being so horrid!" Poppy yelled.

CHAPTER TWELVE

The Cage

"Wherever this cage is going, we can't let Tim go with it." Em was insistent and grabbed the bars of the cage. She pulled with all her might but it was far too heavy for her to move it.

Her sisters joined her, but even with four of them heaving as hard as possible they couldn't slow the cage's descent in the slightest.

"We need to find a different solution," Sally said.

"I hope you realise," Caz said. "That if we don't rescue Tim, all the other girls at school will probably lynch us."

"Personally, I don't see why everyone fancies him so much," Sally said. "After all, he got himself trapped in a cage."

"That's hardly his fault," said Poppy. "The whole point of a trap is to catch people unexpectedly."

"We're wasting time. We need to get him out of

there," Em urged. "Can you see a switch or something?"

They quickly looked around the chamber but it only took a few moments for them to realise that nothing in the chamber resembled one.

"I bet it's up there, where the chain comes out." Poppy pointed to the hole in the ceiling.

"I have an idea," Caz grinned. "Give me a leg-up onto the cage."

Although the cage was descending steadily, it moved slowly enough that the domed top was still a little too high for Caz to reach without help. The others quickly boosted her up and she clambered onto the top, stood upright and grabbed hold of the chain.

"I think you've got about three minutes to stop it," Em said, "judging by its current rate of descent." She'd done the arithmetic in her head and the others knew her well enough to accept it without question.

Caz leapt as high as she could, then started pulling herself up the chain towards the ceiling. She was always great at climbing the ropes in the school gym and this wasn't much different. However, the chain was very old and rusty and made her hands sore by the time she was about half way up.

She paused for a moment and looked down. Tim had recovered a little of his composure, but when she saw his scared face looking up at her through the bars, it was all the encouragement she needed to continue. She increased her effort, ignored her sore hands and headed to the top.

The other three didn't waste time standing about and tried to find another way to help Tim, quickly spreading out around the room. A moment later Poppy discovered a large, thick timber to one side of the room and dragged it over to the cage.

"How will that help?" Sally asked.

"I thought we might use it to lever up the cage so Tim could get out," Poppy replied.

"That's a great idea," Em said. "But there's nothing we could use as a fulcrum."

Sally and Poppy looked at each other and shrugged their puzzlement.

"It's what the lever pushes against to make it work," Em explained.

Poppy felt a little annoyed. "I was sure it would help."

In the cage, Tim started breathing heavily and cleared his throat like he had something stuck in it. He sprawled across the floor and dropped the bag.

"Tim!" Em exclaimed. "Are you okay?"

"I... don't know," he replied. "I feel... weird... and my head..."

"I think it might be dehydration," Sally said looking worried. "Tim, there's some water in the bag. You should drink some straight away."

"But how do I get out of here?" Tim asked as he reached for the bag and opened it. He pulled out a bottle of water and started drinking. Although the girls were still worried about him, at least his mind seemed to be working properly again.

"We're working on it, Tim," Poppy said. "I'm sure Caz will stop the mechanism in no time."

Above their heads, Caz had reached the hole in the ceiling and pulled herself through. The room she found herself in was illuminated by more of the strange glowing substance. She was easily able to make out a large mechanism that mostly consisted of a series of cogs to which the chain was attached. It was slowly unwinding with the cage's descent.

She studied the movement of the cogs and quickly worked out how to wind the cage back up, but the handle that should have been attached was missing. A swift search of the room told her that it wasn't anywhere up here.

Caz poked her head through the hole in the ceiling and shouted down to the others: "Have you seen some kind of handle down there? I need it for the mechanism up here."

"We've been looking around for stuff, but we haven't seen anything like a handle," Sally called up. "What's it look like?"

"I've no idea," Caz replied. "But I think it's pretty big. Oh, wait. I've just spotted it."

"Where?" asked Poppy.

"On top of that standing stone," Caz said and pointed.

"Oh, yes," Em said.

Now they knew where to look it was easy to see it sticking over the edge a little. The stones were about twelve feet tall and although they were roughly carved, there were no hand-holds that would enable them to climb up.

"How do we get up there?" Poppy asked.

"We don't need to," Sally replied. We can use that timber you found to knock the handle down."

"Great idea!" Em said.

"Please hurry!" Tim called out from the cage, feeling that time was running out for him. He took another mouthful of water.

Working together, Sally, Em and Poppy hoisted the heavy piece of wood up the side of the stone and let it fall sideways so that it caught the part of the handle they could see. It struck with a resounding clunk and the handle moved.

"It worked!" Em cried out. "Oh, no!"

It had only been a partial success and although more of it now protruded over the edge, it wasn't enough to overbalance it and bring it down. So they picked up the timber and tried again. This time the handle came down, almost dropping on their heads as it fell to the floor with a metallic clang. The girls scattered to avoid being injured.

Although it was made of brass, its surface was covered in a green patina developed over many years down here. Poppy picked it up with some difficulty.

"How are we going to get this up to Caz?" she asked.

"Good point," Sally replied. "She can hardly climb down then back up while carrying it."

"Don't we have some string in the bag?" asked Em. She shot over to the cage. "Tim, can you give us our bag, please? We need something from inside it."

For a moment he seemed reluctant to pass it up, but then pushed it through the bars for Em to take. The cage and the floor section had now dropped nearly two metres, so he was only just able to do so.

Em turned to the other two and opened up the bag. She pulled out a ball of string, passed it to Sally then rummaged about some more.

"We need something to tie it to or we'll never throw it up there," she said.

Sally nodded and started unravelling the string. "I hope it's long enough."

Em took out the stone ring that Caz had accidentally pulled from the library nook's wall. The size and weight would be perfect for throwing up to the hole. She looked closely at it for a moment and noticed a rectangular protrusion on one part of the outer edge. Although Em wondered what that could be for, she passed the ring to Sally who tied one end of the string to it then gave it to Poppy.

"You do it," she said. "You're always best at throwing."

Poppy felt the weight of the ring in her hand then looked up at the hole in the ceiling. "You ready, Caz?"

"Yeah," Caz replied. "Chuck it up."

Poppy swung her arm back and forth a couple of times before launching the ring upwards. It shot straight towards the hole trailing the string behind it. Caz made a grab for it at the same time as keeping her head out of the way and her fingers closed on empty air.

The ring shot through the hole, missed Caz and bounced off part of the machinery. It almost dropped back through the hole but Caz scrambled for it and managed to grab the string and held on.

"Okay," she shouted down. "I got it."

She hooked the ring onto a protrusion on the mechanism so it wouldn't accidentally fall back through the hole. Below, Sally tied the other end of the string to the heavy brass handle.

"Ready!" Sally shouted and Caz started pulling on the string.

It lifted off the ground okay and they all breathed a sigh of relief that the string was strong enough but the string bit into Caz's hands too painfully and she had to let it go after she'd raised it just a foot.

"Is it too heavy?" Poppy asked.

"No, it's cutting into my fingers."

"Put your socks on your hands," Em suggested.

"Brilliant!" Caz shouted. "Thanks, Em."

She quickly took off her shoes and socks and put the latter on her hands like mittens. It was still difficult to pull up the handle but at least the string no longer cut into her skin. A minute later she'd pulled the handle into the mechanism room and sighed with relief. She put her socks and shoes back on while she caught her breath. She also wound up the string and wedged it into one of her pockets with the stone ring in another.

The handle fit into place perfectly but when Caz tried to turn the mechanism it was incredibly stiff and refused to budge. She glanced through the hole, saw Tim's face again and put her whole strength into it, but still it wouldn't give.

"Come on!" she yelled at the mechanism through clenched teeth. "Turn will you!"

Just when she felt she had nothing else to give, the handle moved by the smallest of degrees. Caz drew breath, ground her teeth and kept pushing. The winding mechanism, now unstuck, began turning a little easier.

The gearing of the cogs was arranged so that one person could lift up the weight of the cage, but that meant it took a lot of turns of the handle to lift it high enough for Tim to fit through the gap. Caz knew she had to push through the pain and exhaustion if they were to free Tim.

"Okay, hold it there," Sally shouted and Caz almost collapsed with relief. But she held the handle in place and waited for the others.

"Hurry up," she muttered through gritted teeth. Although she'd done marvellously well to raise the cage, the whole thing hadn't been designed with ten year old girls in mind.

Sally, Poppy and Em had to lie on their bellies and stretch their arms through the gap between the cage bottom and the edge of the pit. But even then they couldn't quite reach Tim and he was forced to jump up and grab their hands.

It took a lot of effort on everyone's part but they were soon dragging him to safety, pulling him by his hands and clothing through the gap and onto the main floor. Tim shook with relief and all four of them sprawled on their backs to recover.

"You can let go now, Caz," Poppy shouted.

Up in the ceiling room, Caz let go of the handle and dropped to the floor, exhausted, too.

Now it was no longer held in place, the mechanism turned freely and the cage dropped back into the pit with speed, hitting the still descending floor section with an incredibly loud boom. The din reverberated around the room and the adjoining tunnels.

Caz put her hands over her ears and cried out in pain.

The noise had somehow been focused and amplified into the mechanism room where it resonated for ten whole seconds. When it died down her ears were left ringing for a few moments. She moved over to the hole and looked down, pleased to see that everyone was safe and they'd rescued Tim.

Her sisters had closed around him as he sat on the floor, checking that he was all right. Sally in particular was fretting in just the way their mother did when one of them came down with a cold or scraped a knee.

Caz reached for the chain and steeled herself to climb down again, but just before she started the descent another movement caught her attention. One that made her heart sink.

No doubt drawn here by the noise of the cage crashing down, Grisly Gus, holding a net, dashed into the chamber from a side tunnel.

Before Caz could shout out a warning — the others hadn't noticed him — Gus threw the net over them and pulled it tight, laughing out loud as he did so.

"I never thought catching the four of you would be so easy," he gloated.

CHAPTER THIRTEEN

Captured and Trapped

Caz opened her mouth to scream at Grisly Gus to let her sisters go, but it died in her throat when realisation popped into her head. The brute was sure he'd caught all four quads and in the gloom had completely missed the fact that Tim was one of the four kids he'd captured.

But how could she use that to her advantage?

Adults were never as smart as they liked to think, but Caz still had to work out how to save Tim and her sisters. And do it quickly, before Gus realised she was free. If she got things right she'd have the element of surprise on her side.

She watched Gus for a moment while she thought. He was an incredibly strong man, so even with four kids in the net he was easily able to drag it across the floor. Before they disappeared down the tunnel he'd just emerged from, Sally looked at her through the mesh of the net and gave her an "okay" sign with her hand. Caz gave her a thumbs up in reply.

Caz grabbed the chain and readied herself to climb down to the chamber below, but froze when it made a rattling noise. Gus dashed back into the room and looked up at the chain and Caz only just ducked out of sight in time. He stared into the pit, scratched his head then left the room.

Although relieved, Caz knew she couldn't climb down the chain or Gus would grab her for sure. She checked she had the string and the stone ring in her pocket then looked around the mechanism room for another way out.

There was a large stone door at the other side of the room but she quickly realised there was no way to open it from this side. If she was stuck in her for too long she'd lose the chance to rescue the others.

It wasn't easy seeing details in the dim bio-light, but after a moment of searching her eyes grew a little more accustomed to it. She spotted two particularly dark areas of shadow on opposite walls.

She investigated more closely and worked out that each was some kind of small access tunnel. One was located behind the cage mechanism and headed in the same direction as the tunnel Gus had taken.

In spite of the complete lack of light in the narrow tunnel, Caz knew she had no choice but to head that way. She took a deep breath of courage and squeezed through the opening.

"Don't worry," she muttered to no one in particular. "I'm coming."

Once through the entrance, the tunnel became a little larger and Caz hurried along, knowing that she had to catch up with Gus. But after she'd travelled about thirty paces the floor suddenly dropped away in a steep slope. Her feet went out from under her and she slid down on her bum, only stopping when the tunnel levelled out once more.

She'd scraped her elbow on the tunnel wall and thumped the floor in anger. She was about to shout out her rage when she heard a noise — the sound of the net dragging on the floor. She must be close to Gus.

Then she heard Sally's voice. "Let us go, you pig, or you'll be sorry."

"Just shut your whining," Gus replied. "Or I'll really give you something to whine for."

"Typical bully," Caz whispered to herself. "I'll show him."

She hurried along the access tunnel and saw an open hatch in the floor, which explained how she could hear the others. Poking her head carefully through it, she saw that she was directly above the tunnel Gus had taken. He and the net full of kids were still ahead of her and her determination strengthened.

Caz jumped to her feet and raced along the smaller tunnel to get ahead of the slower moving Gus, a plan was formulating in her mind.

It wasn't long before she found another of the hatches, though this one had an old wooden cover wedged into the hole. She tugged on it with all her strength and it came free, but not without a loud creak of wood rubbing on stone.

Down in the corridor, Gus had his head down to pull the weight of the net and he lifted it up at the sound of the cover being freed. Although it was difficult to move in the net, Sally put her hand over her mouth. That noise had to be Caz and she'd be discovered for sure. But Em had other ideas.

"Eeee-ee." She let out a cry of pain that sounded very like the squeal of the trapdoor. "Stop, you're hurting us."

"Do I look like I care?" Gus replied then gave an extra vicious tug on the net which caused all four to give out a yelp. But Em's fake cry had worked and Gus continued down the corridor.

In the tunnel above, Caz could hear the brute getting closer and prepared herself over the hatch hole, standing with a foot on either side of it. For a moment she wished she'd brought the heavy brass handle with her but it was too late to go back for it.

Gus passed directly below the hole and Caz dropped down. She timed it perfectly and landed on his back, which flattened him to the ground and stunned him.

The other four cheered and Caz immediately released them from the net.

"Wow!" said Tim. "That was way cool."

"We knew you'd rescue us," Poppy said.

"Definitely!" said Sally and Em together.

They laughed in joy at their freedom but Gus was already recovering, so the five of them grabbed the net and threw it over him before he could get to his feet. They then pulled it tight and tied the end of the rope to an old torch bracket attached to the wall.

"Serve you right," Caz said and ran down the corridor with the others following behind.

Unfortunately, they hadn't gone very far when Tim collapsed, falling to the ground with a cry of pain. The quads realised it wasn't just a stumble when he lay still and didn't attempt to get up. They helped him into a nearby side room and propped him up against the wall.

"What happened?" Em asked. "Are you okay?"

Tim panted a couple of times and opened his eyes. "Belly cramps. I haven't had anything to eat or drink since yesterday, until you gave me that water, earlier."

"You can have everything we brought," Poppy said and Sally delved into the bag and brought out the remaining food and water.

Slowly, Tim ate and drank his fill, feeling better almost immediately, but the girls gave him time to get his strength back and took a sip of water each to keep them going.

"Sorry for stealing your bag," Tim said between mouthfuls of food. "I was scared and starving and thought I'd never get out of here."

"But you know us from school," Caz said. "Why didn't you stop and talk to us?"

"I didn't realise it was you four," Tim replied. "The light from those torches has a habit of making everything distorted. Besides, you could have been part of the Malprentice gang and I didn't want to get captured by them. I've seen the kind of thing they do."

"There's a gang?" Em asked.

"Wait, Em," Sally said. "It might be better if he explains from the beginning."

Tim finished his sandwich and crisps, wiped his hands on his jeans and took another drink of water before starting on his tale.

"I was out for a ride on my bike," he explained. "On the quiet lanes behind Malprentice Manor. Back Lane and so forth. You know?"

"Yeah," Caz replied. "We bike up there, too."

"Anyway," he continued. "There was nothing unusual going on until I happened to see an old man on the hillside, that place with all the craggy rocks, you know. Well, he seemed like a normal hiker with a backpack until I saw that he was carrying a bow and arrows."

"How weird," said Sally.

"No, the weird part came next. He just disappeared into the hillside like magic." Tim scratched his head.

"Maybe he was one of the Faerie Folk," Poppy suggested.

"Yeah, right," Tim said, frowning. "He was just an old guy. Anyway, I went to take a closer look where he'd disappeared and I found a small cave I've never seen before. So I followed him in."

"Who was he?" Caz asked.

"I've no idea. I've seen him in the village a couple of times but..." he replied, shaking his head. "Anyway, I could hear him in the tunnels ahead and saw the faint glow from his torch. But he moved faster than me and I lost him."

"Oh, no!" Em said. "What happened?"

"I carried on through the tunnels for ages, feeling my way in the dark. Then I found him by accident. He was in a large chamber, but he'd been captured and tied to a stone pillar and looked like he'd been beaten up a bit. The Malprentice gang were threatening him."

"Who's in this gang?" Em was quite urgent in her questioning.

"That butler guy — the one who captured us in the net — he's working with some other men here in these caves." Tim took another sip of water. "Whatever they're up to, they don't want anyone else to know about it."

"Why didn't you go and get help?" Sally asked.

"I tried. But I got lost. I've been trying to find a way out ever since." He fought back tears, trying to stay brave. "I don't know what I'd have done if you hadn't found me."

"Don't worry," Poppy said. "We'll find a way out together."

From down the corridor they heard a bellow of rage that could only have come from Gus. They looked at each with concern on their faces.

"I think the old Grisly got free," Caz said. "Let's go."

"What about Tim?" Em asked.

"I'm okay," he replied. "Thanks to your grub."

They quickly gathered their stuff and put the litter into the bag for recycling. Caz also put the string and stone ring back in, too, then hoisted it onto her back. They moved down the corridor quickly, away from the approaching Gus.

They'd only been running for a couple of minutes when they saw a brighter glow shining around a bend in the corridor ahead. They slowed almost to a stop and heard voices, too. They crept along until they reached the end of the corridor and peered into a large, bright chamber illuminated with industrial electric lights on heavy duty stands.

"This is it," Tim whispered to the girls. "This is where I saw the gang.

For an ancient, underground room it was enormous, with a ceiling three storeys high, supported by a series of stone columns. If there hadn't been so many crates and pieces of machinery cluttering up the place it would have been perfect for indoor sports.

The five of them crept forward to take cover behind some crates. They tried to figure out what was going on, but before they could do so Tim nudged Sally with his elbow.

"Look!" he exclaimed and pointed to the other side of the room.

As he'd previously described, an old man had been tied to one of the pillars that held up the ceiling. His head hung down in either exhaustion or defeat, so they couldn't see his face. Two big thugs stood in front of him, one of whom was teasing him with a cup of water.

"Just tell us where the plans are and you can have a drink," said the man with the water. "It's all we want."

"What do you think is going on here?" Em asked, her curiosity getting the better of her.

"Shh! Listen!" Sally hissed.

The old man shook his head, his face still looking down. He seemed determined to defy his captors.

"Should I rough him up some more?" asked the second of the gang members. "That'll make him talk."

"No," said the first man. "We can wait this out better than him. We're being paid by the hour, remember."

"Oh, yeah." The second man smirked. "Take as long as you like, Granddad."

"Once he gets thirsty enough he'll tell us where the plans are."

"Okay," the old man croaked in a voice that was barely understandable. "I'll tell you what you want to know. I swallowed the diagrams." He lifted up his head and grinned in spite of a split lip. "No one will ever get the treasure, now."

The girls were so astonished at the sight of the old man's face that each of them stood up and cried out loudly at the same time.

"Uncle Rosko!"

As soon as they said the words they knew they'd made a dreadful mistake because the two gang members' heads snapped around with fierce looks on their ugly faces. Another two stepped out from behind some equipment and moved towards the five youngsters.

"Run!" Uncle Rosko yelled, though it hurt his throat to do so. "Get out of here!"

The quads and Tim immediately turned around to race away down the corridor they'd just come along, but blocking their path was the huge, angry shape of Grisly Gus.

They were trapped with no means of escape!

CHAPTER FOURTEEN

Uncle Rosko

"Scarper!" Sally yelled. The quads instantly split up and ran in different directions.

Tim was a second slower in reacting because he didn't know the girls like they knew each other. For the briefest of moments he stared at Gus.

"Where did you come from?" the man growled.

But Tim didn't waste time with an answer. He was light on his feet and zipped away in a flash, just before the Malprentice butler was able to lay his hands on him.

"Grab them!" Gus bellowed. "I've had enough of those little maggots." Then he pointed to one of the men. "You! Stay with the old man."

Gus and three of his men now chased after the kids who weaved around the piles of crates and machinery with agility and precision that couldn't be matched by the much larger adults. Whenever it seemed that one of them was about to be caught, they twisted away in a sudden change of direction or slipped through the narrowest of spaces. Tight gaps the adults couldn't squeeze through.

With each successful evasion, the kids felt more triumphant and began to laugh at the feeble efforts of the five men as they ran rings around them. Unfortunately, they became a little over-confident and Em suddenly found herself trapped between two of the big men who rushed towards her with arms outstretched. In a sudden panic, Em froze in place and couldn't decide what to do.

Then behind her, Tim appeared from between two piles of crates, grabbed her arm and pulled her out of the men's reach. With their quarry abruptly snatched from their grasp, the two men ran smack into each other and fell to the floor stunned.

"Thanks, Tim," Em said.

"No problem," he responded and the two of them went their separate ways again, much more cautiously now.

Looking around for signs of pursuit, Em caught sight of Uncle Rosko, still tied up, and knew that she had to help him. Moving carefully and silently, she sneaked from one area of cover to another and slowly drew closer.

Unknown to her, Caz had a similar idea and was trying to work out how to get near to the old man, but there was the problem of the gang member who stood beside him keeping watch. Caz couldn't get any closer so climbed up a pile of crates to see if that gave her a better view of the situation.

From here she saw what Em was up to and grinned — the sisters often had similar ideas. Checking that no one was looking her way, Caz caught her sister's attention with a wave then signalled to her that she'd cause a distraction. When Em signalled back that she understood, Caz directed her attention to the man guarding Rosko.

"Hey, you!" she shouted. "Ugly-mug! I bet your mother put a paper bag on your head when you were a baby."

"You cheeky little worm!" the man bellowed. "I'll have you know I won bonny baby contests when I was little."

"The judges must have been blind," Caz continued and laughed.

The man's nostrils flared and his eyes bulged like they were about to pop from his head, all the time huffing out lungfuls of fury.

"I bet your dad wanted to sell you to the circus," Caz taunted.

With a final grinding of teeth, the man left his post and dashed towards her.

Caz leaped down from the crates and sped away from him. Em took the opportunity to run over to the pillar the old man was tied to.

"Uncle Rosko, are you okay?" she asked as she pulled at the knots.

"Of course," he replied. "They'd never have captured me if I was still in my prime. I'd have given them what for, outnumbered or not. Did I ever tell you about the time I travelled through Burma?"

"No, but we don't have time for that now, Uncle," Em said. "We have to get out of here."

"Of course, of course," he repeated. "Once I've completed an important little task."

The ropes fell free once Em finished untying them and he rubbed his wrists for a moment while flexing his knees then took a long drink of water from a nearby bottle before speaking again. "Try to keep those men occupied, will you?"

"What?!"

"Please do as I ask, Em," Rosko pleaded. "You'll understand shortly."

Em sighed and nodded and watched as Rosko moved over to a section of wall covered with ornate carvings, symbols and designs. She wondered what on Earth he was about to do.

"I've got you now, you little rat."

Em pretended to jump at the man's words but she'd seen his shadow as he'd crept up behind her, the fool. Twisting away before he could lay a hand on her, she ran straight towards a heavy piece of machinery on wheels. The gap beneath it was a little tight, but Em scrambled under and out the other side before the man could properly react. By the time he went around the machine she'd already ducked out of sight behind some crates.

Sally, Poppy and Tim were having their own games of chase and found that the longer they went on, the easier it was to dodge the men. Being so much older and rather unfit, they became short of breath very quickly.

"Does anyone have any bright ideas?" one of them asked.

"They can't run forever!" Gus snapped. "And when they're caught, I'll teach 'em a thing or two."

"You couldn't catch a cold," Sally yelled and Gus gave chase again.

He quickly realised that Sally saw herself as the leader of the group and decided that she was the best target to concentrate on. Capturing her would be a warning to all of them. But wanting and achieving were two very different things and Sally evaded his advance by leaping over some crates.

Unfortunately, she bumped into Poppy who was racing away from her own pursuer and the two of them fell to the ground in a tangle. The man pounced on them and grabbed their wrists quite forcefully.

The two girls leapt to their feet and each slapped the man hard in the face. He was so shocked by their abrupt attack that they were able to twist out of his grip in opposite directions and sped away before he could react. As he turned around he found himself staring at the angry face of his boss.

"You useless piece of rotting manure!" Gus yelled then turned on his heels to search for one of the girls.

Meanwhile, Uncle Rosko had been busy at the ornate wall. He'd pushed in some sections, rotated others and pulled out various protrusions, all done in a very specific order. Now he stood before the wall and checked the whole thing over before he stepped forward and pushed in two circular sections at the same time, his long arms only just able to reach both of them.

There was a resounding stone clunk from beneath the floor and the whole of the wall section slowly descended into the ground with a grinding shudder that shook the whole room.

While the wall continued its descent, Rosko dashed over to a pile of junk between two stacks of crates. He rummaged through the items — mostly construction tools — and pulled out his backpack, the straps of which he quickly slung over his shoulders. He continued to search the pile and found his bow and a quiver of arrows.

He tested the tension on the bow then fitted an

arrow, drew back and fired it across the room. It hit its mark and one of the men found that his jacket was pinned to a heavy crate by the arrow.

The two men who'd previously run into each other when chasing Em, now saw that Rosko was free and started towards him, though they faltered when he aimed in their direction. However, Rosko's next arrow flew above their heads and they laughed, moving towards the old man again.

But Rosko's aim was true and the sharp arrowhead cut through a rope that held a number of boxes in a net above the men's heads. The net and boxes crashed down, flattening the two men to the ground. They groaned a little before falling unconscious.

A third arrow knocked down an oil lamp and the spilled oil immediately burst into flames, cutting off the fourth man from approaching them. There wasn't any danger the fire would spread out of control but it bought Rosko time.

That only left Gus, but the leader of the group had more sense and was keeping out of sight of the old archer.

"Over here, girls!" Rosko shouted and all five kids dashed to him. "Oh, who's this?" he asked when he spotted their friend.

"This is Tim from school," Caz explained. "He followed you in yesterday and couldn't find his way out again."

"I see," the old man said. "I thought I heard something at the time. Still, the more the merrier." He grinned.

"What?!" exclaimed Tim. "We're in danger, here."

"Never mind that, just go through there." Rosko gave a gesture with his head to indicate the section of wall he'd just opened.

The kids all dashed through, even if Tim did so reluctantly. But Rosko backed towards it slowly, keeping their escape covered with an arrow loaded into his bow. Gus stepped out with his hands raised.

"Come on, Rosko," he said. "You know what you're doing is pointless."

"This is my find," Rosko replied, still backing away, the arrow now aimed at Gus. "I've been researching this site for years."

"This is Malprentice property!" a shrill voice said. "This doesn't belong to you."

Rosko jerked his head towards the direction of the new voice. Edith Malprentice had come down to see what the commotion was about and the look of angry indignation on her face would have curdled milk from fifty paces.

"A find like this should belong to everyone," Rosko responded. "It should be treated with respect, not tunnelled out with heavy machinery."

"It's mine to do with as I please," Edith said. "It's none of your business."

Rosko reached the lowered wall and stepped back into the area it had revealed. The kids stood around him, waiting nervously. He immediately moved over to one side and pressed in one of the decorative tiles. The wall began to rise again.

With the arrow no longer aiming at him Gus dashed forward, but Rosko was too fast and brought his bow around again and the big man was forced to stop. Rosko kept him in his sights as the wall rose.

"Do something!" Edith screamed. But Gus stared into Rosko's eyes, seething, and watched helplessly as the rising wall hid the old man from sight. Gus dashed over and considered clambering through the diminishing gap, but immediately realised he'd be crushed if he tried to do so.

"Open it!" Edith ordered.

"I don't know how," Gus responded.

"Then how did Rosko know?"

"I get the impression he's been down here many times before."

"When this is over, we shall get the police to charge him with trespassing, along with those bratty kids." Edith turned on her heels and stormed towards the exit. "Inform me once you have something useful to report."

Elsewhere, Diz, Conker and Mildred had been placed in an old cell with high stone walls and mouldy straw on the floor. For the hour they'd been imprisoned so far, they'd avoided sitting down because the straw smelled really awful and none of them could bear the thought of their bottoms touching it, even through their clothes.

They'd been grabbed by Gus's men and when they'd brought the three kids before him he'd given orders to lock them up until they found the quads.

Mildred had demanded to see her grandmother, using every bit of haughty disdain she could muster, but Gus had warned the three that if he did so it was likely they'd find themselves with a far greater punishment than the one Gus had in mind. Diz and Conker hissed at her to keep quiet.

They'd been left alone in the locked cell without even a guard to keep watch. Every five minutes or so, Mildred had tried the cell door and given it a good kick of frustration when it still proved to be locked. Eventually she gave up and leaned against the door.

"Do either of you have any bright ideas?" she asked.

The two boys shook their heads but pretended to think about their predicament. In truth, both of them would rather wait it out and accept their punishment than make matters worse. Gus and Gran scared them like no one else in the world.

However, they continued their pretence by looking around the dimly lit cell, examining the walls and scraping back some of the straw with their feet. They could see very little for the only light came through the bars of the cell door and from a small window set into the wall. The latter was way too high to reach and too narrow to climb through even if they could.

Quite suddenly, something moved over Conker's foot and when he looked down he screamed and shook his foot to try and be rid of the beetle he'd spotted.

"Get it off, get it off!" he yelled. "I hate beetles. Get it off."

Mildred laughed, along with Diz, but she crouched down and picked the beetle off Conker's foot. "Aw, are you frightened of the little beetle?"

"They give me the creeps, okay!" Conker folded his arms in anger, as much annoyed with his own phobia as he was with Mildred's teasing.

She looked closely at the beetle and Conker watched her with suspicion, which proved to be perfectly justified when she threw it at him. He ducked and it sailed over his head and into a far corner but he gasped short breaths of panic. There was only one thing worse than a beetle - a beetle he didn't know the location of.

Diz and Mildred laughed even harder as if the whole thing was hilarious. Conker's eyes burned and he turned away because he didn't want the others to see the tears forming in them.

There was another yell but this time it came from Diz who'd seen a spider scuttle up the wall.

"I don't believe you two," Mildred said. "Such tiny things to be afraid of. You won't catch me being afraid of things like that."

"We can't help what we're afraid of," Conker said. "Phobias are irrational. I read it in a book."

"Ooh, get you," Mildred taunted. "Not just a scaredy cat but a swot, too. You'll be making friends with those awful quads next."

They fell into a short, angry silence that was broken by an unnerving squeaking noise.

"What was that?!" Mildred demanded. "I hope it wasn't a rat."

"Why?" Diz asked. "Are you afraid of a little rat?"

The rat made itself known by running across the floor. Mildred screamed so loud and long that Diz and Conker had to put their hands over their ears to protect them. They were relieved when her breath ran out, but she simply drew in more and screamed again, with greater volume and excruciating shrillness. The rat fled from the noise and ran from the prison, escaping through the bars of the door.

Above the cell, the scream resonated with part of an ancient mechanism to such a degree that a restraining peg, weakened by centuries of tension, broke and released the device.

It creaked and juddered with age but the pent up energy, stored for thousands of years, overcame the decades of corrosion and the cell's ceiling began to descend very slowly, accompanied by the sound of grinding stone.

All three of them stared up at the approaching ceiling in disbelief for a moment. Then they screamed.

CHAPTER FIFTEEN

The Ceiling Descends

Once the wall had risen and everyone was safe from Grisly Gus and his men, the quads breathed a collective sigh of relief then embraced Uncle Rosko in a group hug.

"We're so glad to see you," Poppy said. "Mum reported you as missing."

"I suppose I was," Rosko replied. "As far as your mother is concerned I still am. And now you are, too. Still, we're all together and for the moment we have bigger fish to fry." Uncle Rosko liked his little sayings almost as much as Grandma.

"Speaking of Mum..." Sally pulled out the mobile phone and checked it again. "Ah, still no signal." She switched it off quickly because of the low battery and put it away once more.

"The radio waves won't penetrate down here, unfortunately," Rosko said and checked the contents of his backpack. He pulled out a torch, returned the bag to his back, settled the straps on his shoulders and set off down the corridor they were in. His long legs covered the ground with strides the youngsters did their best to keep up with.

"We need to hurry," Rosko said. "If I know Gus Grimshaw — and unfortunately I do — if he can't work out how to operate that secret door he'll probably blow the thing apart."

"What is this place?" asked Em. "Is it a magical lair?"

Rosko laughed. "Only in the sense that nothing like this has ever been found in Britain before."

"Wow!" Sally exclaimed. "So we're the first people down here for millions of years?"

"More like two or three thousand years, but yes." Rosko shone the light of the torch on the walls to highlight the carved decorations. "This whole place dates back to Bronze Age times, but I've no idea why they might have built such a complex set of tunnels and rooms."

"We came down here by accident," Caz said. "How did you discover it?"

"I've been researching the whole area for a couple of years but discovered an entrance on the hills about four months back." He chuckled. "I took me ages to work out how to open that wall. Then about a week ago Gus and his men started bringing equipment in. There must be another way in from the manor house."

"But what are they doing with it?" Tim asked. "All that heavy machinery makes it look like they're going to rebuild the place."

"Or destroy it," Caz retorted.

"Exactly," Rosko said. "They're looking for the

treasure hoard, of course."

"It really exists?!" Poppy exclaimed.

"I have no idea," Rosko said. "I'm interested in the history and archaeology. This could be the most significant find for at least the last hundred years. It could rewrite our knowledge of the area's past."

"You should be a history teacher," Tim said.

"He is," said Em.

"I used to be," Rosko corrected. "Before I retired."

He stopped walking and turned to the others, drawing in a deep breath to start on one of his long stories. The girls loved his tales of how people used to live in the past, but this time he wasn't given the chance to tell whatever he had on his mind.

"Did you hear that?" Sally asked. "It sounded like a scream."

The others shook their heads but fell silent and listened for anything further.

"I can hear a low rumble," Tim said. "But not screams."

Everyone nodded. They, too could hear the rumble.

"It sounds like the movement of heavy stone," Rosko said, a thoughtful on his face. "It's probably nothing."

However, there was no mistaking the next sound — the screams of more than one person, who sounded like they were terrified for their lives.

Poppy pointed down the corridor. "It came from there." She raced off without any hesitation and the others followed behind.

They almost missed the narrow window in the left hand wall, but quickly stopped when they realised the rumbling sound and the screams came from whatever lay beyond.

The window was little more than an unglazed slot in the stone. Too narrow for anyone to climb through, Caz pressed her face up to it. Looking down, she immediately saw who was screaming and turned to inform the others.

"It's the Malprentice kids," she said. "They're in some kind of cell." She put her face back to the narrow window.

"What are you screaming for?" she shouted down to them. They saw her face at the small window and stopped yelling.

"That, you idiot!" Mildred yelled and pointed upwards.

Caz looked up as best she could from her limited viewpoint but saw that the ceiling was descending slowly. "Oh my god! Can't you get out?"

"No," Diz shouted. "Gus had his men lock us in here."

She turned to the others. "They're trapped and the ceiling is going to crush them."

"How fascinating," Rosko mused. "Dreadful, of course, but fascinating all the same."

"This whole place is filled with death traps!" Poppy exclaimed.

"Perhaps they're designed to protect the treasure," Tim suggested.

"Whatever the reason," Em said. "We need to rescue those three."

"Can we find something to stick through the window and hold up the ceiling?" Sally asked.

"We'd never find anything strong enough to hold up that much weight." Rosko stroked his chin as he thought. "We need to find the mechanism that controls it then reverse it. Or stop it at least."

"Not again!" Caz groaned. "I hope it doesn't involve climbing chains this time."

"Well, we can't stand around," Em urged. "Come on!"

"We didn't pass anything on the way here," Tim said. "So the mechanism must be further on."

Rosko gave the torch to Em. "You lot race ahead. I can't run around like you youngsters can. I'll catch you up."

The four girls shot off with Tim reacting a little more slowly again but he soon caught them up as they followed the corridor around a couple of corners. Rosko peered through the window for a moment and saw the ceiling begin to pass by the opening.

The kids hadn't run very far when they came across an opening set into the left hand wall, which revealed a stone spiral staircase that led upwards.

Sally paused for a moment. "Caz, there isn't much time so we have to split up. Can you and Tim check ahead in case this isn't what we're looking for?"

"Okay," Caz said. "Come on, Tim." The two of them raced away immediately.

Sally led the way up the spiral staircase, which was so tightly wound that a large person would have had some difficulty managing the climb. The people who built these stairs must have been a lot smaller than those of today.

They emerged into a small room almost filled by another very old mechanism constructed from stone and bronze. The numerous cogs were arranged in a very complex pattern.

"Why so many cogs?" Poppy asked.

"They'll be arranged to ensure that the ceiling

drops at a slow rate," Em replied.

"But why so slow?"

"Maybe it's designed to make the victims terrified before being crushed to death," replied Sally. "Imagine watching it get closer and closer, but really slowly..."

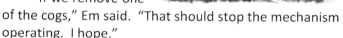

"I think I'm going to have nightmares tonight," Em shuddered.

"How do we stop it?" Poppy looked everywhere. "There's no off button."

"If we remove one of the cogs," Em said. "That should stop the mechanism operating. I hope."

"Our fingers will be crushed if we try that," Sally said. "So we need something to pry one off with."

"There!" Poppy yelled. She pointed to a bronze bar, green with age, which leaned against the wall in a corner of the room. She quickly grabbed it and brought it over to where the cogs were turning. Choosing a small one, assuming it would be easier, she jammed the bar beside it and heaved with all her strength.

"It won't budge," she said. "Give me a hand."

Sally and Em grabbed hold of the bar, too, then all three pushed as hard as ten year olds were able. It resisted for a moment, then the cog popped free and bounced across the floor.

Unfortunately, this resulted in the exact opposite of what they'd hoped for. Instead of stopping the mechanism from working, the cogs to one side of the gap started moving more freely and, judging by the change in the rumbling noise, the ceiling was descending much faster.

In the cell below, the Malprentice children began screaming again as they saw the ceiling dropping more quickly.

"Oh, no!" Sally yelled. "We've made it worse."

But Poppy moved like lightning and rammed the metal bar between two of the rotating cogs. But she wasn't strong enough on her own and the bar simply bounced off the moving cogs before she could ram it in properly.

Sally and Em grabbed the bar alongside her again and swung it back before slamming it between the teeth of the ancient cogs. A couple of them broke off before others bit onto the bar and held tightly in place, jamming the mechanism completely.

The descent of the ceiling had ceased, but so had the screams from below.

"Oh, no!" cried Em. "I think we stopped it too late."

CHAPTER SIXTEEN

The Bottomless Pit

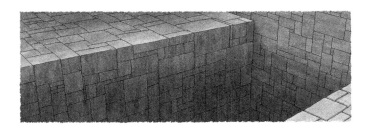

Edith Malprentice fumed as she strode back and forth across the main hall of the manor house. She didn't like kids at the best of times but to have them trample over her property like it was some kind of playground was really too much for her. She picked up a cheap vase from the table by the front entrance and threw it at the door to the cellars.

However, at that precise moment, the door swung open and the vase bounced off the head of Gus who was just returning from below. He recoiled in surprise but other than that it might have been a fly bumping into him for all the harm the impact had. Made of plastic, the vase simply bounced across the floor.

Gus and Edith gave each other an angry glare, then he entered the hall properly and closed the door behind him.

"It would be dangerous to use explosives," he said.

"We'll probably bring the whole complex down and the hillside with it. Including the house. The treasure would be lost for ever."

Edith snorted, ground her teeth and clenched her fists. "This is all your fault!"

Gus's mouth fell open. "How is it...?"

"You should have dealt with those annoying brats better in the first place." She snarled as she spoke and small specks of spit flew from her mouth, such was her fury. "Not only did they escape, they freed Rosko Tremaine, too."

Gus rolled his eyes. "I know you'd like me to do everything, but I can't."

"Are you saying I should find myself a new butler?" Edith narrowed her eyes and her gaze drilled into Gus more deeply, though he wasn't as intimidated as the kids had been.

"Don't tempt me," he growled. "If I go, the men go, too."

"Perhaps one of them can do a better job."

"Hardly." Gus folded his arms. "I brought them in for their muscle not their brains."

For a moment Edith looked like she might burst, but her anger soon abated when her reasoning mind took control and she calmed down. She almost smiled. "Forgive me, Gus. I worry these brats will ruin our chances of finding the lost treasure."

Gus stood in silence. He didn't trust himself to speak further at that moment but his tight fists were more than clear.

"Speaking of brats," Edith continued. "What happened to my grandchildren? Not that I'm particularly interested, of course, but they will inherit the manor one day."

"A few of my men found them," Gus replied through gritted teeth. His anger was only slowly diminishing. "They put them into an old cell to keep them out of the way. Do you want me to bring them up here?"

"Only when you have a spare moment," Edith replied. "No, actually, leave them in there. It might teach the little morons a lesson." She sighed. "I can't believe that grandchildren of mine would turn out so awful."

Gus turned away and said nothing, though he rolled his eyes in a very exaggerated way.

The ceiling's mechanism gave a few last creaks then an eerie silence fell upon the mechanism room and the cell below. Sally, Em and Poppy looked at each other with heavy eyes then came together in a hug.

"We tried our best," Sally whispered. "But saving lives isn't easy."

Em tried to sniff back a tear and failed, which set off Poppy and Sally in turn. The Malprentice kids were pretty horrible but they didn't deserve to die.

"You numbskulls!"

Sally looked at Em who looked at Poppy who looked at Sally then Em. The voice had come from below.

"Mildred?!" Sally shouted. "Are you okay?"

"If you call being nearly crushed okay!"

Down in the cell, the heavy ceiling had come to rest about thirty centimetres from the floor. Mildred, Diz and Conker had lain completely flat but it had come very close to squashing them flat. There were only a few centimetres to spare.

"But at least you're alive," Poppy exclaimed. "Thank goodness!"

"Yeah, right," Mildred complained. "We're lying in stinking, disgusting straw that will probably give us a disease we'll die from."

"What do you expect us to do now?" Em asked.

"Get us out of here!" Considering there was so little room to move, Mildred did an incredible job of yelling.

"We don't know how to reach the cell door," Sally said. "You'll have to wait until your captors let you out."

"Just keep your fingers crossed that you don't need to go to the loo," Poppy said.

"Oh, thanks," groaned Conker. "Now I really need to go."

"Me, too," added Diz.

Mildred clenched her teeth against the sudden urge to pee, too, then after a moment she yelled: "When I get hold of you I'm going to batter the lot of you."

"Some people are so ungrateful," Poppy said and made for the spiral stairs.

"Did you say the toilet thing on purpose?" Sally asked.

"She'd never do that," Em replied. "Not Poppy."

They didn't see the small smile on Poppy's face as she slowly descended the tight spiral staircase.

When they reached the bottom they found Uncle Rosko, Caz and Tim waiting for them. Their uncle was talking about the Bronze Age people who lived in the area.

"What puzzles me," Em said, breaking into their

conversation. "Is how they created all this, particularly the traps. Did they have cogs in the Bronze Age?"

Rosko scratched his head. "That's a good question. You think that it was created much later?"

"That wouldn't explain the designs," said Tim. "Aren't they from the Bronze Age?"

"This is what's so fascinating about this place," Rosko said by way of an answer. "There are so many questions to answer. I suspect that a lifetime of research will be necessary. We still don't know how large the whole structure might be."

"Oh, we saved the Malprentice kids," Sally said, almost as an afterthought.

"We heard," said Caz. "Selfish toads."

"Yeah," Tim echoed.

Uncle Rosko stretched his legs, which creaked at the knees, loudly enough for them all to hear. "We should press on. I suspect there's still an awful lot to do."

Tim groaned. "Really? I just want to go home."

"You don't like our adventure?" Rosko asked.

"It's just... I'm still hungry and thirsty."

"He's been trapped down here since yesterday," Poppy explained.

"Why didn't you say so sooner?" Rosko said. He removed his bag then took a bottle of water from it and a couple of energy snack bars. "They should keep you going for a bit."

He returned the bag to his back then led the way with the torch. The girls followed him closely, so Tim took up the rear, drinking and munching as he walked along.

Caz dropped back a little to speak with Tim. "I know it must be rubbish for you, having been down here for so long, but we can't go back or we'll run into Gus's men again."

"I guess so," Tim said, speaking around a mouthful of snack bar. "But Mum will be worried to death."

She nudged him with her elbow and grinned. "Just think of the essay you can write when you go back to school."

"What do you mean?" Tim looked puzzled.

"The one we always get," Caz explained. "'What I Did in the Summer Holidays'."

Tim's face actually brightened at the thought. "I always hate doing that. I can never think of what to write, normally, but this will make a great essay."

"Exactly!" She grinned again.

The rest of the group had stopped and Caz could see why — the corridor had reached a dead end.

"This is as far as Tim and I got earlier," she said. "Do we need to go back?"

Uncle Rosko shook his head but didn't say anything. His eyes scanned the wall as he counted the stones it was made from, his finger moving in the air like he was touching each one mentally.

After about twenty seconds he stepped forward, placed his hands on two of the stones and pushed hard. The end of the corridor swung away from them like a large stone door and they felt a light breeze on their faces. They paused for a moment before stepping into another section of the underground complex.

This passageway was much wider than the one they'd just walked along and they only had a vague sense of where the far end was situated, but they'd only walked about thirty metres when Rosko brought them to an abrupt stop.

In front of them was a pit as wide as the passage

and it blocked their progress completely. The other side was too far to reach even with a running jump and when they shone a light into its depths it appeared to go down forever. The sides of the pit simply disappeared into total blackness.

A sudden, loud bang made the kids jump. Fearful that Grisly Gus and his thugs had followed them, they all whirled around ready for anything. However, the door they'd just come through had closed of its own accord with a mighty crash.

Rosko ignored the sound and shone his torch light towards the end of the corridor beyond the pit. The beam picked out an ancient wooden door, on either side of which was a stone pillar. The quads and Tim looked on with fascination.

"How do we get across the pit?" Poppy asked.

"This was as far as I got last time," Rosko said. "I've been returning here regularly, making it a little farther each time, learning something new, working out what to do next."

"But..." Poppy felt her question hadn't been answered.

"That's what the bow and arrows are for." Rosko grinned and started unloading his bag, which contained a lot more energy snack bars as well as a number of balls of string, a knife and other bits and pieces. He gave everyone a snack bar while he continued.

"I figured that if I could fire enough arrows into that door, each with a length of string attached, the combined strength of the strings should support my weight and allow me to get across." He now looked unsure. "Trouble is, I've already used up a number of my arrows and I don't know if it will still work."

Sally gestured at herself and her sisters. "Will it be

strong enough to support one of us?"

"Easily," Rosko replied. "But how will that help me?"

"If one of us climbs across, we can take more lengths of string with us," Em replied.

"I like it," he replied. "I should have brought you along from the beginning; you're girls after my own heart. Right, are you any good at rope climbing?"

"Caz is great," Poppy said.

Caz looked at her hands and flexed them a few times. "Yeah, I can do it."

"Excellent." Rosko shared out the arrows. "I need strings tying to each one. They need to be sixty metres long."

"How do we measure that?," Em asked.

"Good point." Their uncle looked around thoughtfully then after a moment he paced across the width of the corridor, counting off his extra-long strides. "The passage is about fifteen metres wide so the string would need to go back and forth across it exactly four times."

"Neat," Tim said. "We can do that."

While the five kids set about their task, Rosko set the torch on the top of his bag, which sat on the ground. He arranged it so it shone on the far wooden door and once satisfied it wouldn't move he took up his bow. He pulled the string back as if he was firing an arrow, getting a feel for the tension and thinking through the action.

It was only a few minutes before the first of the arrows had a string attached to it. Rosko tested the knot then tied the other end of the string to his belt so he didn't lose it over the edge of the bottomless pit. He arranged the rest of the string loosely on the floor near the pit in large loops so it would follow the flight of the arrow without getting tangled up with itself.

He nocked the arrow onto the bowstring and pulled it back. Poppy crossed her fingers and everyone held their breath, willing the arrow to fly true.

Releasing it with a twang, Uncle Rosko watched the flight of the arrow as the string on the floor uncoiled with a whispering whoosh. Unfortunately, the arrow fell way short of the door.

"Oh, no!" exclaimed Poppy.

Rosko laughed. "Don't worry, I can try again." He started pulling on the string, bringing the arrow back to him. "I've got to get my range. I should have done a lot more practicing with strings attached to arrows."

The second attempt almost reached the door. "Practice makes perfect." He grinned.

Tim pulled back the arrow for Rosko while the girls fitted the last few arrows with lengths of string.

This time, Uncle Rosko drew the bow further than he'd done before to create more tension and when he released it he knew it would hit the door with considerable force. Yet, even thought it did so, the head of the arrow simply bounced off the old wooden surface.

Rosko's jaw visibly dropped and he blinked a couple of times.

"What happened?" Poppy asked. "Is the door enchanted in some way?"

"Nothing so wonderful, I'm afraid," Rosko replied. "The wood the door is made from is simply too dense for the arrows to embed into it."

He sat down on the ground and buried his head in his hands. "I was so sure the plan would work I never even considered such a possibility."

Sally looked at the others then back at Uncle Rosko. "Does that mean...?"

"We're stuck here. There's no way forward and Gus's men are behind us."

CHAPTER SEVENTEEN

The Makeshift Rope

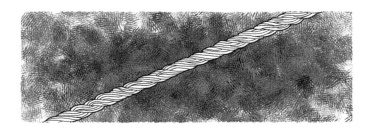

The mood of the group suddenly changed and the excitement of the adventure evaporated like a spilled drink on a hot summer pavement. No one could think of a thing to say.

Caz kicked at a loose stone lying on the ground and it sailed over the edge of the pit. It fell out of sight without making a further sound. She peered over warily then stepped back a little.

Tim retrieved the arrow and gave it to Rosko, who examined it carefully.

"Damn! The tip's bent," he said. "I'm surprised the wood's remained so hard after all the years the door's stood there."

"Does that mean we have to go back?" Poppy asked.

"What, to face Grisly Gus and his men?" Sally added.

"I think we have no other choice," Rosko said and hung his head.

"But this will probably be our only chance to try!" Caz exclaimed. "If we leave we'll never be able to come back now Gus knows you found another way in."

"There must be something we can do," Tim said. "We've got to try at least."

"You've changed your tune," Sally responded with a warm smile.

"Yeah, well... Caz is right — we might not get another chance."

"Okay," Poppy said. "Let's all think hard."

Unseen by the others, Em stood a little apart from the group and looked down to the far end of the corridor, studying it intently. Then quite abruptly, she snapped her fingers and snatched Rosko's torch from the top of his bag. She aimed the beam of light at the area of stone blocks above the door. A grin spread across her face.

"Can you see that?" Em shouted and pointed down the passageway.

"What, the door?" Sally was confused.

"No, above it." Em bounced with tiny jumps of pleasure.

"Stand still!" Caz ordered. "Keep the light steady."

Uncle Rosko screwed up his eyes for a moment and saw the same thing as the others. A circular hole, about 30 to 40 centimetres across had been built into the stonework.

"It's a ventilation hole," he said. "The air has to move through the tunnels and passages."

"Oh, I get it," Poppy said and clapped her hands. She now wore a grin that matched Em's. "You could shoot your arrows through there." She and Em hugged and the others began to understand and smiled, too.

Rosko slapped his forehead. "Well done, Em. I should have seen that myself."

"That doesn't matter," Caz said. "What's important is that we can move forward again."

"Well, maybe," Rosko said. "That's a pretty small target from this distance."

The size of the hole meant that even under normal circumstances, hitting it would be hard. With lengths of string attached to the arrows the task would be much more difficult.

Rosko sighed then set his face into a determined expression. "Faint heart never won fair maiden." Tim looked puzzled but the quads just grinned at each other - their adventure might yet continue.

He took the arrow he'd already fired three times and got ready to shoot again. "Em, put the torch back on the bag, please. Then I won't be distracted by any movement."

She did as he asked, making sure it was secure and pointing at the ventilation hole. Rosko checked the arrow's string wouldn't get caught then pulled back on the bowstring. He took a deep breath, held it, aimed and fired.

The arrow shot through the air and they could barely follow it's movement in the dim light. But they saw it strike the stonework just a few inches below the target hole.

"Aah..." Rosko sighed with disappointment.

"So close!" Em said.

"Great first shot!" said Tim. He pulled on the string and brought the arrow back.

Rosko fired it again and this time it almost touched the passage ceiling at the top of its trajectory, but the aim was perfect and it sailed through the centre of the hole. Everyone cheered in celebration as the string became taut against Rosko's belt.

He pulled on the string slowly and it drew the arrow up against the other side of the hole. Because it was much smaller than the length of an arrow, which was almost a metre long, the shaft of the arrow held in place against the other side. It was sideways on and couldn't pass back through.

Rosko grinned then untied the string from his belt and gave it to Sally. "Hold onto this while I try the rest."

"Okay, Uncle," she said. "I'll move over to the side so I'm not in your way."

The others handed Rosko the arrows one at a time, carefully arranging the strings so they didn't become tangled. He shot them at the target and only missed four times. He did hit the ceiling twice, but one time the arrow bounced off and went through the hole anyway. Soon, all nine arrows had gone through and the strings trailed loosely back down the passage and across the bottomless pit.

Under Uncle Rosko's instructions Sally, Poppy and Em were given three strings each and told to spread across the width of the passage. They then slowly pulled the strings until the arrows had been pulled tight against the other sides of the hole.

"Okay," Rosko said. "Pull them as tightly as you can without breaking them or the arrows." They did so, making gentle tugs on the individual threads until they were satisfied that they were all equally tight.

Tim's face suddenly brightened with an idea. "Are you going to plait them like a pigtail?"

The girls laughed and he blushed. "I have a sister, okay!" he said.

"That's a pretty good idea, Tim," Rosko said. "But that would take far too long." He delved into his bag again and pulled out a strange device with three hooks, a winding handle and lots of small gears.

"This," he said. "Is a rope making gizmo."

They attached the strings to the hooks in three groups of three, ensuring they were all as tight as possible and Rosko pulled on the device with all his strength.

"I'm glad you're here," he said. "You can take turns winding the handle while I pull on the gizmo to keep the rope taut as it's made."

Sally jumped in first and began to turn the handle. "This is easy."

"Only at first," Rosko said. "It will get harder as the tension increases. Caz, it might be best if you don't take a turn if you're going to climb across."

He was right about the difficulty and the kids found themselves taking shorter and shorter turns as the rope twisted into usability. Because they were working everything from one position, the rope itself was rather rough and ready, but it came together pretty well. It soon looked sturdy enough to bear someone's weight. Rosko removed the rope from the twisting device and tied a knot in the end so it wouldn't unravel.

"Can you climb all the way to the top?" he asked as he looked at Caz.

"Yeah, no problem," she grinned.

"Good. I'd like you to cut off the far end and tie it in a knot," Rosko said and gave her his penknife, which she put into a pocket. "Then fasten it to one of those stone pillars."

Caz nodded and tied more lengths of string around her waist while Rosko tied the end of the rope around his.

"We'll all have to pull on it," Rosko said. "So it's taut enough for Caz to climb to the top."

With five of them pulling, the rope stretched gently upwards towards the hole above the door, crossing the bottomless pit on the way.

Caz looked at the pit again and gulped, but took hold of the rope anyway and swung her legs up to wrap around it. She then started moving up the rope, hand over hand and made it look easy to the others watching. But inside she cringed with each movement of her hands. The earlier soreness quickly returned to her hands, but at least the rope wasn't rough like the chain had been.

After a few moments Rosko called out to her. "You're past the pit. That means you're about a third of the way there."

Caz twisted her head to look below her then

swung her legs down and dropped the few feet to the ground.

"What are you doing?" Rosko asked.

"I don't need to climb all the way like that," Caz replied. "Just let the rope go really slack." She ran over to the door and looked up at the hole above it, which was only about twelve feet off the ground.

Uncle Rosko nodded as he now understood Caz's plan. He and the others moved closer to the pit edge and the rope lost its tautness. Caz pulled it so her end hung directly down from the hole above her. Although she'd have to climb vertically to the hole, it would be over a much shorter distance.

Fifteen seconds later she'd climbed up to the hole and the end of the rope. She gripped it tightly with her left hand, her feet coiled around it, too, then pulled out the knife with her right. This was going to be tricky — as soon as she cut through the rope she'd drop to the ground so she had to be ready to brace for impact.

"Here goes," she muttered to herself while the others watched from across the pit.

Uncle Rosko's knife was as sharp as a razor blade and cut through the makeshift rope in a couple of swift movements and Caz dropped like a stone.

Although she absorbed her weight on bent knees and tried to roll after impact, her foot landed on a small, loose rock and twisted her ankle. She cried out in sudden agony and dropped both the knife and the end of the rope, which snaked away from her. In spite of the pain she was in, she lunged for the rope and grabbed the end of it just as it started to unravel.

"Are you okay, Caz?" Sally shouted.

"Yeah," Caz replied. "I just twisted my ankle a bit."

She knotted the end of the rope, together with the

loose strings from her belt, then got to her feet and cried out in pain. "Ouch!" Her injury was a little worse than she'd thought. She hobbled over to one of the stone columns where she paused to take a couple of deep breaths and fight down the pain. Holding the rope, she stared at the stone column and scratched her head.

Rosko saw this and cupped his hands to his mouth. "Use the bowline I taught you," he shouted.

"Oh, no," Poppy said. "Caz was the only one who didn't get to learn it."

Uncle Rosko looked at her for a moment then shrugged. He faced back across the pit and shouted again. "Caz, just concentrate. You can do it."

Caz closed her eyes and tried to picture the actions Uncle Rosko's hands had made while demonstrating the knot, but all she could remember were those her father had taught the quads when they went camping last year.

But suddenly it came clear and she stepped forward, passed the rope around the column and tied the end of the rope to itself. She hadn't remembered the bowline so used a midshipman's hitch instead, which would keep it secure around the column.

"Okay," she shouted then sat down to examine her ankle.

The others worked together, under the guidance of Uncle Rosko, to twist the additional strings around the main rope to make it stronger.

"Do you think Caz is all right?" Poppy asked, almost in a whisper.

"Probably not," Sally replied. "It looks like she sprained her ankle pretty bad."

"We'll probably have to help her along when we

continue." Em looked towards the other end of the passage with concern on her face. "I hope we don't make her injury worse."

Although Diz, Conker and Mildred were uninjured, they were still unable to move beneath the lowered ceiling and things were beginning to get a little desperate. Conker tried his hardest not to cry out loud but his almost silent sobs were heard by the other two.

"What's the matter with you, now?" Mildred asked in her regular nasty manner.

"I need to pee so badly it hurts," Conker wailed.

"Oh, honestly! Boys are such babies."

"Leave him alone," Diz said.

For a moment Mildred was silent, but it was a very short moment. "You only said that because I can't come and get you. Besides, it's not like you to stick up for him."

"Maybe I just want you to shut your whining," Diz replied.

"You're going to be so sorry—"

Her words were halted by a sudden, loud noise from somewhere above their heads. It sounded like something substantial had broken or cracked and the vibrations reverberated through the whole cell and even made the heavy stone ceiling tremble.

"What was that?" Conker asked.

"How on Earth should I know?" Mildred snapped. "I'm stuck here just like you, in case you hadn't noticed."

"I think we're going to die," Diz said. He covered his head with his hands as if that would help him survive.

In the mechanism room above, the tension caused by the bar jammed into the cogs was having dangerous repercussions. One of the cogs had developed a crack across its width and looked like it would give way at any moment. If it did, the ceiling slab would drop the remaining distance to the cell floor.

As if it was trying to threaten them, it trembled again.

"I think you may be right, Diz," Mildred said, her voice reduced to a scared whisper.

With Uncle Rosko bracing the rope for the others, Tim, Sally, Poppy and finally Em made their way across the bottomless pit. They clung onto the rope and edged across before dragging themselves over the lip at the far side, each of them feeling relieved.

Then, with all the children across the gap, a thought occurred to Sally. "How will you get across, Uncle Rosko?"

"Don't you worry about me," he replied. He threw his backpack then the quads' bag over the pit and the others caught them before they could hit the ground. He then moved to the very edge of the pit, re-tied the rope about his waist, held on tightly and jumped.

"Geronimo!" he yelled.

The rope pivoted around the far edge of the pit and he swung down towards the rocky face with his knees bent and ready for impact. He hit quite hard — his creaky knees shooting spikes of pain up his legs — but managed to keep hold of the rope. He immediately began pulling himself up.

It was slow progress — Rosko wasn't as young as he used to be and his rock-climbing days were long behind him. But he knew he had the strength to make it if he kept things steady.

Unfortunately, the makeshift rope had other ideas. It rubbed against the rough edge of the pit and the individual strings began to fray and the first of them snapped with a ping.

All five kids watched in horror as the rope threatened to part and drop Uncle Rosko into the bottomless pit.

CHAPTER EIGHTEEN

The Door and the Island

Sally almost didn't dare look but forced herself to peer over the edge of the pit anyway. Uncle Rosko had nearly climbed to the top, but more threads were fraying and another string snapped as he edged closer.

She grabbed his backpack, tipped out the contents and beckoned to the others. "Come on, take hold of this strap and we'll lower the bag over the edge so Uncle Rosko can grab the other strap." Quickly, but cautiously, Poppy, Em and Tim did so.

Once it was within reach, Rosko grasped the bag strap with one hand. His other remained on the makeshift rope to spread his weight between the two.

Four kids strained with all their might and pulled Rosko a little higher. He slid his hand up the rope then pulled on that again as the backpack was hauled closer to the pit edge. Another slide and pull and Rosko was able to get his hand onto level ground again.

However, the floor was too smooth to grip onto and for a moment it appeared he was stuck in this position. The others pulled on the bag strap again but they couldn't quite get the angle right to get him safely over the edge.

Suddenly, another pair of hands grasped Rosko's wrist and heaved. Caz had limped over, desperate to help and her addition to the team effort made enough of a difference to get him moving again.

The five of them were now able to pull Rosko up and over the edge in a swift but clumsy movement. He rolled over the lip of the pit and lay on his back gasping from the exertion.

Caz also dropped to the floor, grimacing. She was in agony from bracing her feet to help pull up Uncle Rosko — it had aggravated her ankle injury. The others gathered around her but there was little they could do.

"We should have brought a first aid kit," Em said.

"We'll make sure we include one in the bag from now on," said Sally.

Poppy looked worried. "But how can we help her, now?"

"Leave it to me," Uncle Rosko said. He pulled himself to his feet then lifted Caz off the floor. "Grab my bag one of you, please."

Poppy and Em gathered all the items that had been tipped out of the backpack and placed them inside before following their uncle and the others.

Rosko plodded over to the door with Caz in his arms, a little wobbly after the exertion of the rope climb. He nearly stumbled when his foot hit a loose piece of rubble. Only the instant reactions of Tim and Sally, walking either side of him, helped him stay upright.

"I could have limped back here," Caz said through gritted teeth. Although she made a huge attempt to be brave, she was clearly in a lot of pain.

"No limping before I examine your foot," he said, then let her down near the step in front of the door. She put all her weight on her good foot as Rosko helped her sit down.

He wore a worried frown as he knelt in front of her. "Now, this is likely to hurt..."

He unfastened her shoe then pulled it off. Caz let out a gasp of pain then screwed her eyes up tight and clenched her teeth with a fierce strength. Uncle Rosko glanced up, saddened by the tears in Caz's eyes, then pulled off her sock and examined her ankle carefully.

"Is it broken?" Tim asked. The ankle had already swollen quite badly.

Rosko manipulated her foot gently, but even this was painful for Caz. "It's only sprained, thankfully. But it will be painful for a few days." He delved in his bag and brought out a roll of bandage that he quickly bound around Caz's foot while she let out small whimpers of pain through her teeth.

"How will we get her back across the pit?" Poppy asked while Uncle Rosko put Caz's sock and shoe back on.

"We can't," he replied. "Our only chance is to find a way through this door and hope there's another route to the surface."

"And if there isn't?" asked Em.

"We'll cross that bridge when we come to it." Rosko stood up and scowled as he looked around. "I wish we had something to use as a crutch."

"We can all take turns helping her," Tim said. "We can be human crutches."

"But if we're going to move on we need to get this door open," said Sally. "I can't see a handle or anything."

Poppy walked up to it and rapped on the wood with her knuckles. It sounded more like she was knocking on concrete than wood. "I don't think we'll be able to break it down even if we had an axe."

Uncle Rosko moved away from the group and turned his back to hide the worry on his face. He busied himself by coiling the makeshift rope, but his mind fretted on the fact that he may have led the five youngsters into great danger.

Gus finally decided that Edith's grandchildren had spent enough time in the cell and hoped they'd learned their lesson. But when he unlocked the door and opened it he was horrified to find that the ceiling had come down on them.

"Oh my god," he exclaimed. "What have I done?"

"Who's there!?" yelled Mildred. "Let us out of here!"

"Help!" wailed Conker.

"We're trapped!" shouted Diz.

Gus dropped to the floor and looked under the slab of stone, still about thirty centimetres off the ground. He could just make out the shape of three kids in the almost complete darkness.

"Thank goodness you're alive," he said. "I'll fetch a rope to pull you out. Wait right there."

"We're not going anywhere!" Mildred snapped. "And if you don't hurry we'll never beat those quads to the—"

"Shut up!" Conker yelled. "Please get us out, Gus."

Gus jumped to his feet and had just started to race off to get the rope when a dreadful sound came from the mechanism in the room above the cell.

The cogs, into which the bar was jammed, could no longer withhold the pressure from the weight of the stone ceiling. They fractured into dozens of pieces and the bar dropped to the floor. The mechanism ran freely once again.

Down below, the ceiling dropped the remaining short distance and hit the floor of the cell with a deadly thunk.

Gus watched in horror. For a couple of seconds was frozen to the spot as the sound reverberated around the underground complex. He couldn't be sure, but it seemed that there was a faint sound of a splash, which puzzled him. There was no water down here, so where had the sound come from?

He became furious with himself, thinking about something so completely pointless. The true horror of the situation set in and he stared with dread through the cell door at the monstrous slab of stone.

He didn't know which was worse, that the Malprentice kids had been crushed or the thought of what Edith would do to him when he told her.

The bandage on Caz's ankle helped a little, but it was still swollen and she was still in some pain. So she remained seated on the step while the others examined the door that blocked their progress.

"This wood is like rock," Sally said. She pushed on it and the others joined in but the door wouldn't open.

"It must be locked or bolted on the other side," Em said.

"Maybe it's sealed with a magic spell," Poppy suggested.

"There's no such thing as magic!" Tim declared.

"How do you know?" Sally demanded.

"Everyone knows," Tim replied. "This is just a locked door and we need to work out how to unlock it."

"At the risk of showing a lack of family loyalty," Rosko said. "I must agree with Tim. Magic doesn't exist." He became thoughtful for a moment. "Hmm... when you think about it, the achievement of this underground complex is even greater in that context."

"What do you mean?" asked Em.

"This huge place was created with only the simplest of tools." Rosko put his hands on his hips and admired the craftsmanship of the door.

"Maybe it opens from the other side." Poppy said. "Or opens towards us."

"So we'd need to pull it, rather than push it," said Tim.

"But there's no handle," Em sighed.

Sally peered closely at a spot on the frame to the left of the door. "There's a small slot here. Maybe something's meant to fit into it."

"Like a key or a lever, maybe." Poppy looked around on the floor nearby but couldn't spot anything.

"Nnnng!" Caz groaned as her ankle fired electric shocks up her leg. "I can't think straight with the pain from my ankle. I feel like I'm missing something." She slapped the step angrily with the flat of her hand then yelled out in frustration.

Poppy came over, crouched beside her and gave Caz a big hug. "We're going to be fine and you're the toughest of all of us so your ankle will be good as new before you know it."

"Hey!" Sally exclaimed, more than a little indignant. Being very slightly the eldest meant that she liked to think she was stronger and tougher than the other three. Poppy glared at her and Em gave her a light nudge.

"Not now, Sally," Em whispered and Sally hung her head.

In spite of the hug from Poppy, Caz suddenly started crying.

"I'm sorry I can't stop the pain," Poppy said and squeezed Caz again.

"It's not the pain," Caz responded. "We were having such a great adventure, then I injured my ankle. And now it looks as if we're all going to die down here."

"Don't say that," Poppy whispered.

"Why not? Things have been getting worse and worse since..." She paused. "Since I accidentally pulled on that stone ring!"

Caz's head shot up and her wet eyes grew as wide as the grin that quickly spread across her face. She leapt to her feet, almost forgetting the pain of her sprained ankle, and hobbled over to the bag she'd been carrying. She rummaged in it for a minute before she looked up wearing an expression of disappointment.

"It's not here," she said. "The stone ring has gone."

"It must have fallen from the bag," Sally said. "Never mind."

"No, the ring is important!" Caz urged. "I'm pretty sure it will open the door for us."

"You may be right," Em said. "It has a bit sticking out that might fit into that slot."

"Look around," Rosko said. "Perhaps it fell out near here."

After a few moments of searching, Tim pointed and yelled. "Look! There it is."

They looked in the direction he indicated and saw that the stone ring teetered on the very edge of the pit, balanced so precariously it threatened to fall into the bottomless depths at any second.

Mildred, Diz and Conker were completely relieved when they didn't die beneath the crushing weight of the cell's stone ceiling. Although it was a shock when, seconds later, they fell into icy water in complete darkness.

They sank with the momentum of their fall and touched the sandy, silty bottom, but they had the sense to immediately push against it and swim back to the surface. In spite of their many faults they were good swimmers. Their heads broke clear and they gasped for air, more from the shock of the cold than the few seconds they'd spent holding their breaths.

"What happened?" Diz eventually asked as he trod water.

"The floor opened up just before we were crushed," Conker replied.

"All I can say is that whoever designed this place has a horrid sense of humour," Mildred spat. To say that she was annoyed would be like describing Mount Everest as fairly big.

"Can you see anything?" she asked.

"It's pitch black!" Conker spluttered as his head went below the surface again. The cold was affecting his arms and legs already.

"If we don't get out of here we're going to drown," Diz said.

"Like that isn't obvious," Mildred snarled.

Diz turned about on the spot and peered through the gloom. He didn't know if his eyes were becoming accustomed to the lack of light, but he was sure he saw something a short distance away.

"Over here," he said and started swimming in the direction of the shape he'd seen — a patch of darkness that was a tiny bit lighter than all the rest. It almost came as a surprise when, about thirty seconds later, his hand hit something solid.

He stopped swimming and let his feet touch the bottom, which sloped up in front of him. A few steps and he was out of the water completely."

"This way!" he shouted. "I've found dry land."

Conker and Mildred needed no further encouragement and the sounds of splashing from their swimming strokes became hurried then a little frantic. But it wasn't long before the two pulled themselves up on the odd little beach.

"I'm glad I'm out of that freezing water," Conker said. "But at least I don't need to pee any more."

"Me, neither," Diz said.

"Ugh, you're disgusting," said Mildred, though she smirked to herself.

The darkness made Conker brave enough to pull a face at her. "I'm still cold, though," he said.

"'Cos your clothes are soaking wet, stupid," Mildred snarled.

They fell into silence for a few minutes before Diz piped up. "Hey, Mildred, haven't you got a mobile phone?"

"Like I'd get a signal down here!"

"No, but you can use the light to take a look around."

"Oh, yeah," she said. She pulled it from the pocket of her pyjamas and wiped the water from the surface.

Mildred was always spoilt rotten by their parents and even at the age of nine her phone was the latest model and water resistant. So when she switched it on it lit up straight away.

She swung the light around and across the water. They were on a small island in the middle of an underground lake, which was so large the light from the phone wouldn't reach the sides.

Mildred turned the light onto the island itself and all three of them screamed. Her phone abruptly flew from her now trembling hands and into the water's edge, plunging them into complete darkness again.

What they'd seen, in that brief moment of illumination, was that this tiny island was inhabited by skeletons.

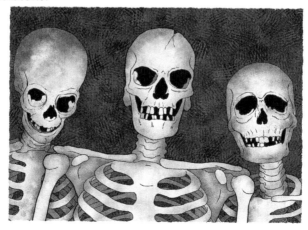

CHAPTER NINETEEN

Thoughts of Treasure

For a moment the quads, along with Tim and Uncle Rosko, simply stared at the teetering ring from their position near the door. Then Tim began to walk rapidly towards it but had to stop after only a few steps.

The ring was so delicately balanced that even the very slight vibrations from his footsteps made it wobble.

"Don't anyone move. Stay exactly where you are, Tim," Rosko said then looked at the girls at something of a loss for ideas. "How on Earth are we going to retrieve it?"

Caz, Sally and Poppy immediately looked at Em but the latter was in deep thought. It took her a few moments to register the stares of the others.

"What?" she asked with wary surprise in her voice.

"You're the lightest on your feet by a mile," Sally said in a quiet voice.

"Yeah," agreed Caz and Poppy in unison.

"No..." Em shook her head.

But even Uncle Rosko nodded. "You've nearly given me a heart attack on a few occasions, you move about so quietly." He grinned to show he meant it in a friendly way.

"Okay, I guess you're right," Em said. "I'll go and get it."

"Might be best to take your shoes off," Uncle Rosko suggested.

Em carefully sat on the step beside Caz, removed her shoes then rose once more, now in her stockinged feet.

As she slowly crept towards the ring, her footsteps soft and silent, she breathed gently and noiselessly, too. It worked — her careful, steady steps had no effect on the balance of the ring and a few moments more would see it safely in her grasp.

She reached the pit edge and stood above the ring for a few seconds calming herself. Then she slowly crouched down and reached out her hand. Her fingers had almost grasped it when Tim let out a sudden, loud sneeze that made everyone jump.

An involuntary reaction to the unexpected noise

made Em's fingers twitch and they nudged the ring before she could stop herself. It then did the one thing no one wanted. It tipped over the edge of the pit.

Mildred, Diz and Conker clung to each other and trembled with fear. Although the underground darkness was scary and discomfiting on its own, skeletons were the last thing they expected. Or wanted.

"We're going to die," Conker wailed. Surprisingly, Mildred didn't belittle him.

They hugged even tighter, not knowing what to do, expecting the skeletons to attack at any moment. Then, when the attack never came, Mildred pushed the boys away from her.

There was a sudden splash in the water.

"What the heck was that?" Conker asked, imagining monsters lurking in the water.

"It's just me," Mildred replied from near to the ground. "I'm trying to find my phone." She groped around some more, splashing all the time. "Ah-ha! Got it." She got to her feet and abruptly sneezed, really loudly. After a moment the sound echoed back.

"This place sounds big," Conker said.

"Hello!" Diz yelled and the word came back as an echo reply.

"Shut up!" Mildred ordered. She fumbled with her phone for a moment and managed to get the light on again, though her hands shook with the cold as she shone it towards the centre of the little island again.

The skeletons were still there, but on closer inspection it was clear they were simply attached to poles stuck into the ground. They were set in a circle around a central cairn with the skeletons facing outward as if protecting the cairn.

There were a dozen of them, completely lifeless, but even dead skeletons were scary. It wasn't just the cold that made them tremble.

At the feet of each skeleton was a small ceramic bowl but whatever they might once have held, there was no sign of their contents now.

"Wh... what is this place?" Conker asked, his teeth chattering.

"This must be where ancient people performed black magic rituals," Mildred said, sounding far braver than she actually felt. "These skeletons were probably sacrificed or something."

"I don't like it here," Conker said. "I wish we could leave."

"Do you think we should swim for it?" Diz asked.

"I'd never make it," Conker trembled. "Perhaps you can swim for help."

"Yeah," Mildred said. "You can do that, right?"

Diz strained his eyes to look for some indication of a distant shore. "I could if I knew which way to go. Can you see anything?"

Conker and Mildred peered through the darkness then both shook their heads without a word. An odd silence descended on the little island.

"Let's look around," Mildred finally said. "We might find something useful."

They squeezed between two of the skeletons, trying not to touch them, and approached the cairn in the centre of the circle. The stones had been built to a height of about four feet and on the top of the squat pile was a bowl carved from stone, the inside of which showed signs of burning.

"I wish we had a fire," Conker said.

"Yeah," added Diz. "I'm freezing."

"Maybe I can start one by rubbing your heads together," Mildred suggested, though the comment lacked her normal venom. The cold was sapping her strength.

Instead of his usual grisly look, Gus Grimshaw appeared rather meek and timid as he slunk into the drawing room and stood in front of Edith Malprentice where she sat by the window. She took one look at him and rolled her eyes in disgust.

"What is it now?" she hissed at him. "More delays? More problems?"

"You could say that, yes," Gus whispered, reluctant to explain in detail.

"Out with it, you fool!"

"There's been an accident." He forced himself to look her in the eye then paused for a moment before continuing. "The kids have been killed. Crushed by the ceiling of the cell they were in."

"Oh my god!" Edith exclaimed. "Still, it only serves them right for trespassing..."

"No, not the Quinton kids. Your grandchildren."

Edith opened her mouth but found that no sound came forth. For a moment she looked like a skinny old fish working her jaw up and down. Then she put a shaky hand to her mouth and drew in a breath so rasping and ragged that Gus thought she was going to faint. She tried to get to her feet but didn't have the strength to do so. She hung her head heavily.

"The poor things..." she eventually said. "Their parents... Oh my god, I'll have to tell their parents!"

"Do you want me to call them for you?" Gus offered.

"Thank you, no." An unexpected tear rolled down each cheek. "I'll do it, once I've gathered myself together. My son will never forgive me."

"No... It's... I'm sorry, ma'am." Gus sidled out of the room and left Edith to her sad thoughts.

Em's mind had no time for any thoughts. She moved with the speed of a striking snake and lunged for the ring as it went over the edge of the bottomless pit. Her reactions were astonishing and she managed to grasp it between the tips of her thumb and index finger. But it was a precarious grasp and she could already feel it beginning to slip from them.

Her lunge meant she was now lying on her belly with her arm over the rough edge and she was reluctant to try and stand in case it caused the ring to go. She held her breath and slowly brought her other hand around, trying to find the right balance between speed and caution. Steadily her arm came around until she was able to wrap her fingers around the ring in a solid grip. She immediately jumped to her feet and held it aloft.

Everyone cheered and all but Caz hugged Em once she'd dashed back to join them. It had been a tense few minutes but she'd done brilliantly. As she sat on the step to put her shoes back on, Caz leaned over and embraced her.

Uncle Rosko examined the ring and ran his fingers

over the shape that jutted from the outer edge. "It looks the right size and shape," he said. He pulled a face and shook his head. "But it feels like too much of a coincidence."

"Using it to trigger the chute in the library might have been by design," Poppy said. "It makes sense to put it there because if a person came down here they'd need the ring."

"That's an interesting thought," Rosko replied as he scratched at the stubble on his chin.

"But that would mean the chute in the secret reading nook was there before the house was built," Poppy continued.

"Which also makes sense if Evil Edith's ancestors hid the Malprentice treasure down here," Sally added.

"Actually, they wouldn't be her ancestors," Tim said. "They would have been her husband's."

"That's right, Tim," Rosko said. "She was Edith Grimshaw before she got married."

"Isn't that Gus's surname?" Caz asked from her place on the step.

"They're distant cousins," Rosko explained.

"Fancy being a butler for a relative," Em said. "You'd think that would be too embarrassing."

"Enough with the history," Sally said. "Let's see if that ring really is a key."

She helped Caz to her feet and they all watched as Uncle Rosko inserted the ring's protrusion into the slot. It was a perfect fit! So he attempted to turn it clockwise. Unfortunately, it wouldn't budge and nothing happened no matter how much strength he used.

"Try turning it the other way, Uncle," Caz suggested.

As soon as he did, the heavy click of a mechanism sounded and the door shifted inward very slightly. Sally pushed on the door and it swung open quite easily despite not being used for many years.

"That'll teach me to make assumptions," Rosko said and gave a wry smile to Caz. He passed the ring to Em and she placed it into the backpack she now carried.

When they stepped through the door it was like entering a very different underground complex. The design and construction were of a much higher standard. The walls were decorated with intricate, detailed carvings and these had been painted with vibrantly coloured pigments, ground from different minerals.

Rosko shone his torch around, back and forth, trying to take it all in. "Oh my word! This is an astonishing achievement — we could be looking at the archaeological discovery of the century."

"How did they do it with simple, Bronze-Age tools?" Em asked.

"Exactly," Rosko replied. "This is beyond anything that's been discovered until now. It's a real treasure."

"So we're going to be rich?" Tim asked with wide eyes.

"We might be famous," Rosko said. "But I doubt that we'll be rich. All the value lies in the historical significance of the place."

Caz looked a little disappointed as she leaned on Sally for support. "We heard there was hidden treasure down here."

Rosko spread his arms to indicate his surroundings. "Isn't this treasure enough?" He shook his head slightly when there was no reply.

He wandered over to the left hand wall to take a

closer look at the coloured carvings but the five kids remained where they were.

Poppy folded her arms and took on a slightly indignant air. "Money isn't important, anyway. Too many bad things happen when people obsess about money."

Em nodded her agreement and even Caz and Sally appeared to be of a similar mind, but Tim was determined not to let it go.

"But a little bit of money wouldn't be a bad thing, right?" he suggested. "Enough for a phone, maybe, or some football boots or..."

The girls laughed, meaning it in a friendly way, but Tim became angry. He tried his best to keep it bottled up, but the laughter didn't stop and his feelings suddenly exploded out of him.

"Stop making fun of me!" he shouted. The laughter died away. "It's all right for you rich kids, but we've never had any money."

"We're not rich," Sally said.

"Compared to us you are," Tim snapped.

"Dad has a fairly good job," Poppy added. "But that doesn't make us well-off."

"Well, my mum has to work two jobs just so we have enough to eat. Finding some treasure would make things easier for us."

The girls fell quiet and looked rather sheepishly. Because their lives were comfortable, it was easy to forget that others didn't have it so good. They quickly apologised but Tim was too angry to acknowledge it.

"What about your Dad?" Poppy asked in a very quiet voice.

"He died," Tim responded and his anger dissolved instantly. He looked away, but not before the girls saw a tear roll down his cheek. "Three years ago it was."

"Oh, Tim, we had no idea," Poppy said then gave him a friendly hug. Such was his emotional state that he simply let her then a moment later embraced her in return. Seconds later, Tim found himself in the centre of a group hug and saw that the eyes of all four quads were moist, too.

Rosko turned away from them. He was proud on the girls but felt it was their moment and their issue to deal with.

"Thank you," Tim whispered and the group broke apart. "But if you tell anyone about this we'll never be friends again."

"Don't worry," Caz said. "You can always rely on us."

The three Malprentice kids were despondent to the point where they huddled together for warmth in the darkness. Such closeness was unheard of between the three of them but they were long past caring.

"We'll never get out of here," Conker sobbed through chattering teeth. "We're going to die."

"Shut up!" Mildred yelled in a voice that was shrill with fear. "Someone will rescue us when they realise we're missing."

"They might think we're dead," Diz moaned.

Mildred pushed the other two away and got to her feet, almost falling over from trembling so hard. But she steadied herself and drew a really deep breath into her young lungs. As soon as they heard this, Diz and Conker stuck their fingers into their ears for they knew what was coming.

With her lungs full to bursting, Mildred turned all that breath into the loudest scream she could manage. Even with their ears bunged up the boys cringed at its piercing nature.

"If no one heard that," Mildred said, "we're as good as dead."

Back in the newly discovered corridor, the group were making slow progress, allowing for Caz's limping walk. Then Sally held up her hand to indicate that they should stop and listen. Nothing appeared to be making a noise, though.

"I thought I heard a distant scream," Sally said.

"It's probably just the wind in the tunnels again," Em suggested.

"Or ghosts," Tim added.

Rosko was supporting Caz and he snorted with derision. "There are no such things as ghosts."

They all started moving up the corridor again, the kids disappointed that ghosts didn't exist. But they'd only travelled a short distance when they got the shock of their lives.

A row of fearsome, threatening figures rose up before them with spears at the ready.

CHAPTER TWENTY

Deeper Underground

Reacting immediately, Tim turned and ran. The quads began to follow, with Caz trying to free herself from Uncle Rosko's support, but the old man stood his ground, showing no fear at all.

Curious about the old man's lack of action, the girls forced themselves to do the same. Caz looked up and saw that her uncle was grinning as he looked at the strange figures.

"Isn't this fascinating?" he said and played his torchlight over them.

The quads spent a few moments taking in more detail and now realised that the figures were not real creatures or monsters of any kind, but artificial constructions.

"What are they?" Poppy asked.

"They look like puppets of some kind, designed to scare anyone who approaches," Em replied.

"Well, I was pretty scared," Sally said. "But only for a moment," she added. All four gave a little laugh as if to say that they all were.

"Can you help Caz a moment?" Uncle Rosko asked, not taking his eyes off the large figures.

Sally took Caz's weight on her shoulders and Rosko walked over to the strange constructions. He pulled a notebook and pencil from a pocket and made notes while he examined them closely.

Rosko was fairly tall, but these scare devices towered above him like metal sentinels. They were nearly three metres in height, made of bronze segments and each had a fearsome mask for a face. Even though it was clear they had no life of their own and could do them no harm, they were still pretty creepy. In the darkness of this underground passage it was easy to imagine they were simply waiting for the right moment to come to life and strike them all down.

Warily, Tim crept back to join the group and avoided the gaze of any of the quads. He sidled over to stand with Uncle Rosko as the latter probed at the sentinels with his fingers and tapped at them with his pencil.

"Fascinating," the old man said.

"Well..." Tim responded, nervously.

Rosko gave him a glance and whispered, "Don't worry, lad. I'd have run away, too, at your age."

"But the quads didn't," Tim hissed back.

"They nearly did."

"But..."

"Listen, Tim. They've grown up in each other's pockets since they were born and at times act almost as they're one person." Rosko chuckled almost silently. "It can take a lot of getting used to."

Tim nodded but still looked a little concerned. "They're hard to work out."

"You shouldn't fret. You'd know if they didn't like you."

Rosko looked the boy up and down as if weighing him up. Such close examination normally made Tim uncomfortable because it was usually due to the colour of his skin, but Tim got the sense that something else was behind the scrutiny.

"I heard what you said earlier," Rosko said. "You're lucky to have such a great Mum."

"Yeah, but she'll be having kittens by now. Worrying about me not going home last night." Tim blinked hard a couple of times and wiped his nose on the back of his hand.

"My niece will be the same." Rosko jerked a thumb in the direction of the girls. "Their Mum. She thinks I can't look after myself. Sometimes it does them good to worry."

"But not this much," Tim replied.

Rosko shook his head, shrugged then looked into the youngster's eyes. "I knew your dad — best carpenter I've ever met. You remind me of him."

Tim became a little choked up again and couldn't reply. Rosko slapped him on the shoulder and stood for a moment before calling over to the girls.

"Come on. We've wasted enough time here."

Rosko stepped around the figures and up the left side of the corridor with Tim close by him. The latter still avoided looking at the girls who walked slowly in a group to the right. Sally and Poppy supported Caz and Em took the lead with the torch and the bag.

They'd hardly gone any distance when there was another heavy stone clunk and the floor vibrated like a large bell, as if struck by a huge clapper.

"What now?" Sally groaned.

"Look out!" Em yelled at the same time.

But before any of them could react, two sections of floor tipped downward in opposite directions. Tim and Rosko found themselves sliding and tumbling to the left and the quads to the right. The group had been split in two.

Thankfully the descent wasn't too great and the slope fairly gentle, but the quads soon found themselves on another hard stone floor.

"Aagh!" screamed Caz. Her sprained ankle took another knock in the tumble and the pain shot up her leg again.

"What happened?" asked Poppy.

"It's pretty obvious," Sally stated.

"We must have triggered another trap," Em explained.

All four watched as the sloping floor rose back into place and became their ceiling. There was no escape that way.

"Someone's trying to kill us before we find the treasure," Caz growled through grinding teeth. The additional pain had understandably increased her grouchiness.

"Where's Uncle Rosko?" Poppy asked.

"We've lost him again," Caz replied. "And Tim."

"They were caught in a separate trap," Sally said.

"They must be on the other side of that wall." Em pointed with the torch. "I think it runs below the centre of the corridor above."

Sally walked up to the wall and shouted as loudly as she could. "Uncle Rosko! Tim!"

A second later they heard a very muffled reply but couldn't work out anything that was said.

"Well, we know they're there," Poppy said. "But we can't hold a conversation with them."

"We need to find them again," Em stated.

Caz ground her teeth against the pain in her ankle. "Easier said than done."

"Did you hear something?" Diz asked. He nudged Conker and Mildred. "I thought I heard shouting."

The three of them stood up, still shivering, and began calling out as loudly as they could. If there was one thing they all had in common, it was shouting really loudly. After a moment they stopped but couldn't hear a reply.

Mildred turned on her phone again and shone it outward from the island, waving it back and forth in the hope that someone would see it.

They yelled again and looked across the lake, trying to see something in the beam of light. Then their cries cut off abruptly — a dark shape moved beneath the surface of the water just off the shore.

After a full half-second of silence, instead of shouts the air became filled with terrified screams.

"Where are those screams coming from?" Poppy asked, a little agitated.

"Not from Uncle Rosko or Tim," Sally replied. "The noise is coming from a different direction. I think."

"It's hard to tell when it echoes around so much," Em said and looked at Caz. But the latter wasn't paying attention and limped over to a stone slab that protruded from the floor next to a small pile of old torches. She sat down to rest her injured ankle. She was about to remove her shoe and sock but Em stopped her.

"That won't help, Caz. And it'll hurt more when you try to put it back on." Em smiled kindly at her sister.

Caz nodded and clenched her teeth to bite back the pain. She still wanted to take off the shoe but knew that Em was probably right. She usually was about that kind of thing.

"Let's find where those screams are coming from," Sally said. "If we help whoever's in trouble they may know the way out. Spread out and listen for clues."

Sally, Poppy and Em fanned out from their current position, each with a burning torch in one hand with new ones taken from the pile by Caz. The latter watched them go and soon realised the room they were in was huge.

Poppy had only walked a short distance when she

heard the sound of gently running water and moved cautiously towards it. A narrow channel had been cut into the rock floor, along which ran the clear water of a small stream.

The torchlight picked out a number of strange fish with huge, bulbous eyes. But when she knelt down on the edge of the channel and brought the torch closer, they scattered in reaction to the unexpected brightness.

"Wow!" she exclaimed, astonished by the speed the small creatures moved. It was hard to imagine there would be any life down here but she couldn't deny the evidence of what she'd seen.

She looked up and down the length of the stream as far as the torch light would allow but there was no sign of where those screams might have come from and the opposite side of the stream was a blank wall of rock.

Em had taken almost no time at all to discover a roughly carved passage that led away from the chamber they'd dropped into. However, when she investigated, it turned out to be a dead end.

Sally, thankfully, had better success. She found another chamber off the main one. The ceiling was covered in the same kind of fluorescent lichen they'd seen earlier and it gave the room an eerie atmosphere. Adding to the creepy feeling was a large stone slab set into the centre of the room like an ancient table.

Dark red stains covered the stone's surface and Sally gulped. She had the feeling they weren't caused by the spilling of ancient fruit juices. It took her a few moments to register that the distant screams were a little louder in here.

Ignoring the table as best she could, Sally saw two doorways at the opposite side of the room and quickly dashed over to examine them. The one on the left showed a flight of stairs that led upwards while the doorway on the right had steps going down. It was from the second doorway the sound of the screaming came.

For a very brief moment Sally was torn with indecision — should she return for the others or take a look down the stairs? The latter won out. She had to check what was down there without wasting time.

A particularly loud scream made Sally falter as she descended the first of the steps. Her hand shook so badly that she nearly dropped her burning torch, but after taking a deep breath she pressed on cautiously.

"Come on," she told herself. "It may be spooky down here but you've got to be brave." She was encouraged by her own pep-talk and picked up her pace a little more.

The bottom of the steps opened up into a much larger cavern that felt damper than the rest of the underground complex. From the light of her torch she saw that she stood on the shore of an underground lake. She was unable to tell the size of it, but the yelling and screaming came from somewhere across the water.

She peered and squinted but could see nothing out there.

Over on the island, Conker spotted Sally's torch, nudged the other two and pointed. "Look! Someone's there. Someone heard us yelling."

"Hey!" Mildred yelled. "Over here!"

Sally heard this but couldn't see anything in the darkness across the water. "Where are you?" she shouted back.

Mildred switched on her phone again and shone it in the direction of Sally's torchlight.

"I see you," Sally shouted. "Are you okay?"

"We're on a small island," Mildred called back. "But we're stuck here and we're freezing."

"Don't worry, I'll help," Sally yelled.

She put the torch on the ground then sat down to take off her shoes and socks. "I hope it's not too deep," she muttered as she picked up the torch again and stepped up to the water's edge.

Sally paused and stared ahead to ensure she was aimed in the right direction then stepped into the water with a sharp intake of breath. It was colder than she'd expected but she continued anyway.

However, she'd only waded a few steps into the lake when her blood nearly froze in her veins — a creature came from nowhere and broke the surface directly in front of her.

As it lunged at her, all Sally registered was a gaping mouth filled with needle-sharp teeth.

CHAPTER TWENTY-ONE

The Monster

Tim woke with a headache and felt groggy, but wondered why the bed he lay on was so hard. Had his Mum woken him? It couldn't be time for school because it was still dark. He tried to pull his duvet over his head so he could go back to sleep but it wasn't there.

Then he remembered he wasn't at home and sat upright, a move he regretted immediately. A wave of lightheaded dizziness washed over him and all he could do was lie down again to wait for the feeling to pass.

The last thing he remembered was the floor tilting beneath his feet and sliding into the darkness beneath. From his headache and grogginess he he must have hit his head in the fall.

He sat up again, more slowly this time, and the dizziness was less severe. He saw the quads' Uncle Rosko crouching in a corner, examining something on the floor in the light of his torch. He couldn't quite make out what it was until Rosko picked up a pale object that he instantly recognised as a human skull.

Tim scanned his eyes about the room and they bulged in growing fear. All across the floor lay numerous skeletons.

"Oh my god!" Tim cried out. He drew in a gasp of air and immediately started coughing — the air was full of dry, dusty flakes he hadn't noticed in the dimness.

Rosko looked over. "Ah, you're awake. Are you all right?"

Tim raised his hand as an affirmative response but he was still coughing and this made him dizzy and his head pound once again. Then his coughing increased again and he had trouble breathing. Rosko dashed over and offered him a bottle of water to drink from.

"Drink in sips," he said. "Until you get your coughing under control."

Tim managed to force the coughing to stop for long enough to drink some of the water, which relieved his problem for a second. He had to repeat the process a few times before his throat was washed clean of the dust and the tickle abated. Although the coughing had stopped he was still dizzy and struggled to focus as he stared at the old man.

"Dizzy..." was all that he could get out. There was a rasping note to his voice that came from a soreness in his throat.

Rosko looked him over. "You have a nasty bump and may have a little concussion. Which is rather unfortunate considering the circumstances."

"What do you mean?" Tim asked, his voice turned into a squeak on the last word.

"There's no door down here."

In the feeble light from the torch, Tim could see that each of the walls was without an exit of any kind. However, higher up the walls was a balcony, complete with stone balustrade, which ran all around the room at a height of about twelve feet. On the back wall of the balcony on one side was a doorway.

"There's one up there," Tim said. "But why is there a balcony?"

"Whatever happened in this room," Rosko replied. "The balcony enabled an audience to observe the proceedings. And judging by the skeletons on the floor..."

Rosko shook his head but didn't finish that train of thought. Tim knew exactly what he meant and the thought made him shudder. He tried to get to his feet and Rosko helped him up, supporting him while he got his dizziness under control. Something crunched lightly under his feet that reminded him of...

"Leaves?" Tim was puzzled. "Why are there leaves down here?"

"They're not leaves," Rosko said.

Tim made the effort to bring his eyes fully into focus and saw that whatever covered the floor was adorned with diamond-like patterns. "Snake skins!" he exclaimed once it sank in.

"Indeed," said Rosko. "They've been here a long time and have become dry and brittle."

"Were people fighting snakes in here?"

"It's hard to be sure, but certainly possible."

"But there are no really dangerous snakes in Britain," Tim said, remembering something from school.

"Judging by the size and pattern of the skin fragments I've looked at, they weren't native species."

"What if some of them are still here?" Tim was

suddenly a little scared and a wave of nausea made him queasy.

"I hardly think so." Rosko smiled. "Not after so long."

Tim breathed a sigh of relief then looked up at the balcony again. "How are we going to get out?"

"I'd hoped you'd be well enough to do a spot of climbing," Rosko replied.

Tim took a big mouthful of water and gave the bottle back to the old man to put in his pack. He looked grimly at the skeleton remains and snake skins. "I'll give it a go."

"Okay," Rosko said with a grin. "If I stand near the wall and you clamber onto my shoulders, you should be able to reach the lip of the balcony."

"Ready when you are." He was still a little shaky and took a deep breath to steady himself.

"Are you sure you're up to this?" Rosko's brow furrowed with concern.

"I'll be fine," Tim replied and forced a smile onto his face. "Anyway, we don't have much choice."

Rosko clapped Tim on the shoulder then moved over to the section of wall below the doorway on the balcony above. He braced his back against the stone wall and linked his fingers for Tim to step into. The boy looked at the old man then up at the balcony.

"Wait," he said. "I won't be able to pull you up."

"No," Rosko agreed. "But we can use our makeshift rope from earlier."

Tim nodded and began the climb, first putting a foot into the cupped hands then, as Rosko raised him a little, he placed his other foot on his shoulder. When he stood with both feet on the old man's shoulders, Tim was in a precarious position pressed facing the cool stone. He inched his hands up towards the balcony edge and followed them with his eyes.

"I can't quite reach," he said.

Rosko pushed with his feet against the ground and stood more erect. Tim's fingers curled over the edge but not enough that he was able to pull himself up.

"A bit further," he breathed.

Rosko grasped Tim's feet firmly, one in each hand, and pushed upwards. Then he raised himself onto his toes, adding a few more inches. The old man's legs and arms shook with the strain, but he knew he couldn't stop. If he did, he was sure he wouldn't have the strength for a second attempt.

He was taken by surprise when Tim's weight abruptly lightened. The boy had gained enough purchase to begin pulling himself up. Rosko extended his arms fully and Tim started working his way through the gap between the balustrade's supports.

But something abruptly appeared from the nearby doorway and the surprise made him lose his grip. He fell from the balcony and landed in a painful heap on top of poor old Rosko.

Although Sally screamed with the shock of seeing the creature emerge from the water, it didn't stop her reacting with lightning speed. She leapt backward then quickly scrambled out of the water and onto the dry shore. Her torch had thankfully fallen away from the water's edge. By the time she turned back to the lake, the creature had vanished beneath the surface once more. A series of ripples were the only sign it had ever been there.

The encounter had been a close thing and Sally's heart pounded quite fiercely. She took a moment to steady herself then rose to her feet and cupped her hands to her mouth to shout across the water.

"I've got to fetch my sisters," she yelled. "I'll be back soon."

Sally pulled on her shoes and socks, grabbed the

torch from where it had fallen then raced up the stairs. She passed through the slab room and over to where the others were waiting for her.

"Where have you been?" Poppy asked. "We were getting worried."

"I found the Malprentice kids," Sally replied.

Em frowned. "I thought they were locked in that cell, trapped beneath the ceiling."

"Yeah, well now they're in the middle of an underground lake and I can't reach them because there's a monster in the water."

"A monster?!" Caz momentarily forgot about the pain in her foot.

"I waded into the water and it nearly ate me." Sally's eager face confirmed her story and her sisters instinctively knew she told the truth.

"What kind of monster?" Caz asked.

"It was so fast I didn't get a proper look at it," Sally said. "I only just managed to jump out of its way in time."

"This could be a great scientific discovery," said Em. "Do you think we'll be able to capture it?"

"I don't want to even try," Sally replied. "You should have seen its teeth!"

"Well, we need to work out how to get past it or we can't rescue the other kids." Poppy was already helping Caz to her feet as she spoke and Sally joined in. Caz winced with pain but was able to move with their help.

Em led the way with a torch and the backpack. She was scientifically excited but naturally nervous at the prospect of encountering the monster Sally had described.

When they reached the two doors in the glowing

slab room, Sally made a suggestion. "Poppy, Can you and Em check up the stairs for anything useful while I help Caz down to the lake. I didn't get the chance to go up there."

"Okay," Poppy replied.

She unlinked herself from Caz then she and Em raced up the stairs. They hadn't gone very far when they reached the end of the tunnel and emerged into another room with a burst of speed.

They came to an abrupt halt at the sight of an unexpected but familiar face poking through a balustrade in front of them. With an expression of shock the face vanished as its owner fell, quickly followed by two cries.

"Agh!"

"Ungh!"

Poppy and Em were on a balcony of some sort and they dashed forward to look over the barrier. They couldn't believe their eyes and gave a laugh on seeing the intertwined figures of Tim and Uncle Rosko. Unfortunately, they both looked in pain and the laugher quickly halted.

"Are you all right?" Poppy asked, now concerned.

"We will be," Rosko replied. "Once you get us out of here."

"How?" Em looked around and spotted a wooden ladder lying on the balcony floor. She dashed over but when she picked it up it simply fell apart. The metal fastenings had rusted and the wood was dry and brittle — it was impossible to use it to help the others.

Uncle Rosko picked himself up and took the makeshift rope from his pack. He threw one end up to Poppy and she tied it to the balustrade with the bowline knot Rosko had recently taught them.

It was only a matter of minutes before Tim and Rosko clambered up, with some help from the two girls, and sat on the balustrade to catch their breath.

"Come on, Uncle," Poppy urged. "We need to rescue the Malprentice kids."

"Give us a minute," Rosko responded. "I'm not as young as I once was and poor Tim took a nasty bump to the head."

Poppy immediately looked concerned and examined the injury to Tim's head, which had now formed into a clearly defined lump. She raised her hand to touch it but changed her mind when she saw Tim's warning expression.

"Where are Caz and Sally?" Rosko asked, suddenly worried.

"They're okay," Em replied. "Although Sally was nearly eaten by a monster."

"I'm sure that must be an exaggeration," Rosko chuckled.

"It's true!" Em's indignation was fierce. "Sally would never lie, especially not to us."

"Very well, let's go and take a look." Rosko got to his feet and looked at Tim. "You up to it?"

Tim nodded. "Yeah... I suppose."

They descended the first flight of stairs and entered the room with the stone table, where Uncle Rosko couldn't help his curiosity and halted to take it in.

"Oh, my word," he said. "Just look at this..."

"Uncle Rosko! We don't have time for this," Poppy said, doing her best to speak the way Sally would have done. "Come on."

She and Em led the way down the second stairway with Tim and a reluctant Rosko following them. When they reached the shore of the lake, Caz was sitting on the ground near the bottom of the steps and Sally was by the water's edge using her torch to peer into the depths.

Caz turned at the sound of footsteps. "Hooray! You found Uncle Rosko and Tim!"

"Sally told us to look for anything useful," Poppy smiled.

"But instead we found them," Em added with a playful grin.

"Hey!" Tim exclaimed, spinning round to glare at her, which he immediately wished he hadn't done. "Ooh, dizzy again."

"Are you okay?" Caz asked.

"I think he has mild concussion," Rosko said. "But he should be fine in a day or two, provided we get out of here."

Rosko walked over to Sally and stared at the water. "What did you see, Sally?"

"It was a monster, Uncle Rosko," Sally declared. "With lots of sharp teeth."

Rosko gave her a dubious smile then stared into the water without comment. Sally seemed to be telling the truth but it puzzled him. He crouched down, scooped up some water in his cupped hand and raised it to his mouth.

"Uncle Rosko!" Sally yelled in astonishment. "The monster might get your hand." Except for Caz, the others came over to see what the commotion was.

Cautiously, Rosko took a little sip of the water then after tasting it for a moment he drank the rest. "It's beautifully fresh. I suggest you all take a drink and refill your water bottles. There's no telling how long it might take to get out of here."

Once they'd done so, Em took some water over to

Caz, too, who was grateful for the cold drink. Then Rosko spoke to Sally some more as he stared through the darkness across the water.

"Am I to understand the Malprentice kids are out there?" he asked.

"I think they're on an island or maybe the other side of the lake, it's hard to tell." She looked up at him in earnest. "I waded into the water to see how deep it was and the monster came at me."

Rosko nodded. "Hold your torch up high a moment."

As Sally did so, Rosko pulled a snack bar from his pocket and opened the wrapper. He then broke off a piece and threw it into the water about ten feet from the shore.

Almost the same split second the piece of snack bar hit the surface, a huge, toothy mouth appeared, swallowed the food then vanished again.

"See!" Sally said. "It's a monster!"

CHAPTER TWENTY-TWO

The Rescue

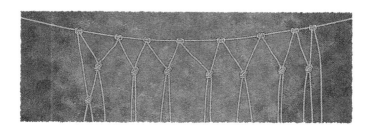

Rosko was completely silent but he looked fit to burst and his clenched lips couldn't hold back the smile that spread across them.

"What?!" Sally roared, her fists clenched tightly. "You saw it, too. It's a monster!"

That was too much for her uncle and a hearty laugh burst out of him with a splutter.

"It's not a monster," Poppy said, frowning at Uncle Rosko while he tried to stop laughing. "It's a huge pike."

"Well, it didn't look like a fish when it attacked me!" Sally wasn't going to give in easily. She fixed Poppy with a hard stare then glared at Uncle Rosko in her most Mum-like way.

The old man calmed himself down and forced a serious look onto his face. "I'm sorry, Sally, I shouldn't have laughed. But after all that's happened I just kind of snapped." He paused and looked at Sally's still furious face. "But Poppy's right, it is a pike and the biggest one I've ever seen."

"How on Earth did it get down here, Uncle Rosko?" Em asked. She'd just rejoined them and stood at the very edge of the lake peering at the dark surface. Her curiosity had pulled her close but not enough to make her put so much as a toe into the water.

"There must be a surface stream that feeds the lake and the pike got washed down here." He thought for a moment. "There must be plenty for it to eat or it would never have grown to the size it has."

"What are we going to do about the island?" Caz shouted over from where she sat.

"None of us can swim over there while that thing's patrolling the waters," Rosko replied.

"So it may be a fish, but it's a monster fish!" Sally exclaimed. She folded her arms and struck a superior pose, which the others ignored.

Rosko cupped his hands around his mouth and yelled across the water. "Hello! Can you hear me?"

The sound echoed around for a few seconds but there was no reply and no sign of any movement. Rosko's face now wore lines of worry and the others reflected his expression. Even Sally, who let go of her indignation. When Rosko shouted again, everyone joined in, but even their combined effort went unanswered.

Over on the island, the three Malprentice kids had taken an abrupt turn for the worse as their shivering became almost uncontrollable. Mildred, due to her illness, was on the verge of losing consciousness and although Conker and Diz tried to remain standing they found it impossible to do so.

"Help!" Conker tried to shout in response to Rosko's call, but it only came out as a hoarse whisper.

Back on the shore, Rosko repeatedly tapped one fist into the palm of his other hand as he strode back and forth. "Something's wrong. We need to rescue them before they die."

"What could be wrong?" Tim asked. He held his head and tried to ignore the pain from his earlier bump.

"Their clothes are likely wet and cold so they could be developing hypothermia. We may not have much time."

"But we can't go in the water and we don't have a boat," Sally said. "How do we reach the island?"

The girls and Rosko looked at each other in the hope that one of them would have an idea.

It was Tim, however, who snapped his fingers with an excited thought. "I have it! We just catch the monster fish to make the water safe to swim in. We have plenty of string."

"But we don't have a fishing hook," Em responded.

"Thank goodness," Poppy said. "I wouldn't want to take one out of a mouth filled with those teeth."

"We can use a net," Caz said.

"We don't have one of those, either," Em said.

"But we have string and I once read a book about making nets." Caz smiled then became annoyed with the surprised look on Tim's face. "Hey! I read all the time."

"No... I mean, yeah... I mean... Can you really make a net just from reading a book?" Tim asked, still pretty dubious.

"Well, I watched some online videos, too." Caz grinned. "It's easier than you'd think."

"Don't you need specialised equipment to make nets?" Rosko asked.

Caz shrugged. "Not for this kind of net. Can I borrow your knife, Uncle?"

Rosko handed it over and Em passed over the ball of string from the backpack. Caz cut a length of about two metres then gave one end each to Sally and Poppy.

"Pull it tight and hold it just in front of me." Caz turned to Em. "Cut me some lengths that are twice this size." She spread her arms to their full extent and Em nodded, taking the knife to and string to begin her task.

As each length was passed to her, Caz doubled it up and tied the looped end to the string held by Sally and Poppy. She spaced each one about ten centimetres from the last until she had twelve pieces attached. There wasn't much string left on the ball

Caz began knotting adjoining strings together in a specific, alternating pattern and a net-like structure began to appear almost straight away. As soon as she'd tied a couple of knots, Rosko grinned and sat beside her. His knowledge of knots helped him grasp the process instantly and he helped to speed things along. He worked on the right half dozen of the strings while Caz did the left. In relatively little time they had a completed net.

Rosko patted Caz on the shoulder. "Well done! Now, let's catch that fish."

Caz started to get up but daggers of pain stabbed her ankle again and she was forced to leave the fishing to the others.

Tim and Em took the net and placed it into the water at the edge of the lake, spreading it out as well as they could. Then they took hold of loose strings tied to two of the corners while Sally and Poppy grabbed the other two. The net quickly became wet and sank the few inches to the bottom. A few feet away a gentle plop sounded as the large fish broke the surface briefly.

"Are you ready?" Rosko asked. Em, Sally, Poppy and Tim each nodded.

"Hurry up," Poppy added. "We need to help those three kids quickly."

Rosko pulled out the snack bar he'd used earlier and dropped a piece into the water over the centre of the net. It worked exactly as they'd hoped and the pike shot into the shallows to grab the bait.

"Now!" yelled Rosko. "Pull!"

Even though they were expecting it, the sudden appearance of the monster fish startled them all and Tim dropped his length of string as it turned to get away.

The three girls recovered in a split second and yanked on their strings. Tim's quick reactions enabled him to gather his loose end and he pulled before the fish could swim off. The four ends were pulled in and the huge pike was captured.

It was about as long as Tim was tall, which was a little taller than the quads. But the way it thrashed and fought against the net it seemed twice that size. Its menacing teeth and eyes were particularly scary and it battled with unexpected strength. The lengths of string began slipping through everyone's hands and threatened to cut the skin.

"It's going to escape!" yelled Sally. "What do we do?"

Rosko grabbed the edges of the net with his big hands and dragged it a little closer so that it was almost out of the water. He gathered up the loose netting and pulled it more tightly so the fish had less room to move and could now barely wriggle. Only its tail was free of the net.

"Tim, grab the tail will you?" Rosko said.

Nervously, the boy did as he was asked, though from his look of fear and disgust he was far from happy about doing so.

Sally let go of her string now Rosko had the net secure. "Come on," she said to Em and Poppy. "We need to rescue the Malprentice kids."

"What about me?" Tim said. "I'm a great swimmer."

"You've had a bump to the head," Em replied. "It's too dangerous if you've got even mild concussion."

"She's right," Rosko agreed.

"Besides," added Poppy. "I bet you don't have your swimming costume with you."

"Like you have yours," Tim snorted.

"Actually, we do," Caz said and pulled the girls' costumes from the front pocket of the bag. "We always keep them in the bag just in case we get the chance to swim."

Rosko beamed proudly, once more impressed by the quads' resourcefulness. "Get changed quickly. I'm not sure how much time we have."

Sally, Poppy and Em disappeared through the dark exit so they could change in private and came back a minute later ready for swimming and dashed to the shore.

"Race you!" Sally said.

"No!" roared Rosko. "The water's cold and you need to save as much energy as you can for the return. Take it steady and keep with each other."

"Sorry, Uncle," Sally said, then she yelped as she stepped into the water. "Co-o-o-old!"

The pike tried to thrash about again but Rosko pulled the net even tighter. Em, Poppy and Sally eyed it with a worried look but quickly waded into the water and were soon swimming out into the darkness.

Caz grabbed Uncle Rosko's torch and shone its beam out towards the island. "I hope this helps them see where they're going," she muttered. "But they're going to be freezing when they get back."

Rosko suddenly looked at Caz then at Tim before returning his attention to the girl. "Caz, I need you to come over here and hold this net for me. There's something important I need to do."

Caz propped the light on top of her bag so it still shone across the lake then hobbled over to the edge of the water. With her feet in the water she hunched down and grabbed the bunched up netting near Rosko's hands. Once he was sure she had a firm grip, he let go and although the fish struggled again it was still firmly held.

Rosko grabbed his knife and one of the burning torches then hurriedly disappeared through the only exit.

Caz stared quizzically at Tim, but the boy only shrugged and said, "He's your uncle."

Caz tightened her grip on the net some more and the fish gave her a belligerent stare that seemed to promise some kind of revenge. A shudder went down her back and she looked away. She tried to spot her sisters in the water as the sound of their strokes grew steadily fainter.

The swimmers made good progress and as their eyes became used to the increasing darkness they found that the light from the shore was just enough for them to pick the island out from the surrounding gloom.

"Nearly there," Sally sputtered between strokes. Em and Poppy didn't respond, saving their energy for swimming.

A few moments later they pulled themselves onto the island and rested for a moment, panting to get their breath back. They didn't register the circle of skeletons, which was probably just as well.

"We can't wait too long or the cold will get us, too," Poppy said and rose to her feet. "We've got to get those three back as quickly as we can."

The Malprentices were difficult to see in the darkness but the three quads fumbled about and quickly found them. They tried to wake them but only Conker made any sound in response. However, all he managed was a rasping gasp rather than anything understandable.

"I hope we're not too late," Em said.

"Won't it be dangerous to take them into the cold

water?" Poppy asked.

"Possibly, but we don't have a choice," Sally replied. "Getting them back to the shore is their only chance of survival."

The girls each grabbed one of the unconscious kids and started dragging them the short distance into the water.

"Remember what they taught us in lifesaving," Poppy said. "Keep their faces above the surface."

Holding them under the chin as they'd been trained, they began the slow process of swimming back to the shore. They knew it would take much longer than the swim to the island, but they also understood that saving the three Malprentice kids rested with them. They couldn't let them down.

They'd covered about half of the distance when Caz spotted them making their way towards the shore, the faint light picking their splashes out of the gloom. She let out a sigh of relief.

"Come on!" she yelled in encouragement. "Keep going."

Unfortunately, her shift in focus from the fish caused a slight loosening of her grip on the net and the monster pike sensed an opportunity.

It writhed with renewed strength and greater determination than it had done previously and Caz and Tim struggled to keep control.

"Hold on!" Tim snarled through his tightly clenched teeth. "Don't let it escape or it'll eat your sisters."

Caz gritted her teeth and clamped her hands even tighter on the net but the fish thrashed about more fiercely still. So much so that the shallow water was a mass of foaming bubbles.

Then the strings of the net began to snap and in spite of herself, Caz let out a short but piercing scream.

CHAPTER TWENTY-THREE

Fish and Fire

"What the heck happened?!" Nate Malprentice was furious with his mother. "They've only been here a day and you couldn't keep them safe that long?"

As soon as Edith had phoned him up with the unfortunate news of the demise of their children, Nate and his wife, Felicity, had raced over to the Manor in their car, hoping it was all a cruel joke on his mother's part. At the worst he expected it to be wild exaggeration. Now the two parents stood in the centre of the drawing room waiting for an explanation.

"I'm afraid they were crushed beneath an enormous slab of stone." Edith looked at both of them from the armchair she was perched on the edge of. She held a cup of tea in her shaking hands and it rattled noisily against the saucer. "We have no idea what caused it to fall." She looked over to Gus standing by the door and he simply shook his head.

Felicity opened her mouth to say something but whatever the words might have been they were completely lost when she fainted clean away and crumpled in a heap on the faded carpet.

Nate and Edith were taken aback and too shocked to move, but Gus leaped forward, scooped her up as gently as possible and laid her on the sofa.

"I feel sick," Nate said and laid a hand on his abdomen, fighting to not throw up. He took a couple of deep breaths and brought the nausea under control, just. He looked at his mother again. "Wait, I thought we agreed you'd keep Mildred isolated from the boys."

"She was, but she escaped. There were..." Edith sighed sorrowfully. There was no point mentioning the Quinton Quads to him.

"Take me there."

"What? Where?" Edith wasn't sure what Nate wanted.

"I want to see where they died."

Gus stared at Nate then rose from where he knelt by the sofa. "I don't think that's a good idea."

"I didn't ask you," Nate snarled. "This is a family matter."

"Nate!" Edith yelled. "Being angry at Gus won't help."

"Whatever, Mother. Just show me where it happened."

Edith rose from her seat with a shaky sigh and put her rattling cup and saucer onto a small table. Gus led the way and they left Felicity unconscious on the sofa.

As they entered the underground chambers, Nate looked around in astonishment. "How is this possible? I lived in this house until I got married and I never knew any of this existed."

"I'd only ever heard rumours myself," Edith replied. "We only discovered it recently."

"But what made you look?"

"I'm running out of money and if I don't find something soon I may be forced to sell the Manor."

"And you're too proud to ask me for help?" Nate looked at her with mixed emotions — he didn't know whether to be angry or disappointed. Then anger began to take over.

Edith dropped her gaze. "I found evidence — clues and a map — of a treasure, hidden beneath the Manor. I hoped it would be the answer to all of my problems."

"But you haven't found it?"

"No," she replied and stared at her son. "Not yet."

Nate snorted his derision and they continued in silence until they reached the door to the cell in which the children had been held. He stared at the massive ceiling slab through the open door and dropped to his knees beside it, crying for the loss of his children. Her knees suddenly weak, Edith held onto Gus for support.

Nate's head jerked up and his sobbing abruptly stopped then he moved close to the stone slab. He reached out and ran a finger along the line where the slab met the floor.

"There's no blood," he said. "How is that possible if they were crushed?"

"What do you mean?" Edith asked with a hint of hope in her voice.

Nate put his nose to the slight gap. "There's a draught coming from under here. And a damp smell, like... underground water."

"How on Earth would you know what underground water smells like?" Gus snapped.

"He does a lot of cave exploring," Edith replied

when her son didn't.

Nate remained on the ground close to the heavy stone, pondering what he might do. Then he recoiled in astonishment, scrambled to his feet and looked at the other two.

"I heard a faint scream," Nate said and pointed into the cell. "It came from somewhere below the slab!"

Although Caz had screamed — partly in shock, partly in fear for the swimmers — she and Tim held onto the net for dear life. Unfortunately, the pike's thrashing about didn't cease.

"It's going to get free!" Tim said. "What do we do?"

"There's only one thing for it," Caz replied. "We have to pull it out of the water until my sisters get to shore."

However, that was more easily said than done. Bigger than either of them, it weighed a lot more, too. But with a well-timed heave they dragged it onto dry land and Caz sat astride it in the same way she'd pinned that bully down at school last term. She was a little too close to the head for her liking, but this reduced the ferocity of its thrashing quite a bit. She ground her teeth against the pain in her ankle.

"Are you okay like that?" Tim asked. "Are you safe?"

"Who knows," she replied. "Just don't let go of your end."

Rosko reappeared in a rush, his arms filled with a large bundle of dry wood. He'd gathered up the remains of the ladder from the balcony room and a few unused torches he'd found. He dropped the wood in a rough pile and hurried over to Tim and Caz.

"Are you all right?" he asked.

"For now," Caz replied. "The pike started breaking the net so we had to bring it ashore."

"It won't last long out of water," Rosko said.

"That won't matter if you plan on cooking it," said Tim, nodding towards the pile of wood.

"What...?   No, that's for a fire to warm the swimmers."   Rosko looked towards the splashing and could see them about forty feet out from the shore.

"We'll be okay," Caz said. "Just light the fire, Uncle."

Rosko immediately set to it, lighting the torches and piling half of the other wood on top. By the time the swimmers reached the shore the fire was burning really well.

He dashed over and helped pull the three Malprentice kids onto dry land then immediately checked for a pulse on each of them. Although he was deeply worried, he was also a little relieved to find that each of them was still alive.

"Oh my god!" Sally exclaimed as she, Em and Poppy flopped onto their backs, their lungs panting like blacksmiths' bellows. "I don't think I've ever worked so hard."

With everyone safe, Caz and Tim released the fish from the net, quickly rolling it into the edge of the water. For a moment it lay there, unmoving, before it sluggishly swam away and disappeared into the dark waters. They walked over to help the others.

"Your foot!" Em exclaimed. "Is it better?"

"I think the cold water just numbed it," Caz replied.

They dragged Mildred, Diz and Conker closer to the fire and laid them down on their sides, then the three swimmers disappeared to change back into their dry clothes again.

"Thank goodness they're only wearing thin summer clothes," Rosko said. "Or we'd never get them warm. The fire should evaporate the water from their clothes fairly quickly."

"I guess we're lucky the air down here is warm," Caz said. She and Tim were pretty wet from holding onto the pike and were glad of the fire to dry off.

"I don't understand," Tim said. "Why is the air warm?"

"The deeper underground you go, the warmer it gets," Caz explained. "It's the opposite of getting colder when you go up a mountain."

Tim nodded. "Shouldn't we move them closer to the fire?"

"We've got to be careful not to warm them too quickly," Rosko said. "Or that could do them a different kind of harm." He watched the state of the fire, ready to add a little more wood to the blaze when it was needed.

Sally, Em and Poppy returned from changing and, after putting their swimming costumes back into the pocket of the rucksack, sat a little further back from the fire than the others. Their exertion and dry clothes meant they'd warmed up already. They sipped on water from bottles and tried to ignore the rumbling in their bellies.

"Watch they don't burn," Sally said, pointing to the Malprentice kids as steam rose from their clothes. "We need to keep rotating them."

"Yes, mum," Caz joked and the others laughed.

A silence fell on the group, broken only by the sounds of the fire as the wood burned and popped and the embers shifted now and again. Rosko fed more wood onto the fire and they all felt surprisingly relaxed in its warmth.

Tim sat cross-legged between Conker and Diz and his head began to drop forward with a sleepiness that crept over him and which he found difficult to fight.

"Wake up, Tim!" Em shouted and everyone jumped at the sudden sound.

"What?" Tim mumbled. "I wasn't asleep."

"It's okay, we're all feeling tired," Rosko said and rubbed his eyes.

"But he can't sleep, not if he has a concussion." Em explained and the others knew she was right.

"I'm so tired, though," he said.

"We'll help you keep awake," Caz said. "We don't want anything to happen to you."

"Indeed not," Rosko said and put the last of the wood onto the fire.

"What's happening?" Poppy asked as she moved closer to Mildred. She and her brothers were shivering uncontrollably.

"How do we get down to the lower levels?" Nate demanded.

"Why? Do you think they're still alive?" Edith sneered.

"I heard a scream. At least one of them is alive." He glared at his mother.

"It might not be them," Edith said. "The Quinton quads are down in those tunnels, too."

"What? Who are they?" Nate grabbed his mother by the shoulders.

"The brats from a nearby house. They're always trespassing and causing trouble."

Nate rolled his eyes and released a sigh of exasperation. "Just tell me how to get down there."

"We don't know," Gus said. "The only way down appears to be through a door we don't know how to open."

"Which is why we hired those layabouts," Edith added and pointed to a group of men standing idly by some equipment.

"We were about to begin drilling through when those damn kids started interfering." Gus started walking towards his men. "We can start drilling now, though."

"Wait," Nate said. "Have you consulted an architect or civil engineer?"

Gus turned back and shook his head.

"Then you don't know whether or not the drilling

might cause the whole place to collapse." He faced his mother. "If it's not done properly every one of us could die."

Rosko crouched by the shivering kids and felt for a pulse on their wrists. "I think the shivering is a good sign. It means they're returning to normal."

Sally felt the sleeve of Mildred's pyjamas. "This is nearly dry already."

"Rub their arms to help the blood circulation," Rosko said.

With six of them and three Malprentice kids, they were able to take an arm each and rub some life into them.

After a few moments, Diz's eyes opened and he looked scared. He could only speak haltingly through chattering teeth. "What's... going... on?"

"We rescued you from the island," Sally explained. "Now we're trying to warm you up."

"I've... never felt... so cold."

Diz tried to sit upright and Rosko helped him do so. The boy turned to face the fire but glanced at his siblings while the others continued to help them. After a few moments, Conker came to with a start but his sister remained unconscious.

"Is she going to be all right?" Conker asked once he realised what was going on?

"She was already ill with measles," Em said. "It's probably harder for her to recover."

The wood Rosko had brought was very dry with age and the fire burned too quickly. It was already on its way to dying out completely and didn't have much more warmth to give them. Conker and Diz had recovered enough to move about again but Mildred was another matter. Although her colour was returning to normal she was still unconscious.

"I think we should leave," Caz said. "We only have a couple of torches left and if we don't get out soon we may become trapped here for good."

CHAPTER TWENTY-FOUR

A Glimpse of the Sun

"Please, Mister, what's going on?" Conker asked, looking at Rosko. He was still shivering and struggling to stay awake. The Malprentices' ordeal had clearly taken its toll on the three of them.

"We're trapped underground and we have to find a way out," Sally said before Rosko could respond, switching into take-charge mode. "Poppy, Em — will you help me with Mildred? Uncle Rosko, her clothes are still a little damp, can we have your shirt, please?"

Rosko wore a long-sleeved shirt over a T-shirt and he gladly gave up the outer garment. He then guided the boys a little way along the shore where they turned their backs on the girls to give them the privacy they needed. Conker watched Tim with a suspicious eye but the latter took no notice.

It was only a few moments later that Sally called out again. "It's okay, we've done it." Helping out with their younger brother had given them plenty of experience changing someone else's clothing.

Mildred now wore the long shirt, which came down to her knees, with the ends of the sleeves well past her hands. Although she was still completely out, her breathing was steady and unlaboured. Rosko walked over and, with the help of Tim, got Mildred over his shoulder in a fireman's lift.

"Will she be all right like that?" Poppy asked.

"It's not ideal, but I can't carry her any other way," Rosko replied. "I just hope my legs are up to it."

Conker was recovering quite quickly but Diz was really struggling. Along with the shivering, his legs and arms felt weak. As much as he hated doing so, he accepted the offered help from Tim and leaned on him for support.

Sally helped Caz to her feet and supported her. The injured ankle hurt again now the numbing effect of the water had worn off. With everyone ready, Em and Poppy grabbed the last two flammable torches and lit them from the embers of the fire.

"I'll take the lead if you follow at the back," Em said.

"Okay," said Poppy. "Just let me know when you want to swap."

Climbing the stairs was a slow process and, for some, a painful one. Everyone was either exhausted, ill or injured and it took a huge effort of will just to reach the balcony around the skeleton pit.

"We've already been here," Tim said. "It's a dead end."

"We're still trapped?" Diz sneered angrily, clearly feeling better. "I thought you had a plan. You're just useless."

"Look, you're alive because of us!" Sally snapped. "I'll put you back in the lake if you want."

"How about I just punch him again?" Caz suggested.

"We could always gag his mouth," Em added.

"Stop it!" shouted Poppy. "We're all stuck down here together so we need to help each other. No one's useless and no one's giving up. This place must have been used regularly, so there's got to be a way out of here that doesn't take us down to the lake. So instead of arguing, let's find it!"

She glared at them, defying any to argue with her. Em grinned widely and bumped fists with her.

"Oh, Poppy," she said. "You're absolutely right. We're getting tired and ratty but we shouldn't let that affect us."

Sally turned to Uncle Rosko. "You know all about this kind of stuff. How do we get out of here?"

Rosko placed Mildred gently onto the ground then, with a wry smile, looked about the strange chamber. "At the moment I have absolutely no idea."

"I knew it!" Diz said and Caz leaned menacingly towards him, her expression helped by the pain she was in.

"However," Rosko continued. "I'm sure we can work something out if we apply a degree of logic to the problem."

"Maybe there's a secret door!" Em declared. "We should examine the walls closely."

She started moving slowly away from the doorway they'd come through, using her torch to examine the surface of the wall. Poppy started doing the same in the opposite direction.

Diz opened his mouth to say something more and

Conker pushed him none too gently. "Shut it, Diz! No one's interested in what you have to say." Diz stared at his younger brother in disbelief.

Poppy and Em worked their way around to the balcony at the opposite side of the chamber where they came together and spotted something at the same time.

"Yes!" cried Poppy.

"Eureka!" shouted Em. She'd been waiting for a chance to use the word ever since she'd read about Archimedes in her book on Ancient Greece.

"You found the door?" Sally asked from across the skeleton pit.

"Not a door, but a faint carving in the wall." Em traced the design with her finger.

"It's a picture of the Sun!" Poppy exclaimed.

"That must mean it's the way out," Caz said.

"How do you figure that?" Tim asked. He couldn't keep up with the quads' rapid thought processes.

"The sun only shines outside," Caz replied. "So it must indicate the way out."

"While I don't want to dash your hopes, it could simply be a design that represents a sun god," Rosko said. "We are dealing with an ancient people, here."

"Why would they worship a sun god in such a dark and gloomy place?" Em asked.

"You could have a point." Rosko became thoughtful for a moment. "Everybody look for other symbols."

"We already checked the walls," Poppy said.

"I know," Rosko agreed. "But there could be symbols on the floor."

"Oh," Em said. "Yes."

The balcony floor was thick with the dust of many

centuries, but even a quick dragging of a foot revealed that it was made up of a series of flagstones, each with a rudimentary symbol carved onto it.

All but Caz, Diz and the unconscious Mildred dropped to their knees and started wiping at the dust with their hands. But within a minute most of them were sneezing and stopped what they were doing.

"Don't be so vigorous," Rosko said. "Then you won't raise so much dust into the air."

"Didn't anyone think to bring a vacuum cleaner?" Caz asked.

"I found a sun," Conker announced. He'd continued wiping away the dirt because he'd had the sense to pull the neck of his T-shirt over his nose, which kept out the dust.

The others came over to look and a clear sun symbol had been carved into the flagstone's surface. Rosko stepped forward and pressed his foot onto the stone slab. A very faint click sounded and everyone looked over to where the sun symbol was carved onto the opposite wall but nothing changed.

"We need to find more of these," Sally said. "If one click doesn't do anything, there must be others."

"How will we know when we've found them all?" Poppy asked.

"Easy," replied Em. "We keep standing on those we find until something happens."

"If nothing happens we know there's more to find." Caz grinned then grimaced at a sudden stab of pain from her ankle. "Ow! I think it's getting worse."

"Sit with Mildred while the rest of us look for the sun symbols," Rosko said.

Caz sighed. She wanted to help but knew it made sense to rest.

"I'm not doing it, either," Diz said. "Cleaning the floor is woman's work."

"Oh, dear," Rosko muttered and covered his face with his hands. He knew the girls well but the boy didn't realise the scale of the mistake he'd made.

Tim and Conker watched open-mouthed as Sally, Em and Poppy grabbed Diz and pushed him up against the wall, jabbering at him in fury. Caz limped over to join in, her own anger beating back the pain.

"Why would you say something like that?" Poppy asked.

"If that's the way you think you must have the brains of a snail," Em yelled.

"Are you a complete idiot?" Sally asked. "Or are you still practicing?"

"Who on Earth put such stupid ideas in your head?" Caz demanded and gave him a poke in the chest with her finger for good measure.

"It was something my Dad said, all right?" Diz said with a trembling voice.

"Well, that makes your Dad an idiot, too," Sally shouted. "You must have inherited it from him."

This was too much for Diz who now became so enraged his face turned red. He pushed the girls away from him then thrust his face close to Sally's and yelled at her.

"My Dad's rich and works hard," he said. "It's not his fault he's always too busy to spend any time with us. He can't help that we've hardly seen him in the past year! He...! He...!"

Diz abruptly turned his back on the girls and leaned against the stone wall, burying his face into the crook of his arm. His body became wracked with intense sobs.

Everyone stared with surprise and were at a loss

for what to do. But after a moment Poppy stepped forward and put her arm around Diz's shoulders. He shrugged her off with his free arm but when she put it around him again he didn't resist a second time.

"We're sorry," Poppy whispered. "We didn't know."

"No one knows, 'cause no one cares," Diz blurted, trying to sniff back the tears.

Conker stood nearby with his head bowed and Caz turned to him. He looked like he might start crying at any second, too.

"Is it true?" Caz asked.

"Pretty much," Conker replied. "He sent us here to stay with Gran because him and Mum are spending time with colleagues for a week before going to Dubrovnik for a fortnight."

"Oh my god!" Caz exclaimed.

"They're not taking you on holiday with them?" Em was horrified at the thought.

"They said we wouldn't enjoy it," Conker sniffed then began crying.

"It's bad enough not to take you with them," Sally said. "But to send you to stay with Evil Edith is too much."

In the background, Tim looked at Rosko with a helpless expression on his face and shrugged his shoulders in a matching fashion. Rosko clapped him on the back then stepped forward.

"It would seem that things have become a little emotional," he said, slowly and calmly. "It's to be expected with everything we're going through, but let's just take a moment to have a drink of water and calm ourselves."

The bottles of water were passed around and everyone took a drink in silence, not knowing what to say. Em began pacing up and down in thought, ignoring the way the others watched her. She then dashed over to the backpack and pulled out their still-damp swimming costumes.

"We can use these as cloths to wipe away the dust," she said.

"Great idea," Caz said.

"You'll ruin them," Rosko warned.

"I don't think anyone will care once we're safe," said Poppy and she took one of the costumes from Em.

Em gave one each to Sally and Tim. "Spread out around the balconies."

All four of them were soon on their knees wiping at the flagstones in a systematic manner. Rosko and the others simply watched, but the work progressed quickly.

The four of them uncovered symbols for snakes, skulls, moons, stars, animals and flowers, along with designs of a more abstract nature they didn't know the meaning of. But for a short while it seemed that they weren't going to find another sun symbol. Then in rapid succession they found another three of them and someone stood on each one. Conker stood on the original one, too, but still there was no sign of any secret door opening.

"I found one!" Diz shouted. Unseen by the others he'd changed his mind about dusting and had grabbed Mildred's damp pyjamas to use as a cloth.

However, it wasn't clear where he was calling from until he emerged from the shadow of the doorway that led down to the lake. With everyone else working on the balconies he had taken it upon himself to check the floor beyond the doorway.

"Okay, let's try again," Sally called out and five of them stood on flagstones bearing sun carvings.

There followed a much louder series of clicks, though at first it seemed that it had no effect. Then the section of the wall adorned with the sun carving rose upward very slowly, rumbling like the belly of a very hungry giant.

"We did it!" Poppy exclaimed and clapped her hands. "We can get out of here!"

But as soon as they moved towards the opening, stepping off the flagstones, the rock door began descending once more.

"This is hopeless!" Sally snarled. "We can only get out if the door is opened but we need to stand on the sun symbols in order to keep the door open."

"If this was a video game," Tim said, "We'd be able to push rocks or crates onto the sun symbols to keep the door open."

Rosko scratched his head. "Unless you've seen something the rest of us haven't, I'm afraid that isn't an option."

"If it was a game I'd switch to the easy setting," Poppy said.

"This is like a game!" Caz exclaimed. "It's a timing puzzle! Five of us have to run for the doorway before it closes again."

"Okay," Tim said. "I'm the school cross-country champion so I should take the symbol furthest away. The one Diz found."

"I'm a sprinter," Sally said. "No one can beat me over this distance."

"She's right," Poppy agreed. "Sally's the best one for it."

Tim opened his mouth to disagree but Rosko stepped in before he could do so. "We don't have time to argue and I've seen Sally run. She can do this."

After a little further discussion they agreed a distance order of Sally, Tim, Poppy, Diz and Em. The others would get Mildred and their stuff into the corridor beyond the hidden door and hold a torch in the doorway so the runners could see to dash around the balconies towards it.

They took their positions and when everyone was on a symbol the stone sun door rose slowly. Caz held the two torches while Rosko and Conker moved the inert Mildred through the doorway and along the corridor beyond. As they placed her carefully on the ground, well away from the stone door, she twitched as if she was going to wake but simply mumbled something incoherent before falling silent again.

Rosko and Conker returned for the two bags and when they disappeared through the doorway Caz followed them through. She passed one of the burning torches to Conker then stood just inside the doorway. She kept well to one side and held the torch out of the way of anyone coming through.

With the furthest distance to run, Sally had insisted that she should start the charge to the closing door. They'd only get one chance at this and she knew she'd have to run like she'd never done before. She breathed deeply and rapidly to get herself prepared.

"Is everyone ready?" she called out and got four positive answers in return. She took another deep breath then, "Ready... Set... GO!"

Sally was off and running almost before she said the word, but the others began their sprints within a half second and their feet pounded on the flagstones as the door slowly descended.

Em was through in a few seconds and dashed past Caz into the corridor. Poppy and Diz almost collided into each other as they reached the doorway at the same time but Poppy adjusted her path slightly and let Diz through before her. Being one of four quads had taught her to react quickly.

The door had descended about halfway when Tim ducked beneath it and headed into the corridor, which meant that Sally had only four seconds to get through the diminishing hole before it would be too small for her to do so. She came around the last balcony corner like lightening and prepared to dive easily beneath the stone slab.

Unfortunately, her feet hit a damp patch of the dust they'd been wiping away and they skidded from under her, sending her sprawling past the opening by a couple of metres.

She scrambled to her feet and tried to make it through the now tiny gap, but she was too late and the stone slab shut off her escape completely.

The skeleton room was plunged into utter darkness.

CHAPTER TWENTY-FIVE

The Phases of the Moon

Sally reached for the door in the darkness and hammered on it so hard with her fists that she had to stop in case she broke a bone. For all the good it did she might as well have tried to lift a mountain.

She sank to the ground with her back to the stone door and tried not to think about how desperate her predicament was. But how could she ignore something when it meant she would be trapped down here forever? She couldn't stop the tears when they began to form.

In the corridor on the other side, everyone stared at each other in the flickering torchlight, their eyes wide, unable to take in that Sally hadn't made it through. Even Diz wore a startled look, which he tried to mask as soon as he saw one of the others turn his way.

"How did that happen?" Poppy asked.

"It was simply an unfortunate accident," Rosko replied and slumped against the wall. "Highly unfortunate."

"But Sally never falls over like that," Em said. "She's always great on her feet."

"Nobody's perfect," Tim said, trying to put a consoling tone to his voice, though it caught in his throat.

"What's important is that she tried her best," Conker offered.

"No!" Caz yelled. "What's important is that Sally didn't make it and we've lost her for good."

"Nate, will you stop for heaven's sake?!" Edith was more than a little annoyed with her son. "Don't you think we've looked already?"

Nate ignored her and continued to examine the walls in the large, main chamber, examining the ornate design Rosko had used earlier. "There must be some way down to the lower levels."

"Of course there is, but there's no guarantee you'll find them safe and well." Edith sat on a small crate.

Nate stepped back from the wall. "We should have taken them with us."

"It's a bit too late to feel you neglected them, now." Edith's natural spite flowed from her like a tap she couldn't turn off.

"I didn't neglect them!" Nate shouted, his fists clenched. But he couldn't face his mother. "I didn't. It just wasn't... right." He wiped a hand across his face leaving a dirty smear, then pointed at Gus. "You, there. Do you know anything about this?"

Gus glared at Nate for a moment before answering in a measured tone. "The old man managed to open the section of wall with the designs on. But I have no idea how he did it."

"What old man?" Nate demanded.

"Rosko Tremaine, the quads' great uncle," Edith replied and waved her arm angrily. "Another interfering wretch. As bad as those brats."

"Not my old history teacher?" Nate gave his mother a puzzled look. "He was down here, too?"

"I'd forgotten he used to teach you. He gave you plenty of detention as I recall." She chuckled.

"This isn't funny, Mother."

Edith sighed and became stern again. "No, indeed not."

Nate walked over to the decorated wall and examined it again for a few moments. "If Tremaine opened this he must have been able to work it out from these symbols."

Gus shook his head. "We don't know how long he spent down here. Or how much research he did. The only answer is to drill test holes in the wall."

"It's too dangerous!" Nate repeated, determined not to take Gus's advice. "The people that built this place were really primitive so there's no telling how unstable it might be."

"It's lasted thousands of years so far," Gus said and folded his big arms. "If we drill out a small hole in the door itself it should be okay."

Unfortunately, although Gus's idea was perfectly sound, Nate would have none of it and dismissed the butler with a wave of his hand. His was the kind of charm he'd clearly inherited from his mother.

Em abruptly slapped her forehead. "Stupid, Em, stupid!"

"What?" Poppy asked, a little startled.

"There must be some kind of switch at this side of the door or no one would ever get into that room." She held her hand out for one of the torches. "Please." Caz handed hers over and Em began to search the walls.

Rosko gave an embarrassed chuckle and rubbed his chin. "I should have thought of that myself. The old grey matter isn't what it once was."

"We've all had a long day, Uncle," Caz responded. Rosko shrugged in a weary manner.

A loud snoring noise startled them and it took them a moment to realise it had come from Mildred, who still lay on the floor. Diz laughed at his sister, which triggered Conker to do the same. Em stared at the two boys with building annoyance.

"Stop laughing!" she snapped. "Sally's stuck and we've got to get that door open."

The laughter fizzled out and Rosko checked Mildred again, putting his hand on her forehead and taking her pulse. "I think the snoring's a good sign. She seems to be picking up and her temperature's better."

Em continued her search and soon found a faint carving on one of the wall's stones. It was hard to make out at first but when she held the burning torch close to the wall and above the design, the shallow angle light made the lines clearer and an image appeared.

"It's a snake," Em declared.

"That must be it," said Tim, coming close to see for himself. "We found some old snake skins at the bottom of that pit."

Em pushed on the stone block but it resisted her attempt to move it, most likely due to the many years it had been out of use. Tim placed his hand next to Em's, adding his his strength to hers, and it slid inward with a grind and a click.

From the moment the door came down Sally was sure she would die alone in the darkness. So she was completely surprised when the stone door she had her back against began rising. She leaped to her feet with immense relief and hurriedly wiped her face, hoping that no one would notice her tears.

As soon as the door had risen high enough, she ducked beneath it and joined her sisters and the others. Poppy, Caz and Em hugged her like she'd been lost at sea for years. They laughed with delight, which made Sally cry again, but tears of happiness this time.

Diz sneered then opened his mouth to say something, but immediately thought better of it and turned away. Only Conker saw this and found himself pleasantly surprised by his brother's action.

"Now we're all together again," Rosko said, interrupting the reunion, "We should start moving on." He picked up Mildred once more, though this time with considerable difficulty and Conker had to help get her into position.

With her torch in hand, Em pushed past everyone and began to lead the way again — her success with the snake switch giving her increased confidence. Poppy took up the rear once more after taking the other torch. Caz gladly accepted the help of Tim and Sally as they took up position either side of her. Diz and Conker trudged along wearily with everyone else.

The group hadn't walked very far when the corridor ended in a set of stairs leading upward. Rosko sighed loudly — his legs weren't looking forward to more climbing. Although Mildred wasn't particularly heavy, the additional force she exerted on his old muscles increased his weariness with each step he took.

Em started bounding up them as if she had unlimited energy, but when she reached the halfway point she stopped for a moment then continued at a more normal pace. Although she'd only climbed about thirty steps, each was much higher than the standard step height everyone was used to. It made a huge difference.

Uncle Rosko also stopped halfway up. The muscles in his thighs had begun to tremble from the exertion. When he tried another step, his leg wouldn't raise him up. He stumbled and almost dropping Mildred.

Conker and Diz were suddenly fearful for the safety of their sister and dashed up the few steps to Rosko's side. They took Mildred from him and supported her weight between them.

Seeing Rosko's plight, Poppy rushed from the back of the group. "Sit down, Uncle. Em, grab this torch, will you?"

Em came back down the few steps she was ahead and took it from her then held both of them up high. She and the others watched as Rosko slumped on the steps and Poppy searched the backpacks. She pulled out some of the water and the only snack bar that remained.

"Take these, Uncle Rosko," Poppy ordered. "You need to get your strength back."

"I was saving the snack for when Mildred woke up," Rosko answered.

"You're the priority, now," Sally said.

Caz nodded her agreement. "We can't make it

without you."

Uncle Rosko shook his head in defeat and smiled weakly, then tore open the snack bar wrapper as everyone watched. But Em frowned and put one of the torches on the step beside her uncle.

"Come on," she said. "Uncle Rosko doesn't need everyone watching him eat. We'll get to the top of the stairs and wait for him there."

Rosko could see they were reluctant to leave him so he waved them away. "Em's right. Just leave me here for a few minutes and I'll follow you."

They began to move off up the stairs, but Diz and Conker struggled with the completely unconscious Mildred, so Poppy grabbed her feet and helped them carry her upwards, which was more difficult than expected on the large steps. However, only a minute later everyone was relieved to have reached the top.

They passed through a short passage and into a circular room with a stone door directly opposite. Em walked over and examined it but there was no sign of how it might open.

Behind her, the others entered the room slowly and stopped in the centre. Mildred was laid on the floor and Caz sat down to give Sally and Tim a breather from helping her. For the moment only Em had any interest in their surroundings and began to examine the walls.

A series of circular stone blocks were set into the walls with fourteen to the left of the door and thirteen to the right — twenty seven in total. Each was painted in black and white of varying proportions.

"The phases of the moon," Conker said as he looked up from where he sat on the floor by his sister.

"Yeah, I know," Em replied. "What do you think

they mean, though?"

Conker shook his head and everyone stared at the symbols for a full minute without saying anything, during which time Rosko entered the room on his hands and knees. He dropped the torch, rolled onto his back and lay there completely exhausted.

"They may have something to do with that," he said, pointing upwards.

Everyone craned their necks to see what he indicated. High above, the circular ceiling was covered with a series of stone spikes that pointed down like a collection of stalactites.

"Oh, no!" Conker yelped.

"That doesn't look good," Sally added.

"Why is this place filled with death traps?" Tim asked, but no one had an answer.

Diz wandered over to one of the disks, an image of a half moon, and pushed on it. It slid in a few centimetres. "Hey, they're like buttons." He started pressing in some more and the others joined in.

Unfortunately, as soon as all were pushed in, a loud clunk shook the whole room, the moon disks popped out and a stone door slammed down to close off the passage through which they'd just entered. The ceiling began to descend with a gut-wrenching rumble.

Mildred, briefly roused by the noise, opened her eyes and she stared at the ceiling. "Not again..." she muttered before her eyes fluttered closed once more and she returned to her slumber.

"We shouldn't have pressed the moons in a random order!" Poppy shouted over the noise. "There must be a specific sequence."

Em moved over to the disk immediately to the right of the exit door. It was mostly black but had a very thin crescent of white on the left hand side and she paused for a second before she pressed it in.

The ceiling ground to a halt and a momentary silence filled the room before Em set to pushing the remaining disks in sequence, moving to her right around the room. The white of the moon's crescent grew wider on the left hand side of each disk until she reached the completely white full moon, next to the now closed off passage. She continued around until the last one was pushed in, the fully black new moon.

But instead of the door opening, as everyone expected, the disks popped out and the noise of the ceiling's descent filled their ears. They stared up in horror.

"What did I do wrong?" Em asked no one in particular. "It should have worked!"

Nate Malprentice gave up trying to work out the meaning of the symbols that Rosko had previously deciphered. He explored all the nooks and crannies around the large chamber, which led him into a small room off the main one where more symbols adorned one of the walls. The design was arranged in a large arc and he moved closer to examine it in detail.

Gus and Edith had left him to it and the big man now sported a large power drill with a long drill bit attached. The kind used to drill holes through thick house walls when cables or plumbing pipes need to pass through them. With goggles over his eyes, Gus placed the cutting end of the bit against the section of wall that Rosko had opened up earlier then looked at Edith with a raised eyebrow.

She paused for a few seconds before speaking. "Go ahead, Gus. Do what you think is best."

He pressed the tool's trigger and the drill bit tried to bounce around on the stone surface but Gus gritted his teeth, braced against the kick and it began to bore a hole. The progress was really slow and the bit hadn't sunk very far when Nate came running over.

"I think I've found another door," he said and led them to the room he'd just been examining.

"I've checked this place," Gus said, his drill still in hand, held like some kind of weapon. "There's nothing in here."

"No, look closer," Nate said. "There's a door. I'm certain of it."

Edith and Gus followed him into the other room and moved right up to the wall he indicated. Although it was only faint there was a distinct line in the rock wall. Edith traced the line with the tip of her right index finger and soon realised that it marked a rectangle the size of a door.

"I have no idea how to get it open, though," Nate said.

However, the potential door was pushed out of their minds when a violent rumbling sound shook the room with frightening reverberations.

"What on earth is that?!" Edith asked, both startled and terrified.

"You were right, Em." Caz and Sally spoke almost in unison and would have laughed if their situation wasn't so desperate.

"You just went in the wrong direction," Sally said.

"If you check the Moon's position in the sky at the same time over a number of nights..." Caz started explaining.

"The Moon seems to move left across the sky!" Em finished off the explanation herself.

"Yeah," Sally added. "You should have begun on the left of the doorway and moved that way."

Em immediately pushed in the first disk to the left of the door. The ceiling stopped descending again so she continued and moved around to her left, pushing disks in this hopefully correct order.

However, she'd only pushed in eight of them when the ceiling began to tremble and dust fell from above. Em worked a little faster but she was only just passed the full moon disk when a violent snapping sound from above announced that the ceiling was descending again.

"Everyone move near to the door," Sally said, leaving Em to finish her task. She helped Caz while Poppy picked up the two packs. Conker and Diz hoisted

Mildred between them while Tim helped Uncle Rosko to his feet.

Em pressed the remaining disks in as swiftly as she could but the points of the stone spikes were getting dangerously close to their heads as she reached the last one and pushed it home.

There was a loud clunk and the stone door opened swiftly, much to everyone's relief, but the ceiling continued down, clearly broken.

It wasn't easy to get through the opening quickly, with the need to help Caz and Mildred, but although there was the danger of becoming panicky they kept their heads and were able to squeeze through. But by the time it was Em's turn she was almost on her knees keeping out of the way of the spikes.

Then, crouched as she was, following Tim and Uncle Rosko ahead of her, her tee-shirt caught on one of the spikes and she stumbled to the floor.

Em lay sprawled out with the spikes getting ever closer.

CHAPTER TWENTY-SIX

The Mystery of the Manor

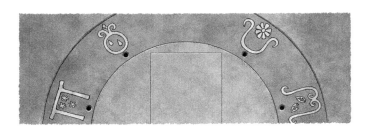

Edith sighed. "A doorway is only useful if you know how to open it, Nate."

"I'm working on it, Mother." Nate stroked his chin in a thoughtful manner, not realising that the gesture made him look pretentious.

"This is ridiculous!" Gus growled. "I'm going back to drilling that wall."

But he was stopped in his tracks by a rapid grating sound that came from behind them. As one they turned and saw that a doorway was now open in the wall opposite the one they'd just examined.

"I was sure the door was in the other wall," Nate said but Gus and Edith took no notice because kids were bursting through the open doorway.

Conker and Diz came through first, carrying Mildred between them, quickly followed by Sally, Caz, Poppy, Rosko and Tim. Edith gasped at the dishevelled, exhausted state of her grandchildren and Nate clenched his fists in anger.

However, before they had the chance to say anything, Em let out a scream from where she'd stumbled in the doorway. Her head and arms stuck out into the room but the ceiling and spikes would crush her legs before she could squirm free.

Thankfully, the quads were lightning fast when one of their number was in danger. Poppy dropped the bags she held and Sally let go of Caz, then each grabbed one of Em's arms and pulled her through the opening just as one of the spikes came down on her left foot.

Poppy and Sally kept pulling and Em's trainer was left behind, dragged off by the spike and pinned to the floor. The foot of her tights were ripped but there was no damage to her foot. The spike had luckily gone between her toes.

Sally and Poppy pulled her upright and she hugged them with a blurted, "Thank-you-thank-you-thank-you-thank-you!" Caz limped over and embraced all three. Their unity had saved them again.

Em looked back at her lost shoe. It was ruined and impossible to recover. "Mum's really going to go ballistic, now," she said and her sisters nodded in agreement.

Rosko shook his head and chuckled but the humour died when he caught sight of the furious looks from Nate and Edith.

"What the heck happened?!" demanded Nate.

"What have you brats done to my grandchildren?!" screamed Edith. "I knew you could never be trusted."

"I'll sue you all for every penny you have!" Nate yelled.

In spite of his exhaustion, Uncle Rosko lunged

forward and roared at the two adults. "Shut up! I've never known such an ungrateful pair of people."

Edith and Nate cowered from the old man and even Grisly Gus was taken aback by the strength of this outburst.

"You want to know what they did to your kids?" Rosko continued, still bellowing. "The girls and Tim saved their lives! If it wasn't for them Diz, Conker and Mildred would be dead by now. Not only that, they risked their own lives to save them."

"You expect me to believe such an outrageous pack of lies?" Edith screamed. "I wouldn't trust anything you or those girls told me."

Rosko lifted his arms and for a moment the quads feared he was going to strike the old woman. But it was just a gesture of frustration — Rosko would never be violent to a woman.

"It's true, Gran."

"Stay out of this, Conker," Nate said almost absently. But Rosko turned and saw it was Diz who'd come forward, still holding onto Mildred, bringing Conker with him. Nate was surprised that his elder son was defending these brats, as his mother called them.

"Dad, I don't care what you or Gran say," Diz continued. "They helped us even though we've been horrid to them." He and Conker looked over their shoulders at the other kids, still with Mildred between them. "Thanks for saving us."

"Yeah, thanks a million," Conker added.

"You're welcome," Poppy said.

"It was nothing," Em added.

"No problem," said Caz.

"We're good." Sally smiled and nodded.

Though Tim said nothing, he grinned and stuck his

276

thumbs in the air.

Nate and Edith looked bashfully at the floor and were struggling to say anything when Mildred raised her head and blinked her eyes in puzzlement.

"I'm starving," she said after a moment. "You know, I had a really weird dream..."

"Gus, carry her upstairs, will you?" Edith muttered.

The big man put down his drill, dashed over to pick up the girl and left the room. They were quickly followed by her brothers, father and grandmother, leaving the rest to their own devices.

After a moment, Rosko jerked his head towards the exit, picked up his backpack and made his way out. But the quads and Tim paused and looked each other up and down.

"I'm glad we're safe," Caz said. "But I'm kind of sorry it's over. The others looked at her in disbelief for a moment then everyone burst out laughing.

"Mum will probably think I'm lost forever," Tim said, losing his smile and looking fearful. "I'd better get home and tell her about the Mystery of Malprentice Manor."

"Wait!" Caz said, her eyes wide. "We haven't solved it completely."

"What do you mean?" Tim was puzzled. "Aren't those underground chambers the mystery?"

"You're forgetting the treasure," Poppy said.

"Remember, it's been hidden for centuries!" Em exclaimed.

"And we still have a puzzle to solve." Sally grinned and pointed at the arch of symbols Nate had been studying earlier.

"They're just ancient symbols on the wall," Tim said. "They don't even look like anything."

"Of course they do!" Poppy said and clapped her hands.

"I know it's obvious to us," said Em to her sisters. "But Tim's not used to seeing patterns in fours like us."

Caz looked at Tim and explained. "The symbols represent the four seasons."

Tim stared and stared but shook his head.

"The one on the left has snowflakes so it must be winter," Poppy explained.

"The water drops and the leaf bud are for spring," Sally said.

"The flower is for summer," said Em.

"And the leaves are for autumn," Tim finished. "Now I see what you mean. I don't understand why I didn't see it to begin with. What do we do?"

"The symbols are arranged in a semi-circle," Sally said. "So I think we're supposed to rotate it."

"How do we do that?" Poppy asked.

"Probably by using these holes," Caz answered. There was a hole beneath each of the symbols and she stuck her finger into the one beneath winter to demonstrate. Although she pulled hard it didn't turn at all. Then she winced with further pain in her ankle.

"We'll never move it like that," Tim said. "We'd never get a proper grip."

Em frowned in thought. "Maybe it was designed for some kind of handle to fit into the holes. Then we'd all be able to grab it at the same time."

"Great idea, just one problem," Poppy said. "We don't have a handle."

"Or anything to use in its place," Sally added.

Tim walked over to Gus's drill. "We can use this."

"That's too big and clumsy," Sally said.

Tim ignored her, bent down and almost wrestled

with the drill, grunting a little as he did so. But after a few moments he'd removed the long drill bit.

"How did you do that?" Poppy asked.

"My Dad was a carpenter and used drills all the time when he was alive," Tim replied. "He taught me a few things." He inserted the bit into the hole beneath the autumn symbol. "What now?"

"Now we pull," Sally said.

"I think we need to get the summer symbol to the top of the arc," Em said.

"Why would you think that?" Tim couldn't see the logic.

"Because we're currently in the middle of summer," Poppy answered.

"And if that doesn't work we'll try something else," Caz said.

There was only enough space on the drill bit for each of them to grip with one hand, but together they pulled. Even exhausted as they were, they heaved with all their might and turned the arc of symbols around slowly to the sound of heavy grinding. Their excitement rose to the point where Caz momentarily forgot about the pain in her ankle and laughed out loud.

As the summer symbol settled into a central position over the faint outline of a door, there was a satisfying click so they immediately stopped pulling. Unfortunately, nothing else happened, even when Tim pushed on the door itself. The girls added their strength to his but it still didn't move in the slightest.

"I think someone's having a joke," Tim said.

None of the girls responded as each was deep in thought, trying to work out what the solution might be.

"Do you think it's like a safe dial and we have to move it through a secret combination?" Sally asked.

"That would be impossible to work out," Em answered. She looked suddenly deflated. "We wouldn't know where to start or how many turns are in the combination."

Poppy jumped and clapped her hands. "I have an idea! Lift me up so I can reach the summer symbol."

Sally and Em each linked their fingers and cupped their hands in front of them and Poppy stepped into one then the other. Sally and Em lifted her as high as they could.

"That's it," Poppy cried out. "Tim, can you hand me the drilling thingy, please?"

"It's a drill bit," he replied, but passed it up to her anyway.

She inserted it into the hole beneath the summer symbol then pushed as hard as she could. It went further in and there was another click. Thankfully it was followed by a grinding of stone and the door slowly swung inward away from them.

It caught Em and Sally by surprise and their

support of Poppy wavered and she began to fall. But rather than crash to the ground, she jumped out of the other girls' hands, flipped over backward and landed on her feet with a flourish, just like in gym class.

"Ta-daa!" she cried.

"Show off!" Caz said, but laughed as she did so.

Sally grabbed the torch from where it had been left on the floor and the quads entered the secret room, closely followed by Tim. As soon as they were in the chamber they stopped in astonishment."

"Wow!" the four girls said in unison.

"Yeah," Tim whispered. "Wow."

The chamber was much longer than it was wide and looked more like a corridor than a room. Down each side were rows and rows of ancient weapons and shields arranged neatly on racks.

"They look brand new!" Em was surprised.

"The air's dry in here," Caz said. "It's obviously preserved them over the years."

"Uncle Rosko should see this," Sally said. "Once we've had a good look ourselves."

They walked slowly down the room, marvelling at each new item they saw. Tim reached out to touch a couple of the weapons, but each time he pulled back, feeling it would be wrong to do so. The way touching the exhibits in a museum is wrong. There was no telling what damage grubby, sweaty fingers could do.

The far end of the room ended in a large pair of wooden doors, plainly made but fitted with bronze handles and hinges. Sally and Poppy pulled on one door each and they swung open as smoothly as if they'd last been used the day before. Just when they thought they couldn't be any more surprised than they already were, their mouths fell open with the sight that lay before them.

The doors had opened on what could only be described as a large cupboard fitted with a number of wooden shelves. It wasn't the cupboard that astonished them, but what lay on the shelves — gold jewellery and valuable artefacts in amazing abundance.

For a few moments, all they could do was stare as the highly polished pieces reflected back the flickering torchlight. They struggled to grasp its true importance.

"We've definitely solved the Mystery of Malprentice Manor, now!" Sally declared and the girls hugged each other. Tim didn't join in — his eyes were glued to the gleaming treasure.

"It must be worth millions," he whispered.

The girls beamed at each other with wider smiles than they'd ever worn before and spoke at the same time. "We're rich!" they shouted. "We're rich, we're rich, we're rich!"

They continued to shout out as they did a little dance — even Caz, hopping on one foot — and soon Tim joined in.

"I think you'll find that treasure belongs to me," Evil Edith snarled. She'd walked up behind them while they were making so much noise. "Every last piece of it is mine!"

The quads and Tim abruptly stopped dancing and shouting and turned to face the old woman. Trust Evil Edith to spoil all their fun.

She glowered down at them then pointed behind her. "Now, get out of my house. Immediately!"

CHAPTER TWENTY-SEVEN

Kids for Breakfast

The last faint glow of the evening remained in the western sky as the quads left the manor and made their way down the drive to the road. Sally and Tim led the way while Em and Poppy helped the limping Caz. Uncle Rosko took up the rear, exhausted and lost in his thoughts.

When they reached the duck pond at the corner of the village green, all five kids stopped, reluctant to part ways. Uncle Rosko passed them by but stopped and turned with a quizzical look. He said nothing but waited for them patiently.

"Thanks for finding me," Tim eventually said.

The girls shrugged then began to beam.

"That was the best adventure ever!" Caz said.

"Even with your injured ankle?" Tim asked.

"You bet!"

"Definitely!"

"Absolutely!"

"Totally!"

Tim laughed. "It did turn out pretty good after you found me and rescued me from that cage. Thanks again."

The girls said nothing but surrounded him and hugged him like he was the best friend they had. For a moment he loved the attention, then became a little embarrassed.

"Er... I've got to go home," he said. "My Mum..."

"Yeah," Caz said.

"I'll see you again." And with that Tim was gone, jogging off home with what remained of his energy.

"If we're ever let out again," Sally muttered.

They set off in the opposite direction to Tim and headed along Church Street, making their way up the hill slowly. Tiredness was taking its toll on all of them.

They were half way along the street when Rosko suddenly spoke aloud, although the girls weren't sure if he was addressing them or not. "Historians and archaeologists will be able to learn so much from that place," he said. "The armour, the weapons... Well, everything."

"I liked the treasure best," Poppy said. "It was so beautiful."

"And valuable," Sally added.

"You'd have thought Evil Edith would've been more grateful to us for finding it," Caz snarled.

"And for saving her horrible grandchildren," Em said.

"They weren't so bad at the end," said Poppy.

"Only because Mildred was unconscious," Caz remarked and they each gave a little chuckle.

"All that treasure, though!" Sally said in wonder,

still finding it difficult to believe. "She could have spared one piece of jewellery or a small artefact. Evil Edith's definitely the right name for her!"

"We should get that pike and put it in her bathtub." No sooner had Poppy said this than she clamped her hand over her mouth, surprised at herself. She never spoke about other people in such a way and her sisters laughed. After a moment she joined in, too, though still a little embarrassed at herself.

The laughter died out when they reached their front gate and they stopped, suddenly nervous, reluctant to go in.

Em gulped. "What time is it, anyway?"

Sally pulled out the mobile phone and switched it on. "It's gone ten o'clock. And there are a million missed messages and calls. All from Mum!"

"I'd rather face Grisly Gus at the moment," Caz said. "Mum will definitely have us kids for breakfast."

Taking a deep breath, Sally swung open the gate and walked up the path to the house. She twisted the door knob and pushed the front door open, but they didn't have chance to enter the house before their parents burst from the living room into the hall.

"Where the heck have you been?!" demanded Mum. "We've been worried out of our minds. Oh my god! Look at the state of you! Em, where's your shoe? Caz, are you limping? Did you even have your phone on? Just tell me where you were. Honestly, you girls are going to be the death of me. Really, I..."

"We found Uncle Rosko," Sally blurted out and gestured over her shoulder with her thumb. But the old man wasn't behind them. He was so deep in his thoughts he'd simply walked down the side of the house towards his home in the converted stable.

"Thank goodness he's all right," Mum said, somewhat relieved. "But you're still in trouble."

Behind her, Dad looked as if he didn't know whether to be outraged or laugh out loud. Their clothes were filthy, scuffed and bedraggled, their faces and hair looked like they'd been scrambling through hedges and Em only wore one shoe. But there was a light in their eyes that lifted his heart. He smiled warmly. Yet Caz...

"What happened to Caz?" Dad asked.

"Just a sprained ankle," Caz replied. "Uncle Rosko said it'll be all right in a few days."

"She fell when she was climbing across the bottomless pit," Poppy said without thinking. Em nudged her and she clamped a hand over her mouth again.

"I'm not interested in hearing your make-believe stories," Mum growled. "Just get yourselves into that kitchen. You look like you haven't eaten for a week." No matter how angry Mum was she never neglected her children's welfare.

The girls sat at the kitchen table in silence, fully aware their mother was both fuming at their disappearance and relieved that they were, in the main, safe and well. She gave them each a yoghurt and a banana to be going on with then set about making some scrambled eggs.

Dad poured four glasses of orange juice then sat at the table with the girls. "Now, where on Earth have you been?"

"We went to rescue Uncle Rosko from Evil Edith," Caz began.

"But got trapped under the Manor with her horrible grandkids," Sally added, talking around a mouthful of banana.

"But we rescued Tim," Caz said. "Then Uncle Rosko."

"There are ancient rooms and death traps down there!" Em declared then licked yoghurt off the lid of the pot.

"And a bottomless pit," Poppy repeated.

"Yeah," said Caz. "And an underground lake."

Em's eyes went wide. "With a monster pike in it!"

"And treasure!" Sally spread her arms wide. "Tons of golden treasure!"

"That we found!" Caz thumped the table.

Mum had finished the scrambled eggs and gave a portion to each of the quads. "I love your imagination and the games you play, but you know you're not to stay out so late. Not to mention the fact that you were grounded."

"But Mum..." the quads said together.

"Not another word," Mum ordered. "Finish your food then a shower and bed."

The girls were too tired to argue and so hungry that they ate more quickly than was good mannered, but for once their parents didn't say anything about it. They'd nearly finished when there was a knock on the front door. The girls looked at each other and started to move.

"You stay there," Mum ordered. "I'll answer the door."

When she'd left the room Dad leaned close and whispered. "Where did you find Uncle Rosko?"

"Grisly Gus was holding him prisoner under the Manor but we freed him," Poppy said.

"But that was after we'd found Tim," Caz added.

Dad groaned and shook his head. "I wish I'd never asked."

They could hear Mum speaking to someone at the front door and the voice that replied sounded scarily familiar. The quads looked at each other in a bug-eyed fashion as Mum invited the visitor in and went into the living room.

"Girls, come in here, please," Mum called out after a moment and the four of them left the table, though Dad had to help Caz, whose ankle had swelled up again.

Sitting in the living room with Mum was Evil Edith.

"I've come to apologise," the old woman said, her voice much sweeter than they'd ever heard before. "For my earlier behaviour. I want to thank you for saving my grandchildren and discovering the Malprentice treasure."

Mum looked shocked. "You mean it's all true? The underground chambers, the lake... everything?"

"Indeed it is," Edith replied. "Although I had no idea about any of it myself until recently."

"They rescued your grandchildren, you say?" Dad asked.

"Not only that, they risked their own lives to do so, apparently." Edith put her hand into the pocket of the jacket she wore. "So I've come to offer them a reward of a hundred pounds." Her hand came out of her pocket filled with ten pound notes.

"Excellent!" Caz shouted.

"Wicked!" Poppy added. "We're rich!"

"Thank you, thank you!" Em said.

"Actually, I'm not sure that's a fair..." Dad began to say but shut up when Mum glared at him, then gave him a nudge for good measure.

Oddly, Sally didn't appear to be as happy as her sisters and became thoughtful for a moment before speaking.

"I think you should keep the money," she said and the other three girls' jaws dropped in astonishment. "But instead, you could give us permission to play in the Forest of Doom as often as we like."

Poppy, Em and Caz were still a little shocked, but as they thought about Sally's idea they began to smile and were soon nodding their agreement.

"But it's dangerous," Edith said.

"Only when trees are being felled," Sally responded. "But you or Grisly Gus could phone up and let us know when that's going to happen."

Surprisingly, Edith chuckled. "Heh heh... Grisly Gus..." She thought for a moment then looked at the girls. "If it's so important you're willing to give up the money, then I can agree to your suggestion."

"Hooray!" the girls shouted as one. "Thank you."

"But you can have the money, too," Edith added.

"Double win!" Poppy yelled. She almost hugged the old lady then thought better of it and the quads went into a group hug instead.

"Thank you, Mrs. Malprentice." Mum took the money from Edith and turned to the girls. "You can have this for spending money on your holiday next week."

"Wait," Caz said. "What about Tim?"

"Yes, he can also play in the woods," Edith said. "And he will get a reward, too."

"Thanks," Caz said.

"One other thing..." Em was a little cautious but continued. "Perhaps you'll let Uncle Rosko study the history of the underground place."

For a moment, Edith had a faraway look in her eyes. "I think he deserves that. We used to be friends when we were young. A long time ago." She turned away.

Mum made shooing motions with her arms. "Right, shower then bed. Now!"

Happy and suddenly exhausted, the quads made their way out of the room and began ascending the stairs. But halfway up they came to an abrupt halt, unable to believe their ears. In the living room, Edith had begun crying.

"I don't know what I'd have done if my grandchildren had died," she sobbed.

"Oh, ah... I'll make a cup of tea," Dad said.

As he made his way to the kitchen he passed the stairs in the hall and saw the girls standing there. He jerked his thumb upward in a silent indication that they should go to bed, but the girls were wide-eyed, open mouthed and unable to speak.

Never, in their wildest imagination, did they expect Evil Edith to have normal human emotions.

Showered and changed, they lay in their beds in the room they shared, completely exhausted but happy.

"What an adventure," Sally mumbled.

"Mm-mm," was all Em could manage.

"And it's only the third day of the holidays," Poppy said then yawned, which triggered the others to yawn, too.

Caz fought her heavy eyes for a moment. "Yeah... what... will we do... tomorrow...?"

The only reply was the light breathing of four sleeping girls.

The End (for now)

ABOUT THE AUTHOR

Steve Ince is a writer, artist, game designer, consultant and speaker with 27 years of development and writing experience, working in a freelance capacity with a variety of clients across the globe.

Steve gained a nomination for Excellence in Writing at the Game Developers Choice Awards in 2004 for *Broken Sword: The Sleeping Dragon* and received a second nomination in 2008 from the Writers' Guild of Great Britain for his writing on *So Blonde*.

Steve's book, *Writing for Video Games*, was published by A&C Black and has sold throughout the world, sometimes used as a text in game writing courses.

Regularly invited to speak at conferences around the world, Steve enjoys sharing his knowledge and experience.

His short film, *Payment*, was released a couple of years ago to critical acclaim.

The Quinton Quads and the Mystery of Malprentice Manor is his first children's novel.

ACKNOWLEDGMENTS

Thanks must go to all those who have been very supportive during my time of writing and illustrating this novel, especially my wonderful partner, June.

Family and friends, too, have been great and without the inspiration of my grandchildren I probably would never have enjoyed creating and writing these fabulous characters and their first adventure.

I'd also like to thank all those who read and enjoy this book. Should the response be positive, the Quinton Quads will return for further adventures in the future.